EAT

A

BOWL

OF

TEA

EAT
A
BOWL
OF
TEA

By LOUIS CHU

Introduction by Jeffery Chan

UNIVERSITY OF WASHINGTON PRESS

Seattle and London

Originally published by Lyle Stuart. University
of Washington Press paperback edition
published by arrangement with Lyle Stuart,
1979. "Introduction to the 1979 Edition" by
Jeffery Chan copyright © 1979 by the
University of Washington Press

Printed in the United States of America

Library of Congress Cataloging in Publication Data
Chu, Louis, 1915-
    Eat a bowl of tea.

    Reprint, with a new introd., of the ed. published
by L. Stuart, New York.
    1.   Chinese in New York (City) —Fiction.   I. Title.
PZ4.C558Eat   1979   [PS3553.H776]   813'.5'4   78-21209
ISBN 0-295-95607-0

TO MY WIFE

INTRODUCTION TO THE 1979 EDITION

First published in 1961, *Eat a Bowl of Tea* is partly a satire on the manners and mores of Chinatown's bachelor society, a community that lay moribund at the close of the second World War, enclaves of old men trapped by racist immigration laws to live out their days in San Francisco, Seattle, Los Angeles, Boston, and New York City. Their allegiances tied to wives and family barred from entering the United States, they found refuge in the backrooms of barbershops and restaurants, at the local tong, in the repartee and rivalries exchanged over a game of mah jong. In this tale of adultery and comic retribution, Louis Chu captures their vanities and illusions, these exiles become the vestiges of those who toiled in agriculture and mining, built the Transcontinental Railroad, and funded the Chinese Republican Revolution of 1911. He finds them fifty years later, bound by popular prejudice and the law to an aging, inflexible fraternity living in New York's Chinatown. Each remains unfailingly that Cantonese peasant warrior, doughty, resourceful, loyal to a sensibility rooted in China that has already evolved in his absence, dogging the disreputable and notorious Quon Gung, patron deity and guardian of low life in general, of actors, gamblers, and hired assassins, in the guise of waiters, cooks, and laundrymen. Chu's work is a vision of non-Christian Chinese-America, certainly the first and perhaps the last portrayal that accurately dramatizes the life and times of Chinese-Americans with a consistency of language and sensibility.

The novel opens with a white prostitute awakening the newly wed Ben Loy; the son of a "bachelor" father, he has been sent to China after World War II to marry. Returning to America with his bride, Mei Oi, he finds himself impotent, unable to make love to his respectable, traditional wife in the environment of Chinatown. Mei Oi is seduced by Ah Song, a gambler and notorious seducer of other men's wives. The affair is discovered; Mei Oi is

1

pregnant, and the cuckold is avenged by his father. Both father and father-in-law must leave New York's Chinatown because of their mutual humiliation, and husband and wife move to San Francisco, where the child is happily received. Ben Loy regains his potency by eating a bowl of tea, a regimen prescribed by a herbalist, and the story ends happily, Ben Loy and Mei Oi in bed agreeing to reunite their fathers at the haircut party for their next child.

In language, the manner and ritual of address and repartee are authentic Chinatown. Chu translates idioms from the Sze Yup dialect, and the effect of such expressions on his Chinese-American readers is delight and recognition. His unerring eye and ear avoid the cliche, the superficial veneer and curio-shop expressions of missionary biographies that precede his work, and he ignores the speech of those obsequious villains and heroes of popular film and television that caricature the Chinese-American population to this day. His narrative consciously makes English out of Cantonese, and his use of the language remains consistent throughout. He does not translate names. The language is active and direct, filled with curses as a product of the predominantly male society, where abstractions are made concrete and literal, and speech must account for the social situations in which each speaker finds himself. When the novel was first published in 1961, reviews of the day found it offensive and the language "tasteless and raw."

> "Go sell your ass, you stinky dead snake," Chong Loo tore into the barber furiously. "Don't say anything like that! If you want to make laughs, talk about something else, you trouble maker. You many mouthed bird. You dead person."

But the linguistic sensibility that lies behind these Sze Yup curses accurately reflects the combative nature of these bachelors who give no advantage in a land of trial, humiliation, and sacrifice. In order to characterize formality between relations, Chu invariably describes the physical distance each maintains from the other. Ben Loy avoids his father to circumvent unnecessary talk. The two fathers-in-law, while lifelong friends in America, must exile themselves to different cities in order to avoid the strain of obligations each owes the other after the problems created by

2

Mei Oi's adultery have been resolved. Overhearing Wah Gay's plan to match his son in marriage, we see the peasant warrior as tactician summarizing his advantages over a friend soon to become a relative.

> To him Ben Loy's marriage was something that had to be attended to sooner or later. The sooner, the better. If Ben Loy should not like Lee Gong's daughter, he could always get another girl and be married. A sense of male superiority came over him and he almost laughed out loud. A daughter-in-law is somebody else's daughter.

The portrayal of a predominantly male Chinatown is not unique. As early as 1896, Sui Sin Fah (Edith Eaton) wrote about the Chinese on the Pacific Coast and sympathetically portrayed Chinatown's bachelor society. Missionary portraits and autobiographies depicting a Chinatown devoid of white characters, save for prostitutes, where gambling and adultery marked the Chinese criminal, unassimilable and pathologically opposed to Western ways, are numerous. For example, Dr. Charles Shepherd, founder of the Chung Mei Home for Boys in El Cerrito, California, produced a novel entitled *The Ways of Ah Sin* (1923) in which he justifies his life's mission to shelter young Chinese-American boys from their heathen parents.

Not surprisingly, in published works variously labeled biography or memoir or guide book—word maps to the "exotic" environs of Chinatown—Chinese-American authors historically have avoided mention of this Chinatown culture that Chu renders so faithfully in his novel. Works such as *My Life in China and America* (1909) by Yung Wing, Garding Lui's *Inside Los Angeles Chinatown* (1948), Pardee Lowe's *Father and Glorious Descendant* (1944), Jade Snow Wong's *Fifth Chinese Daughter* (1950), and Virginia Lee's *The House that Tai Ming Built* (1963) uniformly ignore the existence of a non-Christian bachelor population that represented the vast majority of Chinese-Americans for nearly a century. These works rely instead on stereotyped differences of culture between "East" and "West," wresting poorly formulated notions of dual cultures from English language lessons taught by white missionaries anxious to assimilate the "heathen Chinee'." Such works deny the continuity of Chinese-American culture, its history and evolving sensibility, and sur-

3

render to a model of acceptance that was defined and authenticated by their reading public. Will Irwin wrote in the text accompanying Arnold Genthe's *Pictures of Old Chinatown* (1908):

> I hope that some one will arise, before this generation is passed, to record that conquest of affection by which the California Chinese transformed themselves from our race adversaries to our dear, subject people.

Louis Chu was the first Chinese-American writer to refuse such acceptance.

He was born in Toishan, China, on October 1, 1915. Immigrating to the United States as a young man, he completed his high school education in New Jersey, and went on to receive a bachelor's degree from Upsala College, a master's degree from New York University, and postgraduate training at the New School for Social Research. He was employed by New York City's Department of Welfare and became director of a social center. He served as executive secretary for the Soo Yuen Benevolent Association, and was a well-known figure in New York's Chinatown, where he hosted a radio program called "Chinese Festival." He died in 1970, survived by his wife and four children.

The art of Chinese-America's first novelist is more than that of the journalist or historian or social observer or social propagandist whose works are more accessible because their purpose it to give white readers an acceptable tale of what it is to be Chinese in America. The vision of a Chinatown community in transition, from a bachelor to a family society, that Chu describes in his pioneer work acknowledges the path of social and historical development that community traveled. He details its integrity as an evolving culture, a Chinese-America spread out across the North American continent, at the same time capturing the sense of its community life, the shop-to-shop interiors of Chinatown, the portable coffee from the restaurant next door, the marital problems of a Chinese waiter. So it is that Ben Loy has the opportunity to marry, to raise children in America. His father, Wah Gay, was resigned to his bachelorhood. Wah Gay and his contemporaries, self-styled sojourners, found their own rationale, disparaging their wasted days spent gambling and reminiscing about a China that had already changed in their absence. The thematic irony of

4

the novel is anticipated when Wah Gay slices off Ah Song's ear. Chu invests these old bachelors with a simple male chauvinism that brooks no sympathy, underscoring their lip service to a code of behavior they never followed. Mei Oi's adultery represents comic revenge perpetrated by the wives who remained in the villages of Kwantung while their husbands played mah jong in New York.

There is no question in Chu's narrative about what determines the paternity of the child Mei Oi bears, as if illegitimate beginnings lend strength and continuity to a new generation of Chinese-Americans. In a bachelor society women are scarce, and having children, a family, is difficult. So it is culture, the social environment of a dying generation, that determines paternity in this situation. Further, it is no coincidence that Chu sends Ben Loy and Mei Oi to San Francisco for Ben Loy to reclaim his virility, his paternity, and his wife. His return to San Francisco to make himself anew is not the response of a sojourner. He is a Chinese-American remaking a covenant with Gum Sahn, what the first generation called America, the Golden Mountain. He returns to the city where Chinese-America first began.

To eat a bowl of tea is good Chinese medicine. If Ben Loy is to regain his potency, if the sacrifices of the immigrant pioneers to gain a foothold in American were not to be wasted, the bitter prescription meted to them by an often hostile society would have to be swallowed. Louis Chu, in his art, legitimizes their experience. His sensibility and sense of humor, his ability to capture the language, style, and syntax of Chinese-America, could only have emerged from an organic familiarity with that Chinatown a century old in America.

JEFFERY CHAN

EAT

A

BOWL

OF

TEA

I

In the quiet of the early morning, the buzzer sounded sharp and sudden, cutting the silence like the shrill notes of ten thousand cicadas.

But to the sleeping Ben Loy, a bridegroom who had not worn off the luster of marriage, the noise sounded faint and distant. Buzz . . . buzz . . . buzz. The buzzing flooded the bedroom like subdued sunlight, tugging at the eyes of the sleeper, enticing him to awake. Still on the fringe of slumber, resisting the powerful influence of reality, he clutched at sleep. By now the repeated sounding of the buzzer had invaded his dreams and saturated them with wakefulness, degree by degree. Finally, like a tired man trying to arise from a swamp, he opened his sleepy eyes and stared at the cream-colored wall.

Next to him, still wrapped in sleep was Mei Oi, his bride of two months. His eyes fell longingly upon her soft, smooth face. He smiled. He would not disturb her. So full of innocence and the purity of youth.

He had mistaken the door bell for the alarm clock, calling him for work. Before his marriage to Mei Oi, it had been his habit to be awakened by a Baby Ben every morning, except on his day off. He would set the alarm for 10:30 in the morning, get up leisurely and, in a matter of minutes, would be in the restaurant where he worked and ready for another day. The hardest part had been the getting up. He had come to detest the alarm clock that was always ticking on the night table next to his bed. Yet, every night before going to bed, he would faithfully and carefully make sure that the alarm lever was pulled out.

Now everything had changed. He was a married man. Marriage opened a new vista of life for him. The apartment had become a home, his and Mei Oi's. Not just a place to hang his hat.

The apartment, on the fringe of Chinatown, was slumlike. It had hot and cold running water; but there was no central heating and the toilet was outside in the hallway. Ben Loy was not complaining; he was accustomed to it. He had lived here on and off for seven years, since 1942, when his friend Chin Yuen had invited him to share the apartment.

Wang Ben Loy and Mei Oi had been married in China two months ago; but they had been in New York for only a week. Upon Ben Loy's return to New York with his bride, Chin Yuen had given up the apartment to the newlyweds. He had explained that, since he was a bachelor, he could find himself a bed anywhere. Ben Loy's father had offered to find living quarters for them; but, in view of Chin Yuen's generous overture, Ben Loy happily moved into the apartment with his bride.

The neighborhood was not a fancy one. Catherine Street was like many other streets in the lower East Side, which, instead of flying the flag of excellence, flew the multi-colored washes of its inhabitants. The fire escapes protruding from the front of buildings boasted only of mops and brooms dangling precariously on their rails. Garbage cans were left helter-skelter on the sidewalks, as if a gale had just swished through the middle of Catherine Street.

But it was a place to live. It was home to Ben Loy and Mei Oi.

The spring mattress felt good against his back, after many weeks of bed boards in his native village of Sun Lung Lay. Ben Loy turned slowly in bed, away from his wife. He yawned and rubbed his eyes, hating to get even his hands out of the blankets. Turning again, he threw a fond glance at his bride. The snow-whiteness of her face, even when criss-crossed with strands of long black hair, made Ben Loy want to nudge a little closer and kiss her. Her full lips, rosy even without make-up, looked inviting to the bridegroom. But he was afraid he would awaken her.

From his bed, he glimpsed the outside world through the slots formed by the pink-colored blinds. Sunshine flickered through, but it didn't look like ten o'clock to Ben Loy. It was more like the crack of dawn. He tossed again, turning lazily to look at the alarm clock. Ten minutes to seven! What the . . . But who said it was ten o'clock?

The buzzer sounded again. This time unmistakably, distinctively. From the kitchen. It buzzed three times and stopped.

Goddamsonovabitch! Ben Loy angrily pulled the cover over his head in a futile effort to escape the noise. His wife stirred. Turning to her husband, Mei Oi said sleepily, "Somebody's at the door."

"Never mind that." Ben Loy stuck his head up from under the blanket. "Sleep some more."

Husband and wife stirred and tugged at the blankets, trying to make themselves more comfortable.

Buzz . . . buzz . . . buzz.

"Goddamsonovabitch!"

Mei Oi didn't understand a syllable of it. The covers flew off Ben Loy, exposing his black and white striped pajamas. His black hair was like the feathers of a rooster after a fierce battle. He compressed his lips hard. He sat up in bed.

"What did you say, Loy *Gaw*?" his wife asked sleepily.

"Nothing, oh, nothing." Ben Loy gripped the corner of the blanket and, with one quick sweep of the hand, flipped the cover back on himself again.

"Don't pay any attention to him," he said irritably. "He will go away."

"Who could it be, ringing door bells so early in the morning?" asked Mei Oi. "Must be a crazy man who has no consideration for others." She squirmed closer to her husband.

"Yeah, he must be crazy."

Buzz . . . buzz . . . buzz . . .

"Let me go and see who it is," said Mei Oi, half getting up.

"No, don't go. Leave him alone and he will go away."

Silence gripped the second floor apartment for a moment. You could hear the tiny Baby Ben ticking away on the night table. The sunlight pressed through the pink blinds, flooding the room with a pale brilliance.

Ben Loy turned abruptly to his wife and pulled her toward him. His arms held her like a vise and his legs entwined with hers.

"Never mind the door bell," he said, kissing his wife full on the lips. Again and again he pressed his lips to hers, each time more fervently than the last. He closed his eyes. It was wonderful, just having and holding Mei Oi in his arms. It gave him a sense of possession, of owning. A husband and wife relationship. It gave him a feeling of dignity. Mei Oi was his wife.

Not like those streetwalkers. Filthy, diseased whores!

Then his pleasure in his new wife gave way to the chill of frustration. His passionate kisses became mere mechanical gestures, the pressing of lips together. In a feeble attempt to hide his disappointment, he mumbled to Mei Oi, "I am tired . . . so sleepy."

Ben Loy loosened his grip on his wife's shoulder and stroked her cheeks tenderly, then her hair. He was spent, embarrassed and hurt.

He hoped the buzzer would not shrill again. The sounding of the buzzer brought back memories to him, memories he would like to forget now. His foolish, impetuous, stupid past. His senseless and reckless youth. . . . When the buzzer did not sound again, he was relieved to know that the visitor had surely gone from the door by now. It was a long time till ten o'clock. He would get a few more hours of sleep.

But hardly had he turned away from his wife when the buzzer broke the calm like a spark of lightning. Buzz . . . buzz . . . buzz. Then there were three light taps on the door.

Ben Loy realized now that he would never get rid of the bell ringer by staying in bed. His arm made an arc and the covers flew off. He leaped out of bed, turned and smiled at his bewildered bride and then gently pulled the blanket back over her. "I'll be right back," he said.

As soon as her husband was out of the room, Mei Oi sniffled several times and dabbed at her eyes with her red pajama sleeves. Ben Loy does not love me any more, she sobbed, almost inaudibly. She had been most happy, happy with an ecstatic quality that was beyond expectation or belief. She had had no idea that married love was such a wonderful thing. But this picture of happiness suddenly faded when her bridegroom strangely abstained from any more love-making. At first she had thought Ben Loy was just tired and that he would resume his ardent courtship in a few days. Now it was almost three weeks since he had last charged her body with that wonderful feeling.

Ben Loy walked briskly through the long hall to the door. He unlocked the door and yanked it open. The morning light showed the silhouette of a young woman.

"Let me in, you sleepy head," she said impatiently. "Where have you been all these weeks?" She was about to step inside when Ben Loy raised his hand.

"I can't let you come in," he shook his head.

"Aw, come on, honey," she pleaded. "Just this once." The girl began pushing her way in.

"You can't come in here!" Ben Loy raised his voice. "I have my wife here."

"Ha ha, I don't believe it."

"What's the matter with you? I said I have my wife here!" Ben Loy excitedly pointed in the direction of the bedroom. "There, in that room. My wife!"

"This I'll have to see," she laughed. "You married? Ha, ha, ha . . . Listen, honey . . . will you . . . just this once, huh?"

"No!" Ben Loy almost shouted. The veins on his temples bulged and his face reddened like *Quon Gung's.* "I told you I have my wife with me," he continued more calmly. "What do you want me to do? Kick my wife out of bed and put you there?"

"Do me a favor. I need the money. Let me in . . . just this once and I'll never bother you again."

At this moment Ben Loy's eyes fell on the clothes line strung along the wall in the hallway and now, for the first time, he noticed his wife's panties hanging there. "Here," he said quickly. "Look at these. They belong to my wife!"

The girl stopped short and began backing away slowly. She was a brunette, in her early twenties, whom Ben Loy remembered as one of the girls who had come to his room in his bachelor days. She stared once again at the clothes line. Then she fled down the stairs.

Ben Loy closed the door behind her. A sense of deliverance accompanied him as he tiptoed back to the bedroom.

"Who was that?" Mei Oi asked cheerfully, having recovered from her private eye-drying. "Why did you talk so long?"

"Oh, a crazy man."

"A man? I thought it sounded like a woman."

"No, it was a man. He might have sounded like a woman."

"He must be crazy," said Mei Oi. "Waking people up so early in the morning. What did he want?"

"Oh . . . he . . . he wants to sell me some insurance." Ben Loy climbed back into bed, greatly relieved.

But the encounter made him uneasy. It brought back memories he wanted to forget. It was like the opening of an old wound. Even staying in this apartment seemed an affront to the purity of Mei Oi.

II

One Saturday several months before the wedding, the day had broken humid and muggy. Heavy rain had splashed the sidewalks of New York intermittently during the night. The month of May had just ended. Chong Loo, the rent collector, hobbled down the flight of stairs to the Money Come club house in the basement at 87 Mott Street in New York's Chinatown.

"No money!" Wang Wah Gay, the proprietor, greeted the agent as he came through the door. "Wow your mother. No money today. You come back."

"All right, uncle, all right," said Chong Loo. "I'll be back on the fifteenth." He started to leave. Then he stopped abruptly, with one hand on the door knob. When he turned his head, he gave the impression of having a stiff neck; his whole body swung with it. "Did you see the pugilist master at the Sun Young Theater last night?" he grinned, showing his new set of teeth. The last time he had come around he had not a single tooth.

"Wow your mother," said Ah Song, a hanger-on at the club house. "Go sell your ass."

"Did you hear about the fight last night between a Lao Lim and a Lao Ying in front of the Lotus Tea Shop? This Lao Lim accused Lao Ying of taking his wife out."

"Wow your mother. Why don't you go and die?" said Ah Song, looking up from his newspaper, the Chinese COMPASS, at the mah-jong table.

"Later on the police came and separated the two men," Chong Loo continued. "Heh heh. Women nowadays are not to be trusted."

If the rent collector weren't so old, people might mistake him for a student, with his ever-present brief case. His head was big at the top and tapered off almost to a point at the chin. He had no hair on the dome, but sparsely-scattered long black hair mixed with grey on the circumference.

"Remember a year ago some Lao Tsuey ran down to South Carolina with Lao Ning's wife? She's the niece of the president of the Bank of Kwai Chow," Chong Loo persisted. "Have you heard the latest about . . . ?"

"Wow your mother," said Ah Song, this time a little louder than before.

Across from Ah Song, sitting on the couch, the proprietor, Wang Wah Gay, smiled his agreement. "You many-mouthed bird, go sell your ass."

"Heh heh. See you on the fifteenth, Mr. Wang."

His stooped shoulders and large head and brief case disappeared out the door and he began mounting the steep steps that led to the sidewalk. Wah Gay, from his half-reclining position on the sofa, could follow his exit until the rent collector's unpressed pants gradually ascended out of sight.

"Wow his mother," exclaimed Wah Gay, stretching himself. "He never fails to show up on the first of the month. You don't have to look at the calendar. When he arrives, you know it's the first." He crossed his legs and flicked the ash from his cigar on the tray.

"Chong Loo is all right," said Ah Song. He turned another page of the Chinese COMPASS. The circle of light from the overhanging lamp played on the newspaper. "Wow your mother. That's his job. It's his responsibility to show up on the first of every month to collect rent. Maybe he is a many-mouthed bird but he works for a living."

Ah Song let the newspaper drop flat on the table. Usually he read with glasses, but today he had been looking at the big letters in the advertisements. "Wow your mother, Wah Gay, do you think he's like you, never worked in your life?"

They both chuckled. "You dead boy," said Wah Gay. "You're still young yet. Why don't *you* go to work?"

"Who, me? I've worked more than you ever hope to work, you sonavabitch." Ah Song was a youthful-looking man in his mid-forties, with just a touch of grey at the temples. His neatly combed black hair had the effect of a crew-cut. A white handkerchief always adorned his breast pocket. Even on the hottest days

16

he would never roll up his shirt sleeves or be caught without a necktie.

"When did *you* ever work?" replied Wah Gay. "I've known you for almost twenty years." He pointed a finger at Ah Song. "You sonavabitch, if you ever worked at all, you must have worked when you were a mere boy. Ever since I've known you, you haven't done a single day's work."

"Shut up your mouth. Do I have to tell you when I go to work?"

The basement club house was cool. Compared to the heat and humidity of the street, it was a refreshing paradise. The sudden intensity of the early summer heat had caught everyone unprepared. A few days before, it had been so damp and chilly and windy that Wah Gay had to turn on the gas heater.

The door creaked open.

"Nice and cool here," said the newcomer. He turned and made sure the door closed tight.

"Thought you went to the race track," said Wah Gay.

"I overslept," replied the man. "Might just as well. On a day like this." He looked around the room. "Where is everybody? Still early, huh?" He walked over to an easy chair in the corner and sat down. He took out a cigar and lit it. "You know, on a day like this, I think this is the best place in the city. Nice and cool, with natural air conditioning."

Lee Gong was slight of build, with silvery black hair. He continued puffing on the Admiration which had been given him at a banquet the night before. He and Wah Gay had come over to America from China on the *President Madison* together and had shared the confined quarters of Ellis Island as two teen-age immigrants many springs ago.

In his early days in the United States, Lee Gong worked in various laundries in New York. Later he, himself, owned one in the Bronx. In 1928, he went back to China. He remained there only long enough to marry. Then he returned to the Golden Mountain, leaving his wife in China. He received the news of the birth of his daughter, Mei Oi, several months after he had returned to the United States.

Some ten years later, he sold his laundry. With the proceeds from the sale of the laundry plus his small savings, he had planned to spend the late evening of his life in the rural quiet of Sunwei. The Sino-Japanese War had prevented him from realizing this long-cherished goal. The unsettled conditions of subsequent years in the Far East, which saw Mao Tse-tung grab control of the Central Government of China from Chiang Kai-shek, had weighed heavily in his decision not to return to Sunwei. While there were intermittent periods of peaceful travel in China for those who wanted it, Lee Gong could not bring himself to see anything permanently stable for a retired *Gimshunhock* in China. So reluctantly he remained in New York.

"Ah Song, my boy," said Lee Gong from his easy chair. "You have good results lately?"

"What good results? I haven't been to the tracks for a whole week. No luck and no money."

"Ah Song is a smart boy," said Wah Gay. "He wouldn't go to the races unless he's lucky, heh heh."

"You go to hell." Ah Song folded his paper, got up and stretched his arms. He yawned. Yawning was a habit with him, almost as natural as breathing. "It's so hot you don't want to move."

"You just moved, you sonovabitch," said Wah Gay.

Ah Song ignored the remark and started toward the door.

"Where are you going to die?" Wah Gay called after him. "Be smart. Go get someone down here and start a little game. Where can you go in this hot weather?"

"To the race tracks!" Ah Song slammed the door behind him.

Lee Gong went over to the mah-jong table and sat in the chair that Ah Song had just vacated. He picked up the paper. "That sonovabitch Ah Song eats good, dresses good, and he never works!"

"He's got what you'd call *Life of the Peach Blossoms*," chuckled Wah Gay. "The women like him. He's a beautiful boy."

"Maybe he was born under the right stars."

"Three years ago he went to Canada and I've heard he married a rich widow from Vancouver and she bought him a car and gave him money."

"What has happened to the widow now?" Lee Gong asked, surprised that Ah Song was ever married. As far as he knew,

Ah Song was living the life of a bachelor in New York.

"Nobody knows," the club house proprietor shook his head. "You know Ah Song's type. He never tells you anything. I heard he had some trouble with the police out in Portland when they caught him without proper registration for his car two years ago."

"I've never heard of that," said Lee Gong. "But you don't have to go back that far. Just a year ago he was mixed up with that Lao Woo's wife. Someone saw him and Woo's wife together around Times Square on a Saturday night. Soon the news got back to the husband, who took the matter up with the elders of the Woo Association. The chairman of the Woo Association sent a representative to see Ah Song . . ."

"What happened?"

"Ah Song was squeezed for $1,000."

"Did he pay?"

"Of course."

The afternoon was unusually quiet at the club house, and the two friends found this light talk helped pass the time away.

"This generation of girls is not what it used to be," lamented Wah Gay. "In nine cases out of ten, if the girl were good and honest, no trouble would come to her." Wah Gay got up and started pacing the floor. "You look at this generation of *jook sing* boys and *jook sing* girls. They have no respect for elder people. H'mn, they would call you by name. They would call you Lao Lee even though you are almost twice as old as their old man."

"Regardless what anybody might say," put in Lee Gong. The words seemed to flow out of his mouth effortlessly. "Girls born in China are better. They are courteous and modest. Not like these *jook sings* born in New York. They can tell good from bad." He paused. The newspaper remained unread on the table. "Summer is coming. You'll see them running out on the streets almost naked. You could almost see their underpants."

They both chuckled.

The afternoon moved slowly. Even the sidewalk outside was deserted on this hot, sticky day. The perennial voices of children playing, the roar of their roller-skates against the pavement, were missing. An occasional rumble of passing trucks could be heard in the quiet retreat of the Money Come club house.

"A very deteriorating influence," continued Lee Gong dryly. "This Western civilization." He picked up the Chinese COMPASS again and tried to read it. The only illumination in the room was the circle of light that now played directly on the newspaper. "Nowadays girls go out and get a big belly before they get married."

"Heh, heh," laughed Wah Gay. "What more do you want? One gets a grandchild with a brand new daughter-in-law at the same time."

The door swung open.

Chong Loo, the rent collector, had returned. This time he was without his brief case. Wah Gay had started walking back to the anteroom when he saw Chong Loo enter, and now he came out with an aluminum pot in one hand and a dollar bill in the other.

"Here," he said to Chong Loo, "go and get a few cents' worth of coffee."

Chong Loo, beaming, left with the pot and the dollar. In the meantime, Ah Song returned with two companions.

"You have lucky footsteps today," greeted Wah Gay. "I thought you said you were going to the race tracks?"

"I did," replied Ah Song. "I came back already."

"You big gun."

From the back room, the club house owner brought out six cups and placed them on the square mah-jong table, which was now covered with old Chinese newspapers serving as a table cloth. He rubbed his palms and bent his head forward a little. "You are lucky. You just walked in and we're going to serve you coffee!"

The two men who had just come in with Ah Song were Tuck King, a second cook on his day off, and his roommate, who, because of his generous proportions, was nicknamed Fat Man; but was politely referred to as the Kitchen Master in his presence.

"We were still sleeping when this sonovabitch Ah Song pounded on the door and woke us up," the Kitchen Master said. He removed his Panama hat and put it on a hook on the wall. His right hand automatically went up and smoothed his snow-white hair.

"That's why we came down . . . for coffee," Tuck King laughed. "Share the wealth."

The basement had a refreshing coolness. Not damp. Not muggy. None of the moldy smell of the unused cellar. After coffee, Ah Song spoke out, "Fifty dollars."

Lee Gong poured the mah-jongs on the table, some of them face up, others face down.

"Fifty dollars," echoed Tuck King, sitting down.

"Okay. Fifty."

Leaving the coffee cups unwashed in the sink, Wah Gay joined the others at the mah-jong table. When he walked, he took big steps and his whole body seemed to swing with them. From the sink to the mah-jong table it took him but three steps. In his place on the table were strips of ivory chips which had been divided equally by the others. The mah-jongs now all faced down. Wah Gay added his outstretched hands to the pairs that were already busily shuffling the tiny ivory tiles around. The old army blanket muffled the noise of the blocks clucking against one another. Quickly, deftly, hands moved, setting up the mah-jongs.

Lee Gong picked a pair of pea-sized dice from among the chips and rattled them in his palm. The dice bounced off the mah-jongs and onto the table, where the adhesive characteristics of the blanket acted as a dragging agent and the dice rolled reluctantly to a stop.

"Six."

Ah Song picked up the dice and threw them against the mah-jongs. "Ten."

Next came Fat Man. He watched the dice roll lazily to a two and a one. "Wow your mother!"

The dice rattled once more, this time in the fat palm of Wah Gay. The cubes danced, smacked against each other, and bounced off the stacked-up tiles.

"Eight."

"Ten has it."

Ah Song hit the dice again. "Twelve."

His right hand reached for the mah-jongs in front of him,

counting to himself . . . two . . . four . . . six . . . eight . . . ten
. . . twelve . . .

The mah-jongs thudded quietly against the blanketed table, all face up, in multi-colors of red, green, and blue. Someone let out a thirty thousand.

"Poeng powng!"

"So soon?"

"Wow your mother!"

III

One evening a few days later, the door to the Money Come club house opened and Ben Loy stepped in. No one at the mah-jong table bothered to look up to see who it was. They continued playing as if no one had come in at all. The young man paused at the door, trying to adjust his sight to the basement's dinginess. His steps quickened until he stopped next to Wah Gay.

"Got a letter for you," Ben Loy told his father. From his inside coat pocket he extracted a bluish air mail letter and placed it on the table by the proprietor's elbow.

"Off today?" Wah Gay pocketed the letter, keeping his eyes on the mah-jongs.

"Yes," the young man replied, and left.

The mah-jongs thudded and clucked against one another.

"Poeng powng!"

"Wow your mother. You are dead lucky."

Wah Gay did not get to read the letter until early in the morning, after the mah-jong game had broken up. It was from his wife, Lau Shee, in Sunwei District, Kwangtung Province, China. Even before he opened the letter he was sure he knew what was in it. It was the same old story. Money. For what other subject could there be? His letters from China had been infrequent, partly because he neglected to write home.

To Wah Gay's surprise, this letter mentioned a new matter: The return of their son Ben Loy to Sunwei to get married.

He began to read:

Dearly beloved husband . . . as if I'm talking to you face to face. More than twenty springs have passed since you left the village. Those who go overseas tend to forget home and remain abroad forever. I hope my husband is not one of those. Ben Loy is now a man. It is your responsibility to see that he comes home and makes himself a family. Many veterans are now returning to

Sunwei to take a bride. . . . When you were home you spoke of acquiring a parcel of land between our vegetable garden and the well. . . . Hope your business will be successful enough to permit you to accompany Ben Loy home for a brief visit. . . .

Wah Gay lay alone and pensive on his folding bed, only an arm's reach from the old-fashioned sink that stood against the wall near the doorway. Privacy from the rest of the room was afforded by a wooden partition which reached to the ceiling. A small oblong table stood at the foot of his bed. The mah-jong players had gone. He was all alone now. Each time he had received a letter from his wife he began to relive the past. He knew it was not right to let the old woman stay in the village by herself. He often wondered, during lonely moments, if perhaps some day he and Lau Shee would have a joyous reunion. His mind began to wander to the clouds. . . .

. . . Twenty some springs. It was in 1923 that he went back to China to get married . . . this is the year 1948. Twenty-five springs to be exact, since I left the village. Ben Loy will be twenty-four soon. Those who go back are always the same ones. Thrifty, stay-at-home laundrymen. Every three or four years they go back. Come back and work a few more years and they would be on their way again. The little old woman . . . she is a kind and good wife. Heh heh, I guess she now wants to become a mother-in-law. Women are like that. They all do. When they have a son eighteen or so, you can't keep them from wanting to become mothers-in-law. After daughter-in-law there comes grandson. Heh heh, or they want a granddaughter. But they all prefer boys. Elder brother in Chicago has two grandsons. Women are like that. They want to become grandmothers. . . .

Wah Gay reread the letter again: Dearly beloved husband . . . That night Wah Gay found it difficult to sleep.

24

IV

The following afternoon, when Wah Gay got up at one o'clock, Lee Gong was already there rattling the door knob trying to get in.

The proprietor unlocked the door. "So early today?"

"Yes. I couldn't get any sleep last night."

The two had been friends for many years. Up till ten years ago, they had been friends who rarely saw each other. Wang Wah Gay, after a short stay in New York, had gone out to Chicago, where he became co-owner of the New Canton Restaurant on North Clark Street with his elder brother Wang Wah Lim. Elder brother Lim was in charge of the kitchen; while little brother Gay, because of his greater knowledge of the English language, was a combination manager-cashier-waiter.

On the other hand, Lee Gong's only contact with the restaurant business had been a short three months spent as a dishwasher in a Chinese restaurant on 59th Street. This was when he first had arrived in New York from China and the restaurant since then had changed hands many times.

"I didn't get much sleep either," said Wah Gay. "What was the matter with you? Why didn't you get any sleep?"

"That . . . that young man who was here yesterday," Lee Gong sat down on the sofa and lit a cigarette, "I forgot to ask you his name." He tried to make it sound casual.

"You mean the one who brought me the letter?"

"Yes, that's right," Lee Gong said impatiently.

"That was my little boy." Wah Gay tried hard to keep from laughing out loud. "Come to think of it, it was the first time he has been here."

Lee Gong knew that his friend Wah Gay's son had arrived in this country a few years ago. Other than that he knew nothing. And he had had no reason to want to know more. In spite of the many letters he had been getting from his wife, Jung Shee, in China, urging him to find a suitable husband for their daughter Mei Oi, who was of a very marriageable age—just eighteen—Lee Gong had been of the opinion that his daughter was still young and there was plenty of time to find her a husband.

His many years in America had made him frown on the customary early marriages in China. During idle discussions at the Money Come, Lee Gong had often spoken out against early marriages and dependence upon the support of the parents. While he had expected Jung Shee to keep harping at him to search for a husband for Mei Oi from the Golden Mountain, he had paid little attention to these letters until yesterday, when he saw the young man whom he suspected was Wah Gay's son.

"How many years has he got?" he pursued in earnest.

"This year he is twenty-four."

"A very commendable boy."

Wah Gay was not born yesterday. The moment Lee Gong mentioned Ben Loy he knew what his old friend had in mind. But he didn't want Lee Gong to know that he knew. He was rather proud of his son Ben Loy. He had kept him on the straight path. Any girl would be lucky to have his son for a husband.

"Where does your boy work?" pursued Lee Gong.

"Ben Loy is working in Stanton, Connecticut, at the China Pagoda."

It was almost two o'clock now and Money Come soon had enough players to start a game of mah-jong.

V

The China Pagoda in Stanton had the biggest sign on Atlantic Avenue.

Ben Loy had worked there for two years before he was inducted into the army. After his discharge from military service in 1947, he had returned to work at the China Pagoda, where his cousin, Wang Wing Sim, was manager.

The restaurant was owned by Wang Wing Sim's father, Wang Chuck Ting of New York, who had been president of the Wang Association for twenty consecutive years and was formerly a president of the Ping on Tong. In addition to the China Pagoda in Stanton, Mr. Wang owned the Blossoms Tea Garden at Lexington Avenue and 54th Street, the Wing Shew Herb Company on Mott Street, and the New Republic Noodle Manufacturing Company in Philadelphia. There were other businesses in which he had an interest but did not operate or control.

Wang Chuck Ting and Ben Loy's father, Wang Wah Gay, were born and grew up together in Sun Lung Lay village back in the old country. When Ben Loy had come to New York from his native village in 1941, when he was seventeen, his father had talked to Chuck Ting about a job for Ben Loy in his restaurant in Stanton as soon as the boy had had a year of schooling.

"Working in a small town will be good for him," Wah Gay had confided to Chuck Ting, who had nodded in agreement. "A big city is too full of temptations. You can never tell what will become of a young man like Ben Loy in New York."

For one year Ben Loy had attended P. S. 23 and lived at the Company Room on Mott Street. Then he went to work at the China Pagoda.

Ben Loy was an only son. This fact would add to the anxiety of any Chinese father who considered it his duty to teach his son right from wrong. Moreover, Wah Gay had to do the job alone. And he was held accountable for his son's actions to his wife, Lau Shee, ten thousand li away.

What made the job more difficult was the fact that Wah Gay himself had not set a good example for Ben Loy to follow. The proprietor of a mah-jong shop would hardly be the type to teach the wisdom of Kung fu-tze to the young ones. No one realized that more poignantly than Wah Gay himself. That was why he had asked Chuck Ting to give his son a job in Stanton.

He had hinted to Ben Loy just before he left for Stanton that he should make himself scarce around the mah-jong club house. He had not said so in so many words. He had merely told him that, unless he had urgent business in Chinatown, he should stay in Stanton because the air was better out there. That was all right with Ben Loy. Although Wah Gay was an amiable man and easy to get along with, Ben Loy found it difficult to mingle socially with his father.

In the Chinese scheme of things, father and son don't mix. When a Chinese father and son get together, it is frequently a one-way bawling out. So Ben Loy's philosophy was the less he saw his father, the better.

In such a place as a mah-jong club house, where unattached men usually gathered, the discussion and the language would not be the finest. Ben Loy did not want to embarrass his father or himself. He would not visit Money Come just for the sake of dropping in.

Day before yesterday, on his day off, Ben Loy had dropped in at the Company Room at 90 Mott Street, where the Wangs from the neighboring villages in Sunwei usually gathered on their non-working days. A few lived there. He had seen his father's air mail letter on the wire letter rack in the Company Room and had taken the letter to his father at the club house.

If Ben Loy had not delivered the letter to his father in the basement club house, Lee Gong might never have laid eyes on the young man. He certainly would not have been prompted to visit Stanton two days later. It was the first time he had ever set foot in Connecticut. He had not asked for the restaurant's address from Wah Gay for fear the trip might cause embarrassment.

Having found his way to Atlantic Avenue, he searched for

some sign of a Chinese restaurant. Soon the name, China Pagoda, appeared about a block away on the top of a T-shaped sign with the word *restaurant* on the vertical, diffused with sunlight.

Lee Gong's face broke into a wide grin, like a man who had just made an important discovery. Disliking intensely the brilliant sunshine that was beating down upon the entire town of Stanton, he wasted no time in reaching the restaurant.

The air-conditioned dining room brought a measure of relief to the visitor. Booths fanned out from the two walls, facing each other, with square white-clothed tables in the middle. Some of the booths were emptied of people but not yet of dirty dishes. A young man in a black jacket walked over from the counter near the door and greeted the newcomer with a hello.

"It's so hot out there I wanted to come in and cool off," said Lee Gong. He sat down at a booth near the front of the restaurant.

"Are you from New York?" asked the young man.

"Yes, I came to Stanton to look for a Lao Fung," Lee Gong lied.

"Lao Fung? I don't think I know of anybody by that name in Stanton."

"Oh, he must have moved," said the man from New York. He picked up the menu. "Nothing important. Some eight years ago he borrowed some money from me and I thought . . ."

Ben Loy came out of the kitchen carrying a tray.

"Has that young man been working here long?" he asked, nodding toward Ben Loy, who was serving the dishes at a table along the opposite wall. "Maybe he knows Lao Fung."

"Who? Ben Loy? He came back from the army several months ago. He worked for us before, too."

Lee Gong's hands still held the menu but he was not reading it. "I want a little something to eat," he said. Then, changing the subject, "What is your esteemed family name?"

"My insignificant name is Wang. Wang Wing Sim. And your esteemed name?"

"Insignificant Lee. What is Ben Loy's esteemed family name?"

"He's a Wang too."

"Your beloved cousin."

"Same village. Same village." Wing Sim left for the kitchen to give Lee Gong's order. Beef with tomatoes and one bowl of rice.

Ben Loy crossed over and passed by Lee Gong's table.

"How is business, young man?" Lee Gong called out. He wondered if Ben Loy would recognize him from his brief visit to his father's mah-jong club house.

Ben Loy stopped abruptly and turned. Lee Gong searched the waiter's face for a flicker of recognition. When he saw none, he felt more at ease.

"Business is pretty good," said Ben Loy with a trace of annoyance. He hurried into the kitchen.

As soon as Ben Loy disappeared into the kitchen, the manager returned. "Your order will be ready in a few minutes, Mr. Lee."

"I just want to eat a little bit. Too early to be eating much."

In fact Lee Gong did not care to eat at all, but ordering something gave him an opportunity to sit in the restaurant and find out what he could about Ben Loy.

"That young man seems to be a good boy," he baited Wing Sim.

"Ben Loy is a very good boy," said Wing Sim.

"It's much quieter in the small town," said Lee Gong. Inwardly he was delighted at what he had just heard about Ben Loy. "The air is much better. There are many temptations in a big city. Worst of all is New York."

"That's what Ben Loy's father said about the big city," chuckled the restaurant manager. "He wanted his son to get away from New York so as to stay away from its evil influences."

Lee Gong mentally compared Ben Loy with Wing Sim. Ben Loy was younger and had a fairer complexion, slightly taller. All around a better son-in-law, he told himself. More attractive physically. His daughter Mei Oi would not object to Ben Loy as a husband.

"You . . . you have your family here, of course?" he asked.

"Yes," replied Wing Sim. "My wife and children are here."

The kitchen door flew open and Ben Loy emerged with a large bowl of rice in one hand and the beef with tomatoes in the other. Lee Gong sat watching, privately elated at the thought that his prospective son-in-law was serving him. He decided he liked

30

Ben Loy's gait. A fast, deliberate gait. This would indicate the boy was alert and conscientious. Not lazy or listless. That's what he liked in a young man.

"Here it is, mister," Ben Loy set the dish and the rice down on the table. "We have a pretty good cook here. The beef and tomatoes are cooked Chinese style, with garlic and black beans."

The stranger from New York smiled. He was pleased with the waiter's friendliness.

"An old man like me doesn't eat too much," he laughed as he lifted his bamboo chopsticks for a frontal attack on the beef and tomatoes. "H'mn, good taste."

Ben Loy could see the satisfaction on the old man's face. He wanted to be friendly, hoping to earn a sizable tip. Ben Loy saw no objectionable characteristics in his customer. He wasn't the hard-to-die type. After more than two years in the restaurant business, the waiter could spot the customers who wanted something extra, something for nothing. Ben Loy was always ready for these people. If they asked for kumquats when kumquats were not on the menu, he would point to the menu and say, "Sorry, no kumquats." He was certain this old man was not one of those. Looking at his smooth and uncalloused hands, Ben Loy concluded that the old man was not one who worked at manual labor. His curiosity got the better of him. "Mr. Lee, what is your esteemed profession?"

Lee Gong laughed. "I'm an unemployed citizen of New York."

"You mean you're retired?" asked Ben Loy.

"Pretty soon I'll retire . . . retire to Brooklyn for good."

They both laughed. Ben Loy knew Mr. Lee was referring to the Evergreen Cemetery in Brooklyn.

"The new generation is much better off than when we were kids," Lee Gong continued. "You are lucky to be born in the present generation."

"Well," Ben Loy replied, "there are advantages and disadvantages."

"Look, right now you're working in an air-conditioned restaurant. A few years back . . ."

A couple came in and Ben Loy excused himself. In a few minutes he returned with a porcelain pot of tea. "This is Jasmine tea, just freshly brewed," he said. "We don't offer this brand of tea to everybody."

"Little brother, you have afforded me a big face," said the white-haired man graciously. He felt reassured by the young man's friendliness. He had looked for some resemblance of Ben Loy to his father. He noticed the fullness of the lips, the small nose, and the bushy eyebrows. All bore similarity to the elder Wang. When the young man walked, the swinging gait of the ancient model was remarkably there. Lee Gong was tempted to mention the young man's father as a very good friend of his. But he was a wise old man and he held his tongue. He said instead, "Do you live with your family here in Stanton?"

"I'm not that lucky." Ben Loy shook his head. "Elder brother Wing Sim," and he nodded toward the manager who was at the counter, "he's married and the father of three children, two boys and a girl."

"I bet you have lots of girl friends."

Ben Loy grinned shyly. "I have no girl friends. I'm just like a pig. No girl would like a pig."

Lee Gong finished his lunch and said something about having to go and look for his friend who owed him money. He left a thirty-five-cent tip, paid the bill and left the restaurant.

VI

The following afternoon Lee Gong appeared at the Money Come at 1:30, before anybody else would show up. He had wanted to get there early so he could talk to Wang Wah Gay alone.

"You and I have been friends for many years," Lee Gong began. "I know you just as well as you know me. You know I have no money. But I have a little girl back home in Sunwei."

"Heh, heh," chuckled Wah Gay. "Was that why you asked me who that young man was?" He felt flattered that his long-time friend thought well enough of his son to want him for a son-in-law. "Ben Loy is a good little boy," announced the father proudly. "He's working in Stanton now, a hard working boy."

"I only want a hard working boy," said Lee Gong. "A good boy. And when you want a daughter-in-law, all you want is a good girl, isn't that it?"

"Yes, I suppose it's all that matters." Wah Gay removed the cigar from his mouth and stuck his free hand in his pants pocket. "Heh heh, it's an excellent idea. A good girl. That's all anybody can ask for."

"Our Mei Oi is eighteen."

"But nowadays you would have to get the consent of the young ones," reflected Wah Gay. "You can't just marry them off blindly like in the old days. They have to like each other."

"That's right, I agree with you. No use forcing them into marriage."

Wah Gay thought for a moment. "I'll send the young one home," he said finally. "Tomorrow I'll write a few words to my woman. I'll tell her Ben Loy is coming home to get married. She will be very pleased."

Lee Gong said he would write to his wife too.

Without having broached the subject to Ben Loy, Wah Gay

proceeded to write to his wife, Lau Shee. To him Ben Loy's marriage was something that had to be attended to sooner or later. The sooner, the better. If Ben Loy should not like Lee Gong's daughter, he could always get another girl and be married. A sense of male superiority came over him, and he almost laughed out loud. A daughter-in-law is somebody else's daughter. It should not be too difficult to obtain a daughter-in-law. There are many eligible daughters. Ben Loy would only have to choose. Ben Loy is a good boy. The girl who marries him is very lucky indeed.

The next day Wah Gay airmailed the letter to his wife. A sensation of relief swept over him, for he had wanted to send that letter for a long time. It had taken his old friend Lee Gong to make him pick up the writing brush. He took out another cigar and lit it. His face showed an inward glow.

VII

Ben Loy and Chin Yuen roomed together in a small apartment just across the street from the restaurant, one of two maintained by the China Pagoda for its employees. The living facilities served as an inducement for workers to come to Stanton; for experience had shown that cooks and waiters were reluctant to take jobs in small towns.

One night in the winter of 1942, shortly after eighteen-year-old Ben Loy had started working there, the restaurant closed early because of the blizzard-like weather. Snow had been falling since mid-morning and no one had come into the restaurant since. The cooks and waiters sat around and chatted idly until it became apparent that the weather was not going to let up. Then manager Wing Sim sent them home for the night.

Chin Yuen and Ben Loy went to the apartment, happy at the thought that they had a couple of extra hours to themselves. This was the first time their work schedule had permitted the roommates any leisure time together.

Chin Yuen asked the younger man, "Little brother, do you go in for a little recreation from time to time?" Before Ben Loy had a chance to answer, he added, "I mean such as girls."

"Girls? Where? In this town?" asked Ben Loy, incredulously. He was sitting on the edge of his bed. He proceeded to take off his snow-dampened shoes and socks. He had known Chin Yuen for only two weeks.

"No, no, stupid boy," said Chin Yuen. "Not in this town." Chin Yuen looked like a pocket edition of a fat man with big round eyes. "In New York."

"I have no girl friend anywhere," said Ben Loy, smiling, somewhat taken aback by the conversation. He walked over to the window and looked out. He had never beheld so much snow before. White flakes floated down upon the street, upon the roofs, upon the city, upon the whole landscape, like white-grained rice husks flying from the milling closet. Only this was on a grander scale. All white. Everything was white. The whole world was white.

"Look," he said when he heard Chin Yuen coming toward the window. He pointed to the fast falling snow, which had a musical and rhythmic quality as it glided through the air.

"It's snowing." Chin Yuen quickly turned away from the window. "Haven't you seen it snow before? What is there to see?"

The room was sparsely furnished. No sofa. No chair. When they sat, they sat on the bed. It was not necessary for the boss to furnish these rooms with any degree of luxury. It was a place to sleep, a dormitory. It was unusual for roommates to meet and talk in their room; their hours of work prevented it.

Chin Yuen had just come out of the bathroom and started to get dressed again when Ben Loy asked, "You going some place?" He had presumed his roommate was getting ready for bed.

"Yes. New York. Want to come along? It's going to be a dead night in Stanton." Chin Yuen's mouth twisted into a knowing smile. "You're only young once. Enjoy yourself while you can."

Ben Loy thought for a moment. If he had been working as usual, the hours would have passed quickly. But this way, alone in his room, he would have only the four walls to talk to. If he went with Chin Yuen, no one would find out he had been in New York.

"Don't mention this to Wing Sim," said Ben Loy as he hurriedly changed, excited at the thought of going to New York at this hour.

"Don't be afraid, you dead boy," said Chin Yuen. "Nobody is going to tell your old man."

In less than an hour, with Chin Yuen in charge, the two roommates arrived in New York. From Grand Central, they hailed a taxi to take them to the Hotel Lansing on Fiftieth Street. A small marquee extended over the entrance of the hotel.

As the two walked in, an elderly man with glasses was bending over the desk. He looked up, greeted the strangers and proceeded to register them for the night. "Room 709," he announced to the bell boy, who had come up to the desk. Ben Loy and Chin Yuen followed the bell boy to the elevator and rode up to the seventh floor, where he opened the door to 709. Ben Loy and Chin Yuen looked about the room. One double bed and cream-colored walls. One wash basin in the corner near the window, but no toilet or bathroom. One small dresser. The bell boy went to the window and pulled the shade down. As he turned to leave, Chin Yuen walked over to him and said almost inaudibly, "You have a nice girl?"

The man, who was about fifty years old, in a blue and yellow uniform, knitted his brows, and there was a pained expression on his countenance. He looked sympathetic. Slowly he shook his head. "My friends, on a night like this, I don't know." His hand was on the door knob. He shrugged his shoulders. "They don't come around on a night like this."

Chin Yuen followed the man to the door. Ben Loy was pushing the mattress down with his hands, testing its springiness.

"You try, my friend," implored Chin Yuen, pushing a dollar bill into his palm. "Young one, huh? Nice girl."

The minutes ticked by slowly. The expected knock on the door did not come. Outside the snow continued to fall. The hotel room suddenly became a self-imposed prison instead of a one-night paradise. What could they do but wait? The watch stood still.

"If I had known it was going to be like this," mumbled the disappointed Ben Loy, "I would have stayed in Stanton."

"How should I know it was going to be like this?" said Chin Yuen, feeling a little guilty at having dragged his roommate to New York for nothing. "Maybe some girl will come up. It was never like this before."

Midnight came and went. They stared at the four walls. Should they wait some more or try to get some sleep? In their state of frustration, sleep would not come easy. If they had only stayed in Stanton! They were like two foolish people entrapped on a bed of cactus, squirming to make themselves more comfortable. There was no heart for talk. What a strange situation! Two men waiting. A double bed. A wash basin. Outside the whole world was blanketed in snow. The whole world stood still. Waiting.

Just waiting.

Finally, after what seemed like ten thousand banquets, there came a soft knock on the door. Chin Yuen jumped up. He rushed to the door.

"Do you want to see me?" A middle-aged redhead with a hard smile stood in the doorway.

"Come in. Come in," invited Chin Yuen. Her perfume tickled his nostrils, "Only one?"

"How many do you want?" the woman giggled. She stepped into the room. "Any bathroom?"

"No," replied Chin Yuen. "Outside in the hall."

She walked to the dresser and took off her black coat, which had a fur collar around it, folded it in half and laid it across the top of the bureau.

"Well, I certainly can't take care of the two of you at the same time," she laughed; and her hands went up and touched her hair. She was wearing a thin white sweater over a green dress. She began wiggling out of her sweater. "One of you will have to go outside," she said coyly.

"How much?" asked Chin Yuen, sales resistance lowered from watching the sweater come off.

"Ten dollars."

"Too much money. Too much money."

"Are you kidding?"

"Five dollars."

Her lower lip pushed out and up so that it encompassed the upper lip. Her right hand flew out and reached for her sweater. All this time Ben Loy was debating whether he should go out and lock himself in the bathroom or let Chin Yuen go out first.

"Okay, ten dollars," said Chin Yuen. "Okay, I was only kidding."

The redhead smiled and put down the sweater again. "Now which one of you is going out?" Her eyes flashed from one customer to the other, indifferent to which one to take on first.

Neither answered her. The silence was embarrassing and awkward to the men, but not to the woman. She proceeded to take off her dress, revealing her white nylon slip. Momentarily the men's attention focussed on her disrobing.

Finally Chin Yuen spoke up, "Ben Loy, why don't you go outside first? Maybe there'll be another girl along soon."

The girl pulled her slip up and over her head. She stood in her panties and brassiere. Silently Ben Loy walked out, taking with him a vivid image of the almost naked woman. Chin Yuen kept his eyes on the woman standing beside the bed. He saw her bend forward slightly. The panties slid off her white, well-formed thighs. The flesh-seller had neglected to take off her brassiere and Chin Yuen helped her remove it. Chin Yuen started to unbutton his shirt with hands that shook with nervous energy. In a moment he was completely naked and he hurried to possess her.

Ben Loy waited in the bathroom in a turmoil of excitement and apprehension.

Fifteen minutes later a subdued and weary Chin Yuen stumbled out of the room to call Ben Loy.

"Where's the other girl?" demanded Ben Loy. "Did she come?"

"No, I guess there ain't going to be any other girl," said Chin Yuen. "Go ahead back into the room. She's waiting for you."

Ben Loy went into the room, his blood tingling and exploding inside him. The sight of the naked woman made him forget his embarrassment. He quickly shed his clothes and got into the bed.

The next morning Ben Loy and Chin Yuen woke up at about ten, hurriedly washed and managed to get back to Stanton in time for the lunch hour rush.

The following week on his day off Ben Loy entrained for New York. He had been looking forward to this day. His pleasurable experience at the hotel had allayed all his anxious qualms. Now when he got to the Hotel Lansing, he tried to find the same bell boy who had taken care of him and Chin Yuen. But that elderly man was nowhere to be seen. In his place was a much younger man. Ben Loy followed him to his room on the seventh floor, just as he and Chin Yuen had done the previous week. As the bell boy turned to leave, Ben Loy managed to force out of his mouth, "You have girl? Nice girl?"

"Oh, you want a girl?" the bell boy's face lit up.

"Yeah, girl. Nice girl."

In less than half an hour a young blonde knocked on the door and inquired, "Do you want to see me?"

Ben Loy happily let her in.

His subsequent trips to the hotel were made more pleasurable by the knowledge gained through experience. He stopped looking for the same bell boy. Any one would do. When he was in the mood for it, he even had a second girl come in. In time he came to learn some of the girls' names. He would drop in and ask for his favorite by name.

On these trips he never showed himself in Chinatown, not even appearing at his Company Room. He made the Hotel Lansing his New York headquarters until several months later, when Chin Yuen asked him to share an apartment on Catherine Street. When the women came to the apartment to see Chin Yuen, sometimes they would find Ben Loy there instead. This arrangement suited Ben Loy. He no longer had to go out to look for women. They would come to him.

VIII

Pleased with his conviction that Ben Loy was the right man for his daughter Mei Oi, Lee Gong set about putting pressure on Wah Gay. He would drop in at the club house early in the afternoon to chat with the proprietor about the impending wedding. Did you hear from your wife yet? Have you spoken with Ben Loy about the matter?

Lee Gong had refrained from telling his old friend that he had gone to the restaurant in Stanton to get a closer look at the prospective son-in-law. Did not his cousin Wing Sim say that Ben Loy was a good boy? Did not Wah Gay say that his son was a good boy? Did not Lee Gong, after his own investigation, come to the conclusion that Ben Loy would make a proper and respectable son-in-law?

When Wah Gay saw that Lee Gong was quite impatient about matching their young ones, he summoned Ben Loy to the basement club house for a conference.

It was always an unusual occasion when the old man sent for his offspring. Apprehensive of the usual father-son upbraiding, Ben Loy did not like the idea of going to see his father. He feared that someone had informed his father about his activities in the apartment on Catherine Street. He immediately began to think of excuses and appropriate answers for his father's expected questions.

From Grand Central he took the Lexington IRT down to Chinatown. His father was expecting him; for when he tried the door to the club house, it was already unlatched. He pushed it open and walked in, and just as he did, he saw a man get up and walk out. The man was Lee Gong but Ben Loy did not recognize him.

"You have come out so early?" his father asked.

"Yes, just got here." Ben Loy pulled out a chair at the mah-jong table and sat down.

"How is business in the small town?"

"Pretty good," replied the startled Ben Loy. He had not expected such a pleasant opening conversation from his father.

"You can make a living out there?"

"I guess so." The tone of questioning led Ben Loy to believe that his father was going to get another job for him.

"Ben Loy, as you know," Wah Gay continued, "your father and mother are getting older each day. Each day makes the light of life dimmer for the old folks. I have just received a letter from your mother. She wants you to return home to get married."

Ben Loy did not say anything. He sat silent, thinking to himself.

"If you don't get married when you're young, when would you marry, when you're old?" the father pursued. "I have thought this thing over carefully. Both your father and mother want you to go home and get yourself a woman."

"Next year. Wait till next year." Ben Loy tried to stall for time.

"Next year?" demanded Wah Gay, a pained expression on his face. "Next year the Lord may not be so kind to me. A man of my age lives by the day, not by the year. Regardless of how you feel, you must return home to get married." His voice sounded more severe and curt. "Your mother is crying day and night for your return. You would not want to break her heart by being a disobedient son. It is for your own good, because the *jook sing* girls over here are no good. You can see how they run around. They are useless."

"I'm still young. I can wait a year or two," said Ben Loy sulkily.

"You are not young. You are twenty-four. If you remained unmarried any longer, you will end up with one of those *jook sing* girls, I know. When you do, your old man will be getting a grandchild as well as a daughter-in-law. Then I would have no face to present to my friends and cousins."

Ben Loy twisted his neck and pursed his lips, realizing it was hopeless to try to squirm out of his predicament. He knew that by tradition it was his responsibility to get married, as it was his father's duty to see that he did.

"I'll tell Uncle Chuck Ting to find someone to replace you at the restaurant," announced Wah Gay curtly. "And when you return, the job will be waiting for you there."

He did not mention Mei Oi, because he did not want Ben Loy to know the match had already been arranged. "When you bring your wife over here," he continued, "I'll see that you have a place to live. Leave those things to me. I will take the responsibility."

"Bring my wife over here?" Ben Loy's face lit up. He had assumed that his father's plans were for him to return to China and get married, then leave his bride in Sunwei, while he would return to the United States. "Do you mean you want me to bring my wife to America?"

"Of course," said Wah Gay. "Nowadays everyone does that. Nobody leaves his wife home any more. Times have changed."

"But still, can't we just wait a while?" said Ben Loy. "I have so little money."

"Did I ask you for money?" Wah Gay's face reddened. "Huh, did I?" The old man was angered to think that his son doubted his ability to provide him with a wife. "That's my responsibility. I will see to it that all necessary arrangements are made for your transportation. When you set foot on China, the rest is up to your mother. I don't want you to disobey her. She is your mother."

When Ben Loy left the club house he craved for release of his bottled-up emotions. Maybe he would go to China and see what would happen to him. Sooner or later one has to get married. He liked the idea of bringing his bride to America with him. Not like his father and mother, separated by oceans and continents. As he left, he had told his father that he was going to take a train right back to Stanton. And his father had said, "That's fine. You go right back to Stanton. There is nothing else for you to do in New York."

But Ben Loy stealthily found his way to the apartment he shared with Chin Yuen, to await that familiar knock on the door when Maria or Evelyn or Josie would come.

IX

And so it came to pass that three months after Lee Gong had brought up the subject of marriage for his daughter Mei Oi, Ben Loy sailed on the *President Gordon* for Hongkong and China in September, 1948.

In addition to purchasing ship and train tickets for his son, Wah Gay had made out several foreign drafts totaling a couple of thousand dollars for Ben Loy's trip. He realized that his son, only ten months ago discharged from the army after more than three years of service, would have no savings of his own to speak of. He was happy at the thought that his only offspring was to become a family man at last. It was an occasion looked forward to by all parents. It marked a milestone in the responsibility of family relationship. To Wah Gay and his wife Lau Shee, Ben Loy's marriage would mark a solemn obligation dutifully discharged on the part of the parents.

The elder Wang had feared that Ben Loy, especially after his service in the army, might have become too Americanized to be sent back to China to get married. The possibility of having a *jook sing* girl for a daughter-in-law had always haunted the otherwise easy-going, carefree Wang. He never thought much of these American-born Chinese girls. They are always going out and having a good time. Always new clothes, new shoes, new hats. Expensive perfumes. You needed to be a millionaire to support them. He could not bring himself to approve any marriage which would make his son a virtual slave to his own wife.

More important than his own feelings about the matter, Wah Gay was happy for his wife, whom he had not seen since he visited the village back in 1924. He constantly entertained the desire for a brief reunion with Lau Shee. He considered it a sacred duty. But there was always a tomorrow.

Throughout the years he had received many letters from his

44

wife, who had given up idol worship to embrace Christianity ten years ago. She had been an active church member since. Whenever her husband sent a remittance back home, she would take out a certain amount to donate to the church, saying that her husband had so indicated. This made her feel very proud of him.

In spite of Wah Gay's long absence from home, Lau Shee felt no bitterness toward him. Only sympathy and understanding. Perhaps it was this quality of sympathy and understanding, as exemplified by his wife, that Wah Gay found lacking in *jook sing* girls, which made them objectionable as daughters-in-law.

Lau Shee was not alone in her husbandless existence. There were hundreds and hundreds of women in Sunwei like her, whose menfolks had sailed the wide seas for the Beautiful Country and never returned. There remained, however, always the hope that someday they would come back. When pressed by his wife to return for another visit, as some of the others had done, Wah Gay gave the urgency of business as an excuse.

Maybe next year. Maybe the year after next. And the dutiful wife waited and hoped. She faithfully went to the market place every Sunday and prayed for her husband's return, just as she had fervently pleaded for his return home with the idols at the temples prior to her conversion to Christianity.

Her husband's picture, taken at Bear Mountain many years ago on an excursion, adorned the wall of the main meeting room of the church. It showed Wah Gay a happy and jovial man in a white linen suit. Now, always when he thought of this picture hanging in the market's only church some fifteen thousand li from New York, he would chuckle. His wife had good-humoredly written him that down would come his picture if he ever failed to send money home.

Wah Gay himself had not gone to church since he quit Miss Clark's evening class at P. S. 23. On Sundays he had gone to the nearby First Presbyterian Church, more to learn conversational English than to practice religion.

At that time, he was helping out at Wang Chuck Ting's. Little did he think then that someday he would do nothing but play mah-jong and the horses. Wah Gay was not the type of man to be against anything. Because he himself did not work, that did not mean he was opposed to working. On the contrary, he believed in working, especially for young, able-bodied men. He wanted to see other people work, particularly his son Ben Loy. Young people, he said, should not be so lazy as to prevent them from working. Many times he had said to Ben Loy: "If you don't work when you're young, you're going to find out that you can't work when you're old."

The fact that Ben Loy had worked steadily and not drifted, like so many other young men in a big city, brought a measure of pride and satisfaction to the father. He ventured to think that, after the marriage, Ben Loy would work that much harder because he would have a family to support. Instead of having to keep track of his son himself, he would have a daughter-in-law to take over the responsibility. A year or so after the wedding, a grandson, perhaps. Or a granddaughter? A boy first? Our Chinese people always like boys. But what if it turns out to be a girl? It would not matter. Girls are better appreciated in America than boys anyway.

He had told Ben Loy to tell his mother that he would like to bring his bride to America with him when he returned to New York. He had hinted that, as a matter of diplomacy, he should at least discuss the matter with his mother and let her decide for him. That was the son's filial duty.

The father's own private feeling, however, was that he would rather see his brand new daughter-in-law remain in China, at least for the time being. She would keep the mother-in-law company and look after her wants until, in a few years perhaps, she would pass away. Then Ben Loy could bring his wife over to the Golden Mountain.

On the other hand, he had no desire to see his son follow his own example of leaving his wife in China permanently. He was hoping that, in the remaining years which marked the late evening of Lau Shee's life, she might find her loneliness more bearable with a daughter-in-law to share her tribulations. And some grandchildren too. The house would be filled with tiny, sweet, innocent voices.

During the ensuing weeks, Wah Gay and Lee Gong kept their little secret to themselves. No one at the Money Come even suspected that Ben Loy was already on his way to China, let alone to marry Lee Gong's only daughter. It would have proved embarrassing if one of the principals undertook to cancel the wedding plans. This way no one would know. But deep in his heart Wah Gay felt it was merely a matter of his son liking the girl. It was inconceivable that any girl should find Ben Loy undesirable as a husband. Everything would go through as planned, if the prospective bridegroom approved of the girl.

In addition to the expense money already given Ben Loy in the form of money orders and certified bank checks, Wah Gay had sent a small remittance to Sang Chong Bakery in Sands Market, owned by a cousin from the same village, for forwarding to his wife Lau Shee. In the accompanying letter he had instructed that a gold necklace at least eight *tsing* in weight be ordered from the local jeweler as a wedding present for the bride from the father-in-law. Ben Loy was an only son. Since there were no other sons, the gift would not set a precedent of expense which would have to be followed for each one.

Wah Gay had suggested to his wife that she should feel free to give whatever she wanted to her future daughter-in-law. Rings, bracelets, gold coins, or even another necklace. Those who could afford it would give many gifts to their daughter-in-law. Wah Gay thought a gold necklace was sufficient. Not that his future daughter-in-law did not deserve more, but he felt that so long as he gave her something, it would satisfy the tradition of gift-giving. Anything more would be vanity. He was not a wealthy man and he did not want to pretend to be one.

In the meantime Lee Gong had written to his wife Jung Shee, telling her that Wang Ben Loy was on the way home, that he was twenty-four years old, a very good boy, a very hard-working boy without vices.

In New York the two old heads bided their time and played mah-jong, knowing that any day now they would become relatives.

X

Sands Market faced north, south, and east. The south entrance served as the main gate, through which thousands of villagers passed on each market day, which for Sands Market happened to be *one* and *six*. The market was popularly referred to simply as One-Six, the first and sixth of each month, followed by the 11th, 16th, 21st, 26th, and 31st—these were the market days. Some came to sell a pig, to visit an herbalist, or a midwife. Some came to buy a salt fish. Others came to sip tea and meet friends.

Sun Lung Lay village was immediately to the west of the market, its back almost touching upon the fringe of stores. A half-moon-shaped pattern of bamboo trees acted as a buffer between the village and the shopping area. Their tops swayed and wiggled as the autumn winds rushed at them, speeding through the village and across the green fields. A narrow cobble-stoned causeway wound its way to the main dirt road that led to the gate of Sands Market. But today was not a market day, and the roads were almost deserted.

It was to this village next to Sands Market that Ben Loy, the *gimshunhock*, had returned a week ago. The entire village had buzzed with excitement at the native's return, an occasion rivaling that of a regular holiday. The New Yorker's sudden appearance at the staid, changeless community brought a fresh new look, like a ripple in the village pond.

Ben Loy and his mother, Lau Shee, picked their way quickly along the uneven stones toward the market. They had chosen the 30th day of September for the meeting, because on a Market Day it would be much too crowded for their purpose. During the week that Ben Loy had been home, many relatives had come with greetings and baskets of food for the *gimshunhock*. And many questions too. When is the first-born going to be married? Would he be interested in a school girl eighteen years old over at

Cactus Village? Would he consider marrying a Hongkong girl? There is a girl over at the market—she is cashier at the tea house. . . .

To all these inquiries from friends and relatives, Lau Shee cautioned patience. Ben Loy is going to see a girl recommended by his father first. A girl from the Lee Village. Wait and see if Ben Loy likes her. . . .

As a matter of formality, Lau Shee had engaged a matchmaker, who was none other than her own sister, Ben Loy's aunt. To arrange this initial meeting the aunt had been shuffling between Sun Lung Lay and Mei Oi's New Peace Village, which had been at the next train stop when Sunwei District still had its railroads and locomotives, before they had been disassembled and buried in scattered areas throughout the land to delay the Japanese advances in 1940. Large craters had been dug every fifty feet or so to impede the Japanese jeeps which an invasion was sure to have brought. Now, when Ben Loy and his mother and aunt reached the main road leading to Sands Market, they had to resort to a single file in passing these big holes.

The air of this autumn day smelled of rain and the misty grey of the sky seemed to act as a valve holding the fine film of spray suspended in midair. You could feel it. You could smell it. You could see it. You could sense it. The air, the sky was charged with rain. It only needed a trigger to start the downpour. Casting an anxious eye on the sky, the men and women carrying baskets loaded with provisions began to step more lively. Others on the road bowed their heads and pulled low their wide-brimmed hats against the winds.

South China was much cooler than Ben Loy had expected. He was glad he had brought his topcoat, which he now wore. He had considered leaving this coat in New York because it took up so much space in his luggage.

"This year the cool weather has come early," said Ben Loy's mother when she saw her son pulling up the collar of his coat. Ben Loy said China, being in the south, should have a warmer climate, but his words were lost in the rush of winds.

Noting that it was almost twelve o'clock, Ben Loy and the two women went directly to the Jing Ming Gold Shop instead of dropping off at Sang Chong Bakery first; as was their custom whenever they came to the market. Sang Chong Bakery was owned by a younger half-brother of Wang Chuck Ting. Lau Shee had used the bakery as a mail drop and it was to this store that Ben Loy and Wah Gay always sent their letters. Ben Loy and the two women hurried on to the gold store on the other side of the market, where they were to meet Miss Lee and her mother at noon. When they reached the shop, mother and son stood outside and pretended to look at the display window while Aunt Gim Fung entered the store. She emerged immediately and signaled for them to come in.

After the usual introductory amenities and references to the weather, Ben Loy awkwardly suggested that they go to the Three Star Tea House for "a drink of tea." On the way out, Ben Loy asked the manager to join them; but he politely declined the invitation.

Although it was not market day, the Three Star was rapidly filling up. They found themselves at a table by the corner and ordered tea for seven. In addition to her mother and the matchmaker, the girl's party included her Number Three Aunt.

As soon as they all sat down, the young lady who had come to be inspected unbuttoned her black coat. She did not remove it, because the tea house was without heat. Underneath the coat, she wore a dull blue cotton *long dress*. The girl's lovely features were accentuated by her ordinary apparel, and Ben Loy liked her all the more for her lack of pretentiousness.

His eyes took in the full beauty of Miss Lee's oval face. The soft, clear skin was without blemish, smooth like ivory. Ben Loy's hand moved, as if wanting to touch it to be convinced that it was real. Her eyebrows were like the crescent of the new moon. Her full lips, forming a small mouth, were cherry-red. Her nose was straight and delicate, perfect as a distant star.

"Miss Lee," Ben Loy tried to make conversation, "where did you go to school?" His eyes saw no one else but her. He thought he saw etched on that enchanting face sympathy and understanding, goodness and beauty. He wanted to touch her snow-white hands, which were toying with the chop sticks before her. Her fingers were delicately feminine, not rough and round-tipped

50

like his own. His heart began to throb a song of love. He was enthusiastically in favor of the wedding plans which his father and the girl's father had made for them. But there was something he had to know.

Yesterday his mother had told him of a marriage in which the bride, a beautiful girl, had said nothing at the introductory meeting with her prospective husband. When the future mother-in-law asked her why she did not speak, the matchmaker and the girl's mother both intervened to say the girl was extremely shy, especially when with strangers. The explanation was accepted as satisfactory and, accordingly, plans were set for the wedding. It was only after the wedding that the husband had learned that his bride was mute.

After he had asked the question about her schooling, Ben Loy's eyes fell anxiously on Mei Oi's lips, watching for their slightest movement. They began to curve slowly into a smile. Her eyes stole a furtive glance at the boy from New York, only to learn, to her embarrassment, that he was intently staring at her. Her smooth, unpowdered face reddened and she began staring blankly into her tea cup, as if studying her own reflection.

"At the present time I'm attending the Wah Que School of English," she managed to say, keeping her eyes on the cup.

Ben Loy's face lit up with a wide smile. Ah, she could speak. For a moment he had feared that this might turn out to be another case of the beautiful but dumb bride. What else did he need to know? He had seen that she could walk, she could see, and now she could talk and smile too.

"Our Mei Oi used to attend the Que Jeng Middle School and only recently transferred to the Wah Que so that she could learn more English," her mother volunteered.

Ben Loy's first thought was: So she's expecting to go to America.

"Mei Oi is an excellent student, Mr. Wang," said the Lee matchmaker. "She gets first in everything. No matter what she does, she is first. Always first."

"Mei Oi *is* a very bright girl," added her Number Three Aunt.

"Did your daughter finish middle school?" asked Lau Shee.

"Yes, she did," replied Jung Shee. "She finished last June and has just started at the Wah Que School of English." She paused and wondered if she should continue with what she wanted to say. After a moment of hesitation, she continued, "Nowadays so many school girls are being married to *gimshunhocks.*" She smiled apologetically. "We thought that we might send Mei Oi to a school that specializes in English. So that if she had an opportunity to go to the Beautiful Country, she would know a few phrases."

"Nowadays every girl goes to school," laughed the matchmaker, "because she wants to marry a *gimshunhock.*"

"And every *gimshunhock* wants to marry a girl who can read and write," chuckled Ben Loy.

Stares and whispers soon came from nearby tables. They pointed at the *gimshunhock* with the young lady whose long black hair fell gracefully on her shoulders. Their companions, short-coated, whose wind-swept and sun-drenched complexions blended congruously with the rest of the teahouse customers, were completely ignored. But Ben Loy and Mei Oi were like characters out of story books. The gold prospector from the Golden Mountain. The school girl, the educated girl in the *long dress.* Someone who could read and write among a majority who could do neither.

The matchmaking party abruptly changed their topic of discussion to the impending storm. But hardly a minute had passed when Number Three Aunt spoke up: "You'd make a perfect couple," she beamed at Ben Loy and Mei Oi. "Mei Oi is educated and intelligent and pretty. And Mr. Wang here knows his words and ink. Not only that but he is a *gimshunhock.* If you go to the four corners of the earth, you could not find a better-suited husband and wife." Everyone laughed except Mei Oi, who seemed embarrassed.

"No matter what you do," said Ben Loy's aunt tartly, "there is no need to hurry."

Mei Oi edged over to Ben Loy. "Mr. Wang, when will we meet again?" she asked shyly.

"Soon, I hope," said Ben Loy, flattered by the question.

"We will see how the birthdays come out," said Lau Shee. "See what the red book has to say."

With neither side wanting to commit themselves, the parties returned to their respective homes. It was understood that a future meeting would be arranged through one of the match-makers. Back at home Ben Loy anxiously asked his mother, "Ma, how do you like the girl?"

"The girl seems to be well-proportioned," said the mother. "Not too small and not too skinny. She looks like an alert person."

"Well, do you like her?" persisted Ben Loy.

"Being a church-going woman, I don't suppose I should be bothered with the fortune-teller but your aunt tells me I ought to have Fourth Uncle look at the girl's time of birth." She paused and then added. "There's no harm in that." She pulled out a crumpled piece of red paper from her pocket and showed it to Ben Loy. "Is this the one?"

Ben Loy studied the calligraphy written in thick black ink. Lee: Mei Oi . . . 18 years old . . . 9th hour March 15th.

"Yes, this is it." He handed it back to her.

Lau Shee took the paper and headed for Fourth Uncle's mud hut. When she returned an hour later, she told Ben Loy that, according to the village conjurer, there was no obstacle to such a union.

"Then the thing is settled!" exclaimed Ben Loy, greatly relieved at his mother's findings. "We can go and see her tomorrow."

"Not so fast," cautioned Lau Shee. "We haven't heard from the girl's mother yet."

The following day Jung Shee's matchmaker showed up at the *gimshunhock's* house about noon, excited and out of breath. "The girl's mother said everybody is saying that American soldiers returning to China all have artificial limbs," she announced heatedly. "They are either lepers or are with unnatural legs." She paused to catch her breath, adding that a woman of her age grew breathless from all that walking from Mei Oi's village on such a chilly day. "I told them all this talk about artificial legs and diseases is rumor. You know how people talk. But Mei Oi's mother . . ."

"You go back and tell her my Ben Loy is a healthy boy with two good hands and legs," Lau Shee shouted, pointing to her son.

"She asked me to be sure and take a look at Mr. Wang's legs," said the matchmaker uncertainly.

"You will do no such thing!" screamed Lau Shee.

Before his mother could stop it, Ben Loy quickly pulled both his trouser legs up above his knees. "Here, look. Take a good look," he laughed.

The old matchmaker sprung her neck out like a chicken picking at grains in the open courtyard, and sniffed at Ben Loy's exposed legs. The *gimshunhock* raised his hand and slapped hard at the calf: "See? Flesh and blood."

"Heh heh heh, that's what I've told them right along," remarked the matchmaker dryly and left.

XI

For the next few days Lau Shee was furiously busy preparing to acquire a daughter-in-law. The two matchmakers trekked back and forth between Mei Oi's and Ben Loy's village, making known the respective wishes of the two families. Lau Shee had consulted Uncle Four for a propitious wedding day. He, after looking up the young couple's birthdays in the red book, made calculations with the charts and diagrams that were the secrets of his profession. Then he declared October 16th was the most auspicious day for the wedding.

When informed of this choice, Jung Shee checked the date with her own fortune-teller and gave it immediate approval. Not being a church-going Christian, Mei Oi's mother said she would do her share as she was brought up to do. She would observe all the traditional Chinese holidays and would present, as long as her daughter remained living in her husband's village, all the favors that were customarily a mother-in-law's offering to the bridegroom's household.

Jung Shee did not want to be accused of flouting traditions; for traditions were her world. If she had had a son, she certainly would have liked the girl's family to observe all the holidays when he got married. She preferred to have the bride come in a sedan chair, wearing red instead of white. But she was willing to make some concessions to the young ones, if need be.

Although all their cousins and relatives had been informed of the *new generation* wedding, they brought many baskets of rice, chickens, cloth materials, scrolls and wicker chairs for the couple. The living room bulged with these gifts, creating an atmosphere of festivity. The week before, in preparation for the arrival of these gifts, Lau Shee had gathered several branch-sticks from the trees along the stream and tied them together to make a broom. She had dusted the walls, the ceilings, all the hidden corners.

On the second day of the general cleaning chore, Ben Loy, as a gesture of filial affection, had said feebly, "Mother, let me help you." He had come to realize what a selfless mother he had, always working on his behalf.

She stopped dusting momentarily and smiled fondly at her son. "Ben Loy, you're not used to this sort of work, and you don't know how. Now get out of here before you get yourself all dirty."

Ben Loy half-leaned on the threshold. He told himself that he did not like this old house any more. With America still fresh in his mind, the house represented another age, another world to him. He was critical of his old surroundings. The dirt floor seemed dirty. The doors were narrow and rickety and old. The blackened stove looked like it was ready for the junk yard instead of for cooking. Only the thought that his was a temporary separation made it easier for him to bear his nostalgia for his adopted land.

He remembered well the custom in the village "to beat the dirt" before New Year's. His mother used to holler at him when he was still a boy, "Ben Loy, take these cauldron covers to the stream and wash them!" Or "What are you standing there for? Go and carry me some water!"

But now Ben Loy was a grown man, about to be married. More than that, he was a *gimshunhock*. And *gimshunhocks* don't go around washing cauldron covers in the stream. Ben Loy chuckled to himself as he quickened his steps toward the public square.

The week before, Ben Loy's mother had said she would sleep in the living room, leaving her bedroom to the newlyweds. The son replied that, since he and his bride would be staying home only temporarily, they would sleep in the living room. But Lau Shee was adamant. She would not have it otherwise. Since time immemorial, she explained, the mother-in-law always gave up her own living quarters for the bride and groom when there was no other room in the house.

On the day of the wedding, the sun came out early and flooded the entire market square with a brilliance seldom seen on an October day. The autumn winds disappeared as if by pre-arrangement and a calm settled upon the cluster of stores that made up the market. The 16th was also market day. The usual market day crowds came and went, perhaps in less of a hurry to hustle indoors because of the beautiful weather. The impending marriage of Ben Loy and Mei Oi drew no more than passing interest among the multitude of shoppers. Everyone seemed intent upon business of his own. The market day shopper might be just curious enough to pause for a glimpse of the wedding, then move on in his perennially hurried pace.

Some of the wedding guests mingled in the immediate vicinity of the church on Tsing Dow Road, standing in the sun, chatting, reluctant to go indoors. Everyone seemed on the lookout for the arrival of additional guests; for they peered up and down the street in anticipation. The stiffness and the luster, plus the creases in the material, indicated that many of them were wearing their suits for the first time. After today, this would be their banquet suit, to be worn again on the next holiday.

Other than the holiday attire of the guests, the church could boast of no new decorations. It was like any other store in the row of buildings that lined the street, except that across the entrance were the words *Sunday Auditorium*.

Some of the guests had come from as far as five hours' walking distance. Yok Ling, once a servant girl in the home of Wang Wah Gay and later married off as his daughter to a fisherman in Kwonghoi, had arrived with her three children. Her husband, Boon Tong, could not come because he was away on a fishing junk in Chong-chow, a tiny island southeast of Hongkong. Ben Loy's aunt was busily directing the arriving guests to seats. She was all over the place shouting, "Sit down. Sit down! The wedding will begin soon."

Her husband, Bok Hey, the youngest of the three Bok brothers, had come home from the Phillipines especially for the nephew's wedding. He and his brothers owned the Manila Bakery and this was his fifth trip home. When asked about his frequent trips home, he often remarked: "Oh, going to Manila is just like going to the market." Or "I'm just working for the steamship company."

He was a tanned man in his forties whose black hair was beginning to recede on the forehead. Their three sons, Do Sing, Do Dot, Do Ming, darted in and out of the church. They liked to run down the street to the furniture store and watch the men saw wood. Ben Loy called after them, "Don't go too far away or you'll get lost!" It gave him a feeling of dignity and authority, calling after these youngsters.

"We won't get lost, Loy *gaw*," they said and raced down the street.

Ben Loy stood and watched them until they stopped abruptly in front of the furniture store. He could see them gesturing with their hands and making comments on the various works in progress at the store. He indulged in a fleeting dream that someday he and Mei Oi would have three little boys just like those he was now watching.

The sedan chair carriers had been instructed to bring the bride directly to the entrance of the church. When the bride alighted in her traditionally red Chinese gown, Ben Loy, Lau Shee, the Reverend Young Fen Tung, and the two matchmakers were on hand to greet her. The bride's mother and Lee Hing, the uncle, arrived a few moments later in separate chairs. Lee Hing had recently returned from Rangoon, where he had been abroad for the past seven years. He had come home to pick himself another bride, for his first wife had died from pneumonia the year before. There had been some talk as to who would be married first, the uncle or the niece. But when Uncle Hing learned that Mei Oi was about to be betrothed, he postponed his own plans of marriage until after his niece's wedding.

The bride was escorted at once to the little room normally reserved for the minister's use. A cluster of people soon gathered around her. Mei Oi's mother fought her way out of the room, after cautioning her daughter to stay there until called. In the meantime the two matchmakers were busy yelling for everybody to get out of the room, declaring that everybody was in the way. They shrieked loudest at the children, but none paid any attention to them.

A real surprise had come from Ben Loy's roommate. Chin Yuen had written to his mother in the south coast town of Kwonghoi, requesting her to send *whiskey and rice* to do honor to the marriage of his friend Ben Loy. Chin Yuen's mother herself did not come. The gifts came in the name of Chin Yuen: Two large baskets of old October rice and two large porcelain jugs of whiskey arrived by carriers the day before. Ben Loy was very pleased to receive them, and he smiled to himself: Chin Yuen is a good friend. He has a good heart.

His aunt's three little boys returned to the church area, hopping and skipping happily. A gleam showed on Ben Loy's face, an inward happiness that comes with the knowledge that others are happy and carefree. Watching these youngsters, he again could not help but hope that someday he and Mei Oi would have children of their own. He did not think, however, he would be lucky enough to have three boys in a row, like his aunt.

More guests arrived. Ben Loy was embarrassed because he did not know their identities when they greeted him on arrival. But he did the best he could under the circumstances by nodding and smiling to everyone. When two middle-aged women came in together, he said to them: "Are the children on good behavior?"

They stared blandly at him, because they were childless.

Inside the church, what seemed an empty store suddenly took on the shape of an auditorium. Above the ding of many voices, one could hear, "Please be seated. Please be seated."

The speaker was a young man with curly black hair. He wore a grey tweed suit. He raised his hand high. "Please sit down, everybody. The wedding will take place in just a moment." Someone whispered that he was the minister's aid, a divinity student from Chung Sun University.

Slowly the guests began to take their seats, and soon a quiet settled upon the gathered group. At a nod from the minister, the organist began playing the wedding march.

Mei Oi walked slowly down the aisle on the arm of her father's brother, Lee Hing, who, perhaps because of unfamiliarity with the dress and the role, looked a little awkward. There had been a suggestion that he wear a western suit for his role of giving the bride away, but he finally settled for a borrowed Chinese gown. The uncle's face was almost as flushed as the bride's, as he proceeded toward the altar with Mei Oi on his arm. The upturned faces of many of the wedding guests were turned toward the man in the loosely fitting gown instead of the bride. Here and there were a grin and hushed giggle. And Mei Oi seemed to have difficulty in suppressing a chuckle of her own.

Mei Oi, beautiful and radiant in a red Chinese velvet gown, kept her lowered eyes on the aisle, giving everyone the impression she was a blushingly shy bride. The rouge on her cheeks made the blushing more evident. She was thinking that her uncle would feel more at home with a Chinese writing brush or clucking the beads on an abacus.

Ben Loy, with his Uncle Bok Hey beside him, was already there waiting for the bride. The tall, lanky and tanned Bok Hey presented a marked contrast to the white-faced Ben Loy. Uncle Bok Hey's only experience with the sky-blue gown he was wearing had been to see someone else wearing it on festive occasions. He had borrowed the gown from the village school master.

Ben Loy had deferred to the wishes of his mother and had on a dark brown gown. He began to wonder which one of them was more uncomfortable in the unaccustomed outfits. He thought his uncle looked funny in the gown, and was about to burst forth with a chuckle when he realized that he himself might look equally funny to the people who had gathered there to watch them. A short while ago he had heard a little boy remark, "Look, see how funny he looks!"

Mei Oi was standing to his left. At her closeness Ben Loy's heart throbbed faster.

The elderly Reverend Young Fen Tung, black-robed and bespectacled, began to intone slowly, deliberately, "You, Lee Mei Oi, and you, Wang Ben Loy, have taken a big step along the highway of life. You have undertaken the greatest social act known to man throughout the ages. Marriage is a sacred act and, with the help of God, you two will walk down the highway of life through fog and rain, through brightness and sunshine. . . . Now you have come before the altar of God . . . to be united in marriage . . . and once you are pronounced man and wife, let no man, no man tear asunder. Like many things, my friends, marriage is not all happiness. It is a challenging situation. In times of doubt and sorrow, be a comfort to each other, for together you will succeed. . . . Do you, Wang Ben Loy, take Lee Mei Oi for your beloved wedded wife? . . . And do you, Lee Mei Oi, take for your beloved wedded husband Wang Ben Loy?"

60

Ben Loy nervously slid the diamond ring on Mei Oi's finger and, somewhat stiffly, kissed her.

Back in the village, since the early morning hours, the *small-borns* had been busy preparing the wedding banquet. When the bride and bridegroom arrived home in sedan chairs after the church ceremony, the tables were already set and some of them overflowed into the public square. The unusually warm weather made the guests comment over and over again how kind the Lord had been and what a propitious day it was.

The banquet lasted two hours.

XII

Mei Oi had met her father for the first time at Idlewild Airport when she and her husband arrived from San Francisco. She had not known which one was her father until the white-haired, slightly-built man wearing a brown, double-breasted suit that needed pressing edged forward and called out, "Mei Oi!"

"Papa!" Mei Oi was trying to find some resemblance between this man and the pictures that she had seen of him back home, pictures that had been taken a long time ago. Her father placed an arm around her shoulder, "Daughter, daughter!"

"She's air-sick," volunteered Ben Loy. A gust of wind raised and lowered everybody's hair.

The larger man with a cigar in his mouth next stepped forward. His hand went up to his mouth and the cigar dropped out of sight. "*Ah Sow*," he bowed slightly.

Mei Oi blushed. "*Lao Yair*," she bowed, assuming this man was her father-in-law.

Ben Loy's father, Wah Gay, extended his hand to his new daughter-in-law; but Mei Oi failed to take it, whereupon he quickly switched it to his son. "Loy, how are you?"

"Ah Loy!" Lee Gong shook hands with his son-in-law.

They hailed a taxi and headed for Manhattan. Mei Oi was sick from the plane ride. To her the trip downtown was an endless stream of turns and stops. Turns and stops. She only half-heartedly answered her father's question about her mother and the village. Her father-in-law thoughtfully put out his cigar.

"We must give a banquet to celebrate the wedding," said Wah Gay as the taxi rolled down Second Avenue toward China-town. "After all, you, Ah Loy, are my only son." He turned to the bride's father, "You, my good friend . . . you have only this

62

little girl . . . heh heh. It's only right we should give a banquet in honor of the marriage."

Later that day Wah Gay and Lee Gong brought noodles and won ton, telling the young ones that these were good for Mei Oi's upset stomach.

XIII

Still unnerved by the prostitute's early morning call, Ben Loy got up at ten that morning to go to work for Chin Yuen, who was ill. He was not anxious to go back to work so soon after his return to New York, but Chin Yuen was a good friend. He did not want to leave Mei Oi.

"Are you sure you'll be all right?" he asked tenderly.

"I'll be all right," she said from her bed. "You go ahead and go to work."

"If anybody should come, just ignore him," he said. He was afraid someone else might come to the apartment. When he had shared the apartment with Chin Yuen, loose women came to the apartment at all hours. He was ashamed of his past and he certainly did not want his wife to learn about it.

Left alone, Mei Oi slept until noon. When she tried to get up, the four walls of the bedroom whirled before her. The floor underneath her feet shook like a hog just out of a mud puddle in the village square. The effects of the plane ride from Hongkong to New York were still with her. She had been ill the day before and had eaten little since. She sank down on the edge of the bed. Her elbows rested on her thighs, supporting her forehead with her hands. The ceiling swayed back and forth. Back and forth. Mei Oi closed her eyes tightly, holding back her tears.

The physical illness was just a temporary inconvenience, Mei Oi knew. In another day, or at most in a few days more, the dizziness from the plane ride would disappear. The giddiness came only when she stood up. As long as she remained in bed, she was relatively immune to the ill effects of the trip.

In the early morning when the buzzer had awakened her, she had been warmly receptive to Ben Loy's ardent kisses, hoping that they would lead to the act of love. Aside from the physical pleasure she would have derived from the union, it would have indicated to her that her man still loved her. When Ben Loy had turned away, she felt unwanted and useless. She had tried to console herself with the thought that her husband was being considerate and did not want to make demands upon her when she was still sick from the trip. But his monk-like behavior had begun even before she set foot on the airplane.

The first few weeks of her marriage had been happy; for Ben Loy was considerate, masterful and understanding in his role as a bridegroom. It was only when they had gone to the hotel in Hongkong that the sudden change in him had occurred. The first night at the All Seas Hotel Ben Loy had failed miserably at making love. He was no more successful on subsequent nights. She had hoped his lack of ardor was only temporary and that soon she would again enjoy him as a husband.

After what seemed like the trekking of a thousand li, Mei Oi slowly opened her eyes. A relative calm had returned to the room. The walls no longer whirled and the water buffalo beneath the floor had gone. She could see the windows and the dresser clearly now. The bluish linoleum floor looked nice and smooth and shiny. The large pendulum that was their bedroom had run out of momentum. Soon it would be stilled completely and Mei Oi would see things in their true perspective.

She flopped over on her stomach and buried her head in the pillow. Sobs, like a baby's whimpers, came to her freely and unashamedly in her solitude. Her heart had wanted to cry out for the past few weeks, but she did not want to cry in front of her husband.

A few short weeks ago she was still a girl. Her mother's daughter. Now she was a woman and a wife. She had looked forward to her marriage with excited anticipation. Like many girls of her own age, she had hoped to marry a *gimshunhock* and come to America to start a new family. Her mother had often said to her: "Mei Oi, I hope you will marry a *gimshunhock* and go to America with him. Then you will see him in the morning and at night."

It was obvious her mother was thinking of her own husband, Mei Oi's father, who had left her to return to America months before Mei Oi was born. Mei Oi was too shy to show any outward emotions during this discussion of marriage with her mother. But inwardly she had wanted very much to marry a *gimshunhock* and come to the Beautiful Country and raise a family. To her mother she would only say modestly, "I'm not that fortunate."

She knew she wouldn't marry a farmer. A farmer's wife worked from dawn till dusk out in the fields. She could see all around her farmers' wives toiling incessantly, gathering firewood, turning the earth, planting, harvesting, exposed to the elements in all sorts of weather. Cracked hands. Calloused feet. A face bronzed and lined and hardened by the wind and sun. Not a pretty picture, but a common one. Marry a school teacher? Not Mei Oi. There was this common observation. Unless you're poor, you would not be teaching.

After many months of anxiety and waiting, there had come a letter from her father, Lee Gong in New York, informing her mother that he was sending home a prospective son-in-law in the person of one Wang Ben Loy.

And now that she had married Wang Ben Loy and come to New York, the greatest and most beautiful city in all the world, she should be happy, very happy. A whole new panorama of fertile fields lay before her. Youth. Dreams. The future. All that a girl from New Peace Village in Sunwei could ever hope for.

But today her frustrations and heaviness of heart dwarfed even the discomforts of her illness from the plane. Mei Oi, the bride of two months, lay alone on her bed, troubled and uncommunicative, separated by ten thousand li of oceans and mountains from her mother, whose love and encouragement she urgently needed now. Over and over she asked herself: What did I do to Ben Loy to make him stop loving me?

Finally, exhausted by tears and emotion, she fell asleep again.

When she awoke in mid-afternoon, she felt better. The ill effects of the plane ride seemed to have been washed away by her tears. She got up and stretched and yawned. Cry some more? How much can you cry? Who can hear you cry? And who cares when you are ten thousand folds of mountains away from home? Go ahead, Mei Oi, she told herself, go ahead and cry. And see who will pity you.

That night when Ben Loy came home from work it was almost

one o'clock in the morning. Mei Oi was waiting up for him. She had bathed and powdered her skin with talcum, in anticipation of her husband's return. When the lock on the door finally clicked, she was tense and full of expectation. Her heart pounded furiously against her ribs. But she wore a bright smile on her face. As she hurried from the bedroom, where she had been resting, to the living room to meet Ben Loy, she was like a little school girl let out for summer vacation.

"Loy *Gaw*," she said daintily, coming up to him and taking his coat and hat. "Was business good today?" She kissed him on the cheek.

"Not bad," replied Ben Loy, pleased with Mei Oi's attentions. "I was not familiar with where the things were and that made it difficult."

"I understand," said Mei Oi. She timidly took his hand and guided him to the sofa. "Today is the first time you went to work since you married me." She nestled closer to him, still holding his left hand with her right.

Mei Oi's mind flashed back to her wedding night when she had stood before the brand new wash basin, which was part of her dowry, and washed her face and hands many times, wanting to delay the consummation of her marriage. Ben Loy was sitting by the edge of the bed, a ready and eager bridegroom. When he saw she was dallying, he had strolled over to her and carried her to the bed. With gentle hands, he had first unbuttoned her coat, and then untied her trouser string and, over her weak protestations, pulled off her pants.

"Do you remember our wedding night?" Mei Oi asked, full of excitement. She placed her head on his shoulder and wrapped her arms around him. "At first I was afraid but you made me very happy. Do you . . . Loy *Gaw* . . . do you want to make me very happy tonight?"

"I am tired," said Ben Loy. He took his wife in his arms and kissed her mechanically on the lips. He stroked her long black hair. "It was hard work at the restaurant. I am sleepy and tired."

Trying to fight back her tears, Mei Oi abruptly got up and walked to the bedroom. It took her a long time to fall asleep; but Ben Loy was snoring within minutes after he got into bed.

67

XIV

Wah Gay went ahead with plans for a marriage banquet. He had considered not having the party at all, but he dismissed the idea quickly. After all, Ben Loy was his only son. During the father's many-times-ten-years in New York, he had been invited to all kinds of celebrations: Weddings, hair-cut parties, departures for China, new arrivals from China. During the days when two Chinese opera companies played to standing room only, he was frequently invited to sit down and dine with the stage celebrities after the show. Now, with the return of Ben Loy and his bride, it was only fitting that the brand-new father-in-law invite his friends and cousins to celebrate the auspicious occasion. The banquet at the village did not count, according to Wah Gay. This was New York, where another set of friends and cousins waited expectantly.

This probably would be only the beginning, for what would be more proper and natural than to celebrate the birth of a grandchild in another year or so? Wah Gay beamed when he thought of a yet-to-be-born grandchild. He would become a grandpa. Just thinking about it made him happy.

With two hundred and fifty invitation cards in raised gold letters already sent out, Wah Gay once more settled down to relax at his favorite pastime and occupation. Normally in-laws among the Chinese would shy away from the gaming tables when the other was present, in order to avoid any possible embarrassment. But as far as Wah Gay and Lee Gong were concerned, the marriage of their offspring placed no such restriction on their social activities. The two continued to play mah-jong just like old times.

There was, however, one added chore for Wah Gay. A steady stream of invited guests would come in to congratulate him, each bearing a red envelope containing money. To the bearer of each envelope, Wah Gay would say, "Heh heh, there's no need for this, old friend." He would hand each a red printed thank-you card and a cigar. He kept the thank-you cards handy, right next to the mah-jongs. When he had received fifteen to twenty of these money-bearing envelopes, he would tie them with a rubber band to keep them more orderly. Soon his desk in the back room began to bulge with these envelopes and their contents. Wah Gay himself would not open them. He would turn them over to his son and daughter-in-law after the banquet.

The day of the banquet broke clear and sunny but, toward the latter part of the afternoon, the sun began to fade and patches of clouds floated eastward. An hour before banquet time, a slight drizzle began to descend upon Chinatown. The neon lights on Mott Street came on earlier than usual. The streets and sidewalks soon were wet. A semi-darkness commenced creeping upon this city within a city.

Automobiles and taxis stopped and crawled. Started and stopped. People darted in and out of traffic. Umbrellas bobbed up and down. Neon lights flickered in the distance. The wetness of the asphalt pavement reflected the lit-up pagoda roof of the Grand China Restaurant.

There had been no mah-jong playing for Wah Gay this afternoon. He and Lee Gong had been sitting idly in the basement club house until 5:30, when they trotted over to a cigar store on Chatham Square to pick up cigarettes and cigars for the banquet. Wah Gay found out, when he called to check, that the liquor had been delivered to the restaurant by Wing Lee Wei Company.

When the two fathers arrived at the restaurant, Ah Song, the club house hanger-on, and Chong Loo, the rent collector, were already there. Wah Gay had asked them to help out at the banquet. Chong Loo tore a small opening in each package of cigarettes and placed one to a table. Ah Song instructed the waiters to open a bottle of Haig and Haig and a bottle of Johnnie Walker for each table. Outside in the vestibule, the flowers which the florist had delivered a few minutes earlier awaited attention. Ah Song asked one of the waiters for a flower vase with which to decorate the head table.

Dinner at six, show up at seven. That's a prevailing Chinese custom. Although the invitation card said six o'clock, in all probability the dinner would not start until sometime after seven. Ben Loy and his bride did not arrive until a few minutes after six. Mei Oi's face was flushed slightly from the brisk walk to the restaurant. Her red satin Chinese gown fitted her snugly.

The moment the couple entered the restaurant, Ah Song appeared at the doorway with roses for Mei Oi. He proceeded to pin the flowers on Mei Oi's gown, while the bridegroom stood by awkwardly. From where they sat watching, the respective fathers-in-law were open-mouthed at the scene. The bride's face reddened noticeably.

Wah Gay, his face flushed, and mindful of Ah Song's reputation with women, was angry at himself for having asked Ah Song to help out. Ordinarily the incident itself would have been nothing scandalous; but Ah Song was famous for this sort of thing.

Wah Gay leaned over to Lee Gong and whispered, "That sonovabitch Ah Song is no damned good." They hoped that not too many of the guests had seen the episode. It had occurred in the vestibule, screened off from the rest of the dining room by a partition.

Ben Loy quickly steered his bride toward the head table, where no guests had been seated yet. Wah Gay now stood by the entrance, welcoming the arriving guests, while Lee Gong was sitting nearby, content to let his old friend play the host. Wang Chuck Ting, also sitting nearby, had been asked by Wah Gay to be master of ceremonies. Now, as Ben Loy and Mei Oi approached the head table, the president of the Wang Association got up and nodded to them. He shook hands with Ben Loy and bowed slightly to the bride. The seating of the bridal couple created a babble among the guests as they whispered comments on the bride's beauty.

After having seated Mei Oi at the head table, Ben Loy joined his father at the reception line. Children were running helter-skelter in all directions. Waiters were bringing ice cubes and ginger ale for the tables. The manager came out of his cashier's cage and walked over to the microphone, which was at the left of the head table, and tested it by counting into it.

The guests continued to stream in, reaching a crescendo at

70

about six-thirty, and then began to taper off. Smoke filled the dining room rapidly.

The drizzle, light as it was, had brought out an assortment of umbrellas and these were evident everywhere throughout the large dining room. As the room became more fully filled, the waiters had to twist and turn to make their way through the zig-zagged pattern of round tables, which were much too close together. Shortly after six-forty-five, the stream of arriving guests had dwindled to a trickle. Those who had arrived early were getting restless. There was much turning of heads and frequent consultation with their watches. The late arrivals were expecting the commencement of speeches momentarily. Wah Gay, now seated at the head table, looked in the direction of the doorway to see if anyone else was coming in. Then he consulted his watch. Five minutes past seven. He leaned over and whispered into Wang Chuck Ting's ear.

The President of the Wang Association, a man in his seventies, who would look quite at home with a vest pocket watch and a gold chain dangling across his slightly bulging stomach, slowly got up and walked over to the microphone. "Uncles, brothers, aunts, sisters, and honored guests, little brother appreciates the privilege tonight to welcome you all on behalf of our host, Mr. Cousin Wah Gay. He has set these inadequate tables for you as a token of thanks and appreciation for your generous gifts. Although his beloved son, Mr. Cousin Ben Loy, and Mr. Lee Gong's daughter, Miss Lee Mei Oi, have been married in the old country, Mr. Cousin Wah Gay is not one to forget his friends and cousins and relatives in New York. On the occasion of the marriage of his son Ben Loy to Miss Lee, he wants to share this happiness with you all. . . . Now I would like to introduce to you the President of the Wang Association, Mr. Cousin Fook Ming, to say a few words . . ."

The guests stirred in their seats and applauded politely. Some craned their necks to see who was going to talk. Many were indifferent. A man almost directly opposite the banquet chairman got up and walked over to the microphone. He was a pale, thin, bespectacled man in his late fifties. Actually he was a Vice-President of the Wang Association, but, in keeping with custom, he was introduced as President. "First of all," he began, "I want to introduce to you our host, Mr. Cousin Wah Gay."

Wang Wah Gay got up and beamingly acknowledged the applause.

"Mr. Lee Gong, father of the lovely bride."

Lee Gong got up and bowed to the upturned, smiling faces.

"The bride and bridegroom, Mr. and Mrs. Ben Loy."

The newlyweds rose and waved to the guests. The applause was by far the loudest.

"And now I would like to introduce some officers of the Wang Association . . . Mr. Cousin Ping Wah, Treasurer of the Association . . . Mr. Cousin Won Duck, Chinese Language Secretary . . . Mr. Cousin Kuen Jay, English Language Secretary . . . Mr. Eng Ho Soon, President of Ping On Tong . . ."

The obliging audience applauded everybody who rated an introduction. Many consulted their watches for the second and third time. Children drained dry their glasses of water. Here and there a mother cautioned her restless youngster to keep quiet.

Wang Chuck Ting next introduced Wang Doo Ott, Second Vice-President of the Wang Association, but he, too, was introduced as *the* president of the Association. "On behalf of Mr. Cousin Wah Gay," began Vice-President Doo Ott, "the bride and bridegroom, I want to thank you all for the many gifts, for the monies, thank you for your time. By your presence here tonight, you have given our host a big face. . . . Please drink heartily."

Wang Chuck Ting again got up. "I invite you to drink many drinks and to use your chop sticks generously. We all hope that by this time next year, we will once again lift up our glasses and drink many drinks."

Another round of applause broke out among the guests. At the head table, Ben Loy gazed at the carnation in his lapel, while Mei Oi opened her pocketbook and took a quick glance at the tiny mirror. Ben Loy eyed her longingly. He was very proud of her tonight. He thought she looked very lovely in her red gown.

Someone at the table said, "Next year we will drink to the first baby."

Embarrassed, Mei Oi lowered her eyes and focused them on

the chop sticks in front of her.

Wang Chuck Ting continued, "Today is an excellent day for a holiday. The rain and wind will bring good fortune and good luck to the newlyweds."

When the toastmaster finally sat down he turned to Ben Loy. "Little brother, how did you come to pick such a lovely bride?" Ben Loy mumbled that the bride had been already picked out for him by his father. To this Wang Chuck Ting chuckled, "I wish *my* father had been so good at picking himself a daughter-in-law!" Laughter broke out at the table. Hardly had the laughter died down, when Chuck Ting opened his mouth again. "Heh heh, next year around this time, we'll drink again. We'll drink to their first-born."

A shy smile appeared on Mei Oi's face, now fully flushed. Ben Loy tried to suppress a grin.

A few late comers straggled in and, after looking around, found seats without too much inconvenience to the rest of the guests. The pandemonium of the crowd blended with the clinking of ice cubes being gingerly dropped into glasses. Wah Gay cheerfully picked up one of the bottles and started pouring for his distinguished guests. He even poured one for his new daughter-in-law, who feebly protested that she did not ,drink. Right away a chorus of protests arose from the other guests.

"If you never drank before in your life," said Wang Chuck Ting, "tonight you must drink, for tonight is a big holiday."

The crimson of Mei Oi's face deepened. From a nearby table, unnoticed by Mei Oi, Ah Song stole repeated glances in her direction.

By the time the waiters brought out the *little dishes*, the guests were famished. They attacked the food with enthusiasm. Soon the sweet and pungent spareribs, the one-thousand-year eggs, the spiced gizzards, and shrimp chips were gone. Next the waiters brought out a large bowl of soup for each table. Ben Loy gazed at the thick shark-fin soup sprinkled with powdery Virginia ham. After a moment's hesitation, he picked up the small ladle in front of him and began serving the guests.

"Let's not stand on ceremony," Chuck Ting protested. He reached over and picked up Wah Gay's bowl. "Here, fill up your father's first."

"Don't forget the bride," someone said. Ben Loy sheepishly picked up Mei Oi's bowl.

"I just want a little," she said.

Chuck Ting raised his glass. "Let's drink to the bride and bridegroom."

The soup was followed by *Wor Shew Up, Bird's Nest Chicken, Lobster Egg Roll, Mushrooms, Squabs* . . . all in rapid succession amidst clinking glasses. The guests toasted many drinks. And gradually stomachs were moving closer toward the edge of the table. Wah Gay cupped his hand to his mouth and whispered to Lee Gong, "Let's go."

Each took with him a cup and a bottle. They stopped at their own table. "A drink of many thanks to you," said Wah Gay and Lee Gong, raising their cups. "Good fortune all year round!"

"Good fortune all year round!" the guests rose with their glasses in response. The two hosts moved on quickly to the next table, then the next, until they had gone around to every table, thanking the guests, pouring drinks for them. Many of the guests jovially predicted that they would drink again next year at the haircut party of the first grandchild. Wah Gay and Lee Gong laughed happily at these predictions.

As soon as they returned to their own table, Wah Gay signaled to Ben Loy and his cousin, Wing Sim, who had come from Connecticut for the festivity and was sitting at the next table with his wife, Eng Shee. It was time for Ben Loy and Wing Sim to make the rounds. After a hasty huddle to decide what brand of whiskey to take along, they started off with a first stop at the head table, with Wing Sim pouring the drinks and Ben Loy doing the toasting. Earlier Wing Sim had suggested that he carry two bottles, one to be filled with tea for Ben Loy. But the bridegroom shrugged this precautionary measure off, saying that he would not get drunk.

Ah Song got up and glanced in the direction of Ben Loy. He walked over and was about to join the two cousins when Chuck Ting intervened. "Ah Song, there's no need for you to accompany them. They'll manage by themselves."

Ah Song retreated to his own table, but not without another

furtive glance at Mei Oi.

Chong Loo joined the bridegroom and Wing Sim with a tray full of chopped betel nuts and now offered these to the guests. The married adults at each table took a piece of the chopped nuts wrapped in red paper and left a tiny envelope of money on the tray. Before moving on to the next table, Chong Loo scooped up the red envelopes and stuffed them into the brown paper bag carried for this purpose, and replenished the tray with the chopped nuts.

While all this was going on the waiters continued to bring out additional dishes: *Abalone, Chicken Guy Que,* and many others.

Mrs. Wing Sim, who was not many years older than the bride, now accompanied Mei Oi for the tea ceremony. On a little round service tray, the older woman carried ten cups filled with tea, first to the head table. Mei Oi stood next to her, holding her folded fan up to her chin.

"Drink tea, sirs," announced Mrs. Wing Sim, extending the tray to the center of the table. The guests rose, each picking up a cup of tea and sipping it. The cups were then put back on the tray. Most of them were still nearly full. Little red envelopes began dropping onto the tray beside the cups. Ben Loy's aunt, Mrs. Wang Wah Lim, was ready with a brown paper bag to receive the red envelopes. She had flown in from Chicago especially for the party.

As soon as the cups were refilled, the hostesses moved on to the next table. At each stop, the same refrain greeted them: "Heh heh, next year we will drink again." And Mei Oi would raise her fan a little higher.

When the tea ceremony was over, Ah Song walked briskly to a waiter's stand in the back and brought back several boxes of cigars. He proceeded to pass out the cigars to the men at each table.

By the time the guests were ready to leave, it was close to nine o'clock. Ah Song was holding the door open. Wah Gay, Lee Gong, and Ben Loy stood by and smilingly nodded to the departing guests.

"Thank you many times, great uncle."

"Thank you."

"Thank you, Mr. Wang."
"Thank you, Mr. Lee."
"Today you have given me a big face."
"You have a kind heart."
"Thank you for the big face."

XV

Long before the banquet got under way, Ben Loy had decided he must make a supreme effort to assert his prerogative as a husband. His relationship with Mei Oi, he told himself in retrospect, had deteriorated in the last few weeks because of his lack of manliness. Tonight he must regain the prestige he had lost in the eyes of his wife. The drinks at the banquet gave him added courage. It was not only to celebrate his wedding that he had been drinking so jovially. He was also preparing himself for the night with Mei Oi. His normally pallid complexion was flushed from the strong drink.

Mei Oi put away the umbrella and removed her coat. Ben Loy took her hand, gently pulling her toward the sofa. He kissed her hands, her arms, her throat, her cheeks, and then her lips. She responded with delighted fervor to his kisses.

From the sofa, the two young lovers, with their arms around each other, glided into the bedroom. Apprehensively, Ben Loy realized that, in spite of all the tender love-making, his manliness had not yet asserted itself. He hoped that the sight of Mei Oi's lovely ivory body would kindle the power to possess her. They began to undress. His pleasure at seeing her take off the red satin gown was mingled with anxiety.

When Mei Oi was completely nude, Ben Loy went to her and clasped her with all his strength, desperately pressing his naked body to hers. He showered her with kisses. He stroked and kissed her in all the secret places of her body, making her gasp and writhe. Still his manliness would not come.

"I'm sorry, *Moi Moi*," said Ben Loy sadly, sick with guilt and humiliation. He hadn't called her *Moi Moi*, little sister, for a long time.

"I am sorry too, Loy *gaw*." She began to cry. The wedding banquet suddenly became meaningless. Ten thousand banquets could not make up for the ignominy of this one night. "Maybe . . . maybe you should go and see a doctor," she sobbed. "Maybe he can help you."

Ben Loy was powerless to comfort Mei Oi. He got up from the bed and went to the living room. He lay on the sofa, hoping that sleep would come. Why, he wondered, had he been so full of fire with the whores at the Hotel Lansing and could give no pleasure to this lovely, gentle girl whom his father had chosen as his bride? He lay in misery, bitterly ashamed of his impotence.

It was a long time before the sobbing in the next room died away.

XVI

To Mei Oi the novelty of New York soon wore off. Chinatown turned out to be less glamorous than she had pictured it. Buildings are buildings everywhere. New York lacked the intimacy of a rural village. She could not go over to Lane Four to borrow a porcelain dish for her cooking. In the village there is always something going on. Market days. Weddings. Hair-cut banquets. Planting. Harvesting. The Moon Festival. There is a oneness, a togetherness. A sense of belonging. A proud identity. In a village everybody knows everybody else.

New York for Mei Oi was a strange land. She knew no one outside of her immediate family. There was no one to visit. Ben Loy's aunt lived in Chicago, and Wing Sim's wife lived in Connecticut. She was alone at home while her husband worked. Added to this loneliness, she was sorrowing over the abrupt termination of her brief honeymoon. What had begun in the ecstasy of love was lost. Love had tumbled off the high pedestal of married bliss. As a pathetic substitute for ardor, Ben Loy usually took his wife to see a movie uptown on his days off. Sometimes, but seldom, he would take her to one of the local Chinese theaters when the film was exceptionally good. Other times they would go shopping or sight-seeing around New York. They saw the Statue of Liberty, the Empire State Building, the Museum of Natural History, Times Square. All these they did not have in rural Sunwei.

Ben Loy wanted to please his wife. If she hinted that a dress in a window looked nice, he got it for her. During the six months since her arrival in New York, he had bought her an expensive watch at one of the credit jewelers uptown. Wah Gay, acting the part of the proud father-in-law, had given her a diamond ring and a pair of gold bracelets. Ben Loy had given her a hair dryer, too. On his days off he even cooked for her.

But the gestures of affection from her husband could not make Mei Oi a happy woman. She was restless. One day after dinner she said to her husband, "Many women from China are now working in sewing shops in Chinatown. May I go out and get a job too?"

"I don't want you to work," replied Ben Loy firmly, taken aback by the suddenness of the question.

"Other housewives can work, why . . ."

"When a group of women get together," said Ben Loy, "they do nothing but gossip. And when they do, there's bound to be trouble." The request made him feel insecure. If his wife worked, he reasoned, she would come in contact with all sorts of people, both good and bad. He had heard of a woman who ran away with the boss of a sewing shop not long ago.

"I'll just keep quiet," said Mei Oi, disappointed. "I won't talk to them."

"That's what you say," retorted Ben Loy.

"It's a lot easier to pass the time away when one is working," said Mei Oi, dabbing at her eyes with a handkerchief. She ran from the kitchen to the bedroom, leaving the dishes undone in the sink.

"*Moi Moi*, please don't cry." Ben Loy hurried to her side.

"I'm not like others," she burst out crying. "Others are kept busy with their little ones."

Ben Loy put his arms around her and kissed her, stroking her soft black hair until she was quieter.

"Promise me one thing," she sobbed. "Promise me you'll go to see a doctor."

"I'll go next week," he replied sullenly, more conscious than ever before of his inadequacy. "Don't worry, I'll go."

"Go and ask your father if I could go to work too," she managed between sobs.

"Okay, I'll go next week," said Ben Loy.

The next week, when Ben Loy dropped in to see his father, he found him alone in the clubhouse. "Got a letter for you," he said.

"*Ah Sow* is well these days?" the father asked, accepting the letter.

"Hao, hao," replied Ben Loy.

He motioned for Ben Loy to sit down. "*Ah Sow* has come home for about six months now . . . more than six months," he began slowly. "Do you have any news for me?"

"What news should I have?" retorted Ben Loy irritably. "What news do you want?"

"I'm referring to your wife," said Wah Gay, rather gravely now. "Maybe *she* has some news for me." He waited for Ben Loy to answer. But the son only stared at the blank wall, then at the doorway, as if he wished someone would come in to interrupt the conversation.

"Your mother in her last letter to me asked me the same thing," continued the father. "Asked if I have any news for her concerning you two. Both your mother and I are getting on in years. We are not getting any younger each day. By giving your mother a grandson, or even a granddaughter, you would make her very happy. I think you should consider your mother's happiness, and mine too. . . ."

Ben Loy, without saying anything, got up and began edging toward the door. He saw nothing but the bleak dirty cement steps leading to the street.

"If you don't want children when you're young, when do you want them?" the father called after him. "When you're old?"

"What's the difference?" retorted Ben Loy. "You can have them any time you want!" He stormed out of the basement.

As he walked back home, anger made his face flush. If he had known the old man was going to bring up such a topic, he certainly would have stayed away from the club house. Forgotten was his task of finding out from his father if he would permit Mei Oi to go to work. He was in no mood to consult a doctor right now either. He did not feel like going home to Mei Oi, but there was no other place for him to go. When he opened the apartment door, Mei Oi was sitting by the desk in the living room.

"What are you doing, writing letters?" he asked perfunctorily. There was no trace of irritation in his voice.

"Just a few lines to mother," she said, looking up. "Haven't written her for a long time." She was about to get up from her

81

chair when Ben Loy approached and kissed her squarely on the lips, then on her cheeks, on her forehead. She disengaged herself and pulled away. "Did you talk to *Lao Yair?*"

"What's the difference whether I talk to my father or not?" he said. "You know he would say no."

"What did he say?"

"Oh, nothing. I just gave him the letter and left."

Mei Oi disappeared into another room. She reappeared a few moments later. "I almost forgot. Did you see the doctor?"

"No." Ben Loy scrutinized her from top to bottom. She had changed into a blue Chinese gown with a large silver dragon design on the front. He had always admired these sheath dresses on other women, but he never thought that some day he would see his own wife wearing one of them.

"You promised you would see the doctor."

"Okay, okay. I said I would and I will."

"Help me with this button." Mei Oi walked over to the full length mirror on the closet door. She lifted her chin high. She let her fingers drop. "Here, you snap this on for me."

Ben Loy took hold of the collar and struggled with the hook and eye. "There, I've got it!"

Mei Oi turned to face the mirror again. She inspected the collar. She spun around and glanced at the curves reflected in the mirror. She tugged at the lower half of the dress and wiggled a little bit. Her schoolmates back home had told her that when she came to America she would be wearing nothing but western clothes. Now she was glad she had brought several of these Chinese gowns with her. From what she had learned of American dresses they were either too tight, too small, too long, or too short. And she was not familiar with the sizes. As a school girl in Sun-wei she had worn nothing but two-piece Chinese suits. She remembered how she and her classmates used to chuckle when they saw a girl wearing a tight-fitting gown. To them, at the time, a girl in a clinging gown was just plain naked. But Mei Oi had come to love these tight-fitting dresses.

She sprayed some perfume on herself. She smelled good and

looked good. Ben Loy reached to pull his wife to him, to hold and kiss her, but she pushed him away firmly.

They went to a movie uptown. Mei Oi had discovered that the movies had a relaxing influence on her; so that, after a night out, her inner frustrations became less compelling.

XVII

Irritated by the constant reminders from Mei Oi that he consult a doctor, Ben Loy reluctantly stopped by the East Broadway office of Dr. Long the following week. The doctor was sympathetic.

"You said when you first got married in the village," the doctor wanted to make sure, "you were quite adequate?"

"Yes, sir," replied Ben Loy.

"When you came out to Hongkong with your wife and stayed at the All Seas Hotel, you found yourself incapable of an erection?" Ben Loy nodded embarrassedly. "Yet before your marriage, you had been quite adequate with a prostitute at the same hotel?"

"That's right, doctor."

"H'mn." The doctor assumed a pensive pose. "Maybe what you need is a change of scenery. Go away. Go away for a vacation and see what happens. Very often the cause is psychological."

When Ben Loy got home that afternoon, Mei Oi was very anxious to talk to him.

"What did the doctor say?" she asked as soon as her husband stepped inside the door.

"That doctor talked nonsense," said Ben Loy. "He told me to take a vacation. Go away to some other place for a while, he said."

"The doctor said to go away? Where?" Mei Oi was puzzled by Ben Loy's report.

"Anywhere. Just go away," said Ben Loy.

"Are *we* going away?" asked Mei Oi innocently.

"Going away?" Ben Loy wore a startled expression on his face. "What for?"

"But you said the doctor . . ."

"Oh, never mind him. He's crazy. He thinks you can just pack up and go away." He wrinkled his nose.

84

Weeks passed before Mei Oi brought up the subject of going away again.

"Loy *Gaw*," she said disarmingly. "I have never been to Washington, the capital of the country. It would be fun to see the sights."

Coming from his wife's pretty little mouth, it did not sound like going away to Ben Loy. It was just a visit to Washington. When he realized that he himself had never been to the nation's capital, he agreed to make the trip. He had told himself that someday he would like to see Washington. He decided the time was now. He called his friend Chin Yuen and asked him to work one day for him, the day preceding his day off, so that he would have two days in Washington.

Ben Loy and Mei Oi registered at a hotel not far from Union Station. They went sight-seeing in the daytime. The Lincoln Memorial, the Government Printing Office, the Congress, the Washington Monument, the White House . . .

During their brief stay in the nation's capital, Ben Loy and Mei Oi were happy and carefree. They held hands. They dined in different restaurants. They went window-shopping. Once again they were like a couple of honeymooners.

When night came, they were exhausted from the strenuous activities of sight-seeing. But they were happy and relaxed.

When time came to go to bed, Ben Loy held no feeling of inadequacy. The daytime excitement of the various tours had made him forget his inadequacy. He simply did not have time to think of his past. The bed now merely represented a continuation of the exciting tours on his itinerary. With the cooperation and understanding of Mei Oi, he rediscovered his manliness during his first night in Washington. He was elated. He was also puzzled because the doctor's advice had proven valid. His only regret was that he had to return to New York the following day.

To his dismay and disappointment, he fell back into the old rut of incompetence at his own apartment on Catherine Street in New York.

"Loy *Gaw*," pleaded Mei Oi, "please go back and see Dr. Long again."

XVIII

Ben Loy waited for his turn at the doctor's office. It was to please his wife that he now found himself thumbing through the pages of a torn magazine, sitting opposite a lady who had followed him in. Momentarily he turned from the magazine to the lady. Young, fairly good looking, of medium build. Shapely legs. Her skirt was slightly above her knees. The well-proportioned legs drew his attention and reminded him of one day in Calcutta.

He had been on a tour of Calcutta's *Chininagar* with two other GI's when they had wandered into a tiny novelty store just off the fringe of Chinatown. At first the conversation was that of a shopkeeper and a potential customer. As Ben Loy and his companions turned to leave, the lady proprietress said in broken English, "My friends, wait. You wait a minute."

She called out something in Hindustani to someone in the back room. Almost instantly a dark-skinned girl came out. She looked no more than sixteen. She had a ready smile and nice shapely legs. She beckoned to Ben Loy. "Come. Come here. I want to show you something."

The twenty-one-year-old Ben Loy had followed her behind the bamboo curtain.

"Aw, com'on. Let's go!" said Ben Loy's fellow soldiers. "We ain't got all day."

But Ben Loy ignored them and followed the girl. As soon as they were shut off from view by the curtain, the girl flipped open her dress, revealing her whole naked front. "See? Nice, huh?"

Ben Loy followed her to another room . . .

The door opened and the doctor stepped out. "Who's next?" he called.

Ben Loy's eye jumped from the lady's shapely legs back to the pages of the magazine. A man got up and followed the doctor in. The door closed. Ben Loy's eye went back to the lady's legs.

... Two hours later that same afternoon in Calcutta, Ben Loy and his buddies went to another section of the city. There was nothing else to do. Just killing time. On a street corner a youngster came up and accosted them. "Hey, Joe, you likee Chini goil?"

Ben Loy was delighted at the mention of Chinese girls. He had had them all. All different colors and shapes. "Chinese girls? Are you sure?"

"Sure, Chini goil. You come with me. You come." He was a mere boy, about ten or eleven.

Ben Loy and his companions followed the boy to the second floor of a building in a busy section of the city. Coming in from the sun-drenched streets of Calcutta, it felt like entering a cave. The boy called out something and a woman opened the door. They all went in. The woman brought out a girl, but she was not Chinese. She appeared to be Indian.

"You Chini?"

The girl shook her head.

"But the boy said . . . what the hell. A woman is a woman." Ben Loy followed the woman to a wooden bed. . . . Then at the Four Seas Hotel in Hongkong . . . the boy had brought him a different girl every night . . . yet when he came to Hongkong with Mei Oi and stayed at the same hotel . . . he was impotent.

If only he had been less lustful in his youth, he probably would not be in this room waiting to talk to the doctor now. He could have been so happy with Mei Oi, but . . .

He took a last look at the lady's legs before going into the doctor's examination room.

"My name is Wang, doctor," Ben Loy began. "I was here a few weeks ago . . ."

The doctor looked at him blankly; then a flicker of recognition expanded on his face. "Oh, yes," he nodded. "I remember."

Ben Loy began telling the doctor how during his first night in Washington with his wife, he had regained his strength; that when he came back to his apartment in New York, his old condition returned. "It's all my fault," he continued sadly. "Running after women—the many times I've had gonorrhea and syphilis."

87

"You should have thought of these things a long time ago," the doctor shook his head. "Am I to understand that you are completely impotent now?"

"Almost," replied Ben Loy. "Sometimes I wake up in the middle of the night and my manliness has returned. But at almost the very instant that I . . . possess my wife I have my . . . you know . . . it is all over. My wife does not have a very satisfactory husband," he concluded sadly.

"You have no venereal disease now?" the doctor asked.

"No."

"Are you sure?"

"I think so."

The doctor gave him a thorough examination. He prescribed some tablets for him to take each day and told him to return in two weeks. "Maybe this will help bring back your vitality."

"What about my impotence, doctor, is that a temporary thing or . . . ?"

"Sometimes it is and sometimes it is not," said the doctor. "Come back in two weeks and we'll see. I told you before that sometimes it's psychological."

When he left the doctor's office, Ben Loy was more dejected than he'd been when he entered. He had hoped that Doctor Long would tell him that his impotence would vanish after the medication. The dread possibility of permanent incapacity dawned on him and the thought began to torment him.

Instead of going directly home, he turned into Mott Street. At 91 Mott Street he went up the stairs. A white-haired man in a tan cardigan sweater opened the door in answer to his knocks on apartment two on the second floor.

"Hello," he fidgeted awkwardly. "I want you to look at my sickness."

"Come in." The old man indicated a chair for the caller. "Sit down."

The room was illuminated by the sunlight coming in through the windows of the adjacent room. Ben Loy sat down. The first thing he noticed was the sink, almost directly opposite him, next to the door. Presently the elderly man pulled the light cord and the glow from a 60-watt lamp added to the illumination of the room. He threw a tiny pillow about the size of a brick on the table in front of Ben Loy. He pulled up another chair. The herbalist placed three fingers on Ben Loy's upturned wrist, now resting on the little pillow, feeling the pulse. After several moments, he felt the pulse on the other wrist. He bowed his head and closed his eyes. The moments ticked by slowly. Finally the herbalist lifted his fingers from the wrist. "Kidney weak," he announced thoughtfully. "Kidney weak."

"Yes, I know," said Ben Loy. He wondered if it had been a waste of time to come to the herbalist's. He was now told that his kidney was weak.

"Eat something that would supplement your diet," said the herbalist, who practiced the art of feeling the pulse under the name of Nee Ho. "You need to take some gingsing." Nee Ho took out a pack of cigarettes and offered one to Ben Loy, who declined politely. He lifted his head and blew away the smoke.

"Not right away," he continued. "You have to eat some invigorating tea first. Perhaps after several brewings, you can start taking gingsing. But not before that. Your system is too cool to accept gingsing now."

Ben Loy did not take the prescription to a Chinese herb store. He thought the inter-mixing of medicine might be harmful. If all the modern sciences in America could not bring relief to his marital difficulties, how could he expect a herbalist to work miracles for him? On the other hand, there are undoubtedly tested remedies within the herbalist's realm of knowledge that are good for many ills. He folded the prescription neatly and put it into his coat pocket. He went to the Doyers Street Pharmacy to have Dr. Long's prescription filled. He would give Dr. Long's tablets a trial.

When Ben Loy finally got home that afternoon, Mei Oi had already finished cooking the rice. "What did the doctor say?" she asked, trying to conceal her anxiety.

"He gave me some tablets to take," said Ben Loy. "I don't know if they're any good." He did not mention that he had also gone to the herbalist's.

In the evening, after dinner, he and Mei Oi went to the movies.

XIX

After two weeks of taking Dr. Long's tablets, Ben Loy was eager to find out if they had had any beneficial effects on him. On the eve of his next day off, instead of taking one tablet, as prescribed by the doctor, he took two, one at noon and one after dinner.

When bed time came, Mei Oi was nervous and sympathetic. In a way, the outcome of this effort meant even more to her than to Ben Loy. If her husband's impotence proved to be permanent, she would face, in effect, a life of widowhood. She would be trapped and bitterly frustrated. If she had not loved her husband, it might have been a different matter, but she had been inextricably in love with him since that first meeting at the market place.

"*Moi, moi,*" he said tenderly, "regardless of what the future holds, I want you to know that I love you dearly. I'm sorry things have turned out this way."

"I'm sorry, too," said Mei Oi.

Ben Loy gently pushed her onto the bed.

Fifteen minutes later, the chagrined husband mumbled awkwardly, "I guess the tablets didn't do me any good."

Mei Oi kissed him on the forehead. "Maybe you ought to try one of those herb doctors," she said dejectedly. Her eyes began to brim with tears.

"As a matter of fact I did go to one of them," said Ben Loy. "A Dr. Nee Ho. I still have his prescription with me. I'll have it filled tomorrow."

The next day, before going off to work, he stopped by the Strong Body Herb Company on Pell Street to have Nee Ho's prescription filled. Then he took the package of herbs home, giving Mei Oi instruction to start brewing it at ten P.M. so that, when he came home at midnight, the tea would be ready for him.

A few days later he took the same prescription to the herb store and got it filled again. Although no noticeable benefits had manifested from his taking the herbs, he was willing to *eat* another bowl of tea. After the second eating, there was still no sign, however gradual, of returned vitality to Ben Loy.

XX

When July rolls around in Sunwei, there is no better way to escape the heat than to find one's self a spot under the banyan trees in the public square. In New York, where people are plentiful and trees are scarce, there is no banyan tree. And even if there were, Mei Oi could never get up early enough to reserve a spot under it for herself.

One particularly hot July afternoon, eight months after her arrival in New York, Mei Oi opened all the windows wide to let more air into the apartment. Even with the windows wide open, the air hardly stirred. Disappointed, she walked to the front door and opened it. Immediately a rush of wind pushed past her, flooding the apartment with a new coolness. Mei Oi was thrilled at this new discovery. She stood by the open door, inhaling deeply the fresh air. But as soon as she walked back to the apartment proper, even with the door open, the breeze vanished. Experimentally she returned to the front part of the ·hall and immediately the breeze rushed at her.

Why not get a chair and sit down by the door and be cool? she asked herself. She walked quickly to the kitchen ·and brought out a straight-backed chair. Placing the chair squarely in the doorway she sat down to enjoy a cool afternoon. She lifted the bottom of her dress above her knees. It was cooler this way.

She had been using this resourceful cooling system for about a week, when one day, as she was sitting thus in the doorway, she noticed someone coming up the stairs. When the bobbing head came up higher, she saw it was Ah Song's. Even before he took another step up, her face had become crimson. The doorway was several feet away from the top of the stairs. As soon as his eye level came up to the landing, he could see a figure sitting by the open door. Any uncertainty about the person's identity soon evaporated as he approached the landing.

"Oh, hello," said Ah Song, with just a trace of surprise in his voice.

"Oh, it's Uncle Song," said Mei Oi, quickly pulling the hem of her dress down over her knees; but it was too late for Ah Song not to have seen her exposed legs.

"It's terribly hot today, isn't it?" Ah Song was in a dark cord suit.

"Yes, it is." She got up. "That's why I'm sitting here. There's no breeze inside." She stood awkwardly in the doorway.

"I . . . I was just going upstairs to see a friend . . ."

"Yes," Mei Oi nodded. She wished Ah Song would continue upstairs. When he just stood there and grinned at her, she felt embarrassed; and, after a moment of hesitation, invited him in.

"Ben Loy is at work," she said after they were seated in the living room.

"Oh, is that so? And you're home all alone?"

"Yes," replied Mei Oi uneasily. This was the first time she had been left alone with a man other than her husband. Ah Song was practically a stranger. Even when she was with her own father she would blush.

"What time does Ben Loy get home?" asked Ah Song.

"Some time after midnight." She wished he would go away instead of asking so many questions. He was not at all like that beggar man who used to come to her house in Sunwei and call out over the top of the half doors: *Good little girl, have a kind heart and give me something to eat.* She would always give him something. Even when the pot of rice was all gone, she would pester her mother to part with some taros or potatoes.

"Does your father-in-law ever come up to visit you?" Ah Song pursued. He pulled out his cigarette case and lit a cigarette. He puffed at it leisurely and contentedly. His left thumb and forefinger went up and touched his nose. He did this many times. Each time he did this the big diamond on his second finger sparkled in front of Mei Oi; so that she could not help but notice it.

"No, very seldom." Mei Oi shook her head. She was already getting alarmed at Uncle Song's obvious intention to stay. She had asked him to come in as a matter of courtesy and had not expected him to accept her invitation. If someone had seen him even near her apartment, she could be ruined by gossipy talk. And never again would she be able to lift her head to face either Ben Loy or her father-in-law.

"Uncle Song," she continued, her face frantic with fear, "you must forgive me; but, as you know, a woman alone having a male visitor . . . it's . . . well, it's the sort of thing that is not done. I'm sorry, it's all my fault. I asked you to come in. Now I must ask you to leave. Please come back when my husband is home."

"Don't be afraid. I won't stay long." Ah Song almost chuckled. "This is New York, not China. You can have male visitors if you want to."

"But . . . but what would people say?"

"Nothing. What *can* they say? We're not doing anything wrong." Ah Song's left hand went up, touched his nose, then came down and adjusted his tie. "What kind of life do you have here? Your husband goes to work and you stay home to stare at the four walls!"

"But I'm married to him," protested Mei Oi.

"Ben Loy will do whatever his father tells him to do. He's that way." Ah Song took great relish in revealing this to Mei Oi. He felt that the more derogatory things he could say about Ben Loy the better it would make *him* look in the eyes of Mei Oi. He knitted his brows and sought additional ammunition to throw at this young wife who, to him, was just a country girl who found herself in a big city. "Do you still think you're married to Ben Loy? Your husband was a regular customer at the local whorehouses. Everybody knows that but you and Wang Wah Gay!"

"No, no, it's not true!" Mei Oi cried.

"My dear girl, you have been badly misinformed." Ah Song tried to suppress a chuckle. . . . He got up and started pacing the floor. "I'm sorry if I've hurt you by telling you the truth, but somebody has to tell you sooner or later."

Ah Song was very pleased with the turn of events. He had always enjoyed seeing a woman cry. Now, when sobs came to Mei Oi, he was particularly pleased. He believed that he held the power to sway the emotional outburst of this young girl to suit his fancy.

"Please don't cry," he said, wiping away the tears with his own handkerchief. His arm was now around her, comforting her. The delicateness and warmth of her flesh . . . the mere touch of her sent his heartbeat soaring. The large diamond on his finger blinked dazzlingly bright as he held the handkerchief in his hand.

"Please, I'm all right now." She gently lifted his arm and pulled away from him. "Will you please leave now?" She dabbed at her eyes with her own handkerchief.

"In just a moment." Ah Song followed her to another part of the living room. "After I've told you how much I love you!"

"What . . . what did you say?" Mei Oi was shocked.

"I've loved you ever since I first saw you at your wedding banquet at the Grand China Restaurant," continued Ah Song. "Day and night, no matter how hard I tried, I couldn't get you out of my mind!"

"How can you stand there and tell me these things?" Mei Oi managed to blurt out between sobs. "Don't forget: I'm Ben Loy's wife." Good or bad, she told herself, still she was Ben Loy's wife. Today was the first time she had ever heard anything bad said of her husband.

"Yes, I know," said Ah Song. "But I also know that in this country divorce is a common thing. If a woman doesn't love her husband, she can get a divorce and marry another man." He shrugged his shoulders and turned his palms up.

"But I don't want to divorce my husband. . . ."

"I love you. Marry me. I can give you a life that Ben Loy cannot hope to give you in a thousand years." Ah Song's imagination began to fabricate a fantastic family background. "Very few people know this, but my family in Canada owns a lot of land; in fact a great part of the State of Montreal . . . of course you've heard of Montreal. We own the biggest hotel in Toronto. My family owns the biggest theater in . . . in Vancouver . . ."

These names were vaguely familiar to Mei Oi, for she had heard of them before. She was immensely impressed; but she could not understand what Ah Song, with *his* family background, would be doing in New York. She was tempted to ask him when he resumed, "Some years ago, when my mother wanted me to marry a girl I didn't love, I left home, and I haven't been back since. From time to time my mother writes and pleads with me to go back. But I haven't wanted to go back. I liked this bachelor life. But since I've met you . . ."

He walked over to Mei Oi and placed her hands in his. "I no longer have a desire for this old life. I . . . I want to take you home with me as my bride." He patted her hands fondly. "My mother will love you, I know. You will never have to sweep a single room." He peered at her tearstained face briefly, then sat down beside her at the couch. "The last time I was home, my mother had eight servants."

"Please go now," said Mei Oi.

"My mother is the old-fashioned type. I know she would shower you with diamonds and jades and gold necklaces."

"Come and visit us when my husband is home," Mei Oi sobbed and buried her head in her palms.

Ah Song put his arms around her. She tried to move away but he held her tight. "But I love you, don't you understand?" Instinctively he bent his head and kissed her on the cheek. She jumped up, walked a few paces away and whirled.

"Please leave me alone!" she implored.

"I just want to tell you I love you." Ah Song gestured with open arms.

"You've already told me that. Please leave now before somebody comes." She started walking toward the door, hoping he would follow her. But he only straightened his tie and peered at himself in the full-length mirror in the living room. It reflected a nonchalant, cold, and calculating individual. He would get what he wanted, he told himself.

"Can I borrow the use of your bathroom?" he asked flippantly, trying to delay his departure. Mei Oi did not answer him. She stood by the door, sulking.

"The toilet is outside," she finally said in a loud voice. She placed her hand on the door knob, anxious to see Ah Song leave the apartment.

"Brew me a cup of tea and I'll leave," called Ah Song from the living room. He was still admiring himself in the mirror.

Reluctantly Mei Oi returned, making her way to the kitchen in silence, a prisoner in her own home. She did not want to make a disturbance that would expose Ah Song's visit to her apartment. She wanted him to leave quietly, undetected, just as he had come. If she had known he was like this, she would never have let him take a single step over the threshold. She was hoping that, if she did what he wanted her to do, he would leave peacefully.

Inside the kitchen she let the water run into the white-enameled pot, then put the pot on the range for the tea. When she turned to sit by the kitchen table to wait for the water to boil, Ah Song appeared in the kitchen doorway. She stared blankly at him.

"You'll feel better after you've got to know me a little more," grinned Ah Song. He knew she would not dare make an outcry; because if she did, she would place herself in a scandalous position. He knew, too, that he was free to stay as long as he liked because her husband would not be home until midnight. He would take his time with this naive country girl. He walked over and helped himself to a seat.

"After all," he resumed, "what does a woman want in a husband? Good looks, money, position. A life free from worry. *My* mother would never interfere with the life of *her* daughter-in-law—if she had one. And my father—he leaves the women-folks alone. He never bothers my mother."

Ah Song waited for Mei Oi to say something; but she was quiet, resting her chin on the palm of her hand, her elbow on the table top. Once in a while she glanced back at the pot. Once more Ah Song put his diamond-ringed hand to his nose. "We live in a big mansion . . . great big mansion, several blocks big . . ." He made a wide arc with his hand.

Unwillingly Mei Oi followed his every word and gesture. She mentally compared her present existence to that of mistress of a mansion with servants and acres and acres of land.

"I wish you would leave," she said dejectedly. "My husband may come home early today. When he went to work, he complained of a headache." She stared at Ah Song hopefully.

"I'll leave in a few minutes, after I have my cup of tea. That is, if that's no trouble to you."

Mei Oi got up, walked quickly to the shelves and returned with a container of tea. Just as she turned to face the pot, the trapped steam started to escape from the lid. She gingerly flipped open the lid, threw in a fingerful of Jasmine tea leaves, and quickly let the cover down. After a moment, she picked up the pot and started pouring its contents into Ah Song's cup. After she had replaced the pot on the range, Ah Song grabbed her gently by the wrist. "Mei Oi, I love you!" he almost pleaded.

The cry of *I love you* was a mixture of sweet and sour music to Mei Oi's ears. She was flattered and frightened.

"Please don't say any more," she said. Her hand pushed away the hand that had held her wrist, and Ah Song reluctantly let go.

"Believe me, little sister, ever since I first saw you, I have had you in my mind day and night." He shook his head. "It's torture to love someone who doesn't even know you exist."

Mei Oi nervously took a seat opposite Ah Song. "You have no right to talk to me like this," she protested, trying to conceal the quiver in her voice. "I'm a married woman."

"My mother has a right to acquire a daughter-in-law as much as anybody else," said Ah Song. "Fate has brought us together. We must not fight fate, but welcome it."

This sort of talk bewildered Mei Oi. Her attitude toward Ah Song was becoming less harsh. She saw in him a little boy wanting something—desperately begging, pleading. Like that beggar man in Sunwei.

"Uncle Song, I'm Ben Loy's wife," she began.

"Yes, I know that. I also know that I love you. Don't you understand?"

"No, I'm afraid not," she shook her head. "I'm a little confused." When she saw that Ah Song was staring at her, she quickly lowered her eyes.

Ah Song thought he saw an opening. Swiftly he was out of his chair and next to Mei Oi. He was on his knees, his hands holding hers.

"Please believe me," he whispered, "I love you so much, I'd

98

do anything for you. My mother would feel honored to have you for a daughter-in-law." He put his head close to hers. "You are so beautiful, Mei Oi. I love you, I love you, I love you!"

Mei Oi said nothing. She could not think clearly. Ah Song's hands reached out to wrap her in his arms. He kissed her on the cheeks.

"Please don't," she tried to push him away; but he tightened his grip.

He kissed her full and long on the lips. Then again.

"Please don't." The protest was almost inaudible.

He pressed his lips over her face, whispering, "I love you, I love you!" Finally he lifted her from the chair and carried her into the bedroom.

"Uncle Song, please leave me alone. . . ."

Ah Song's heart was throbbing madly. Drops of perspiration appeared on his forehead. He gently dropped her on the large double bed and lay down beside her.

"Please don't . . . please don't. . . ."

The bed springs squeaked under their combined weight. The neatly-made bed was quickly disarrayed.

"I won't hurt you . . ."

"Please don't . . ."

"I love you. I won't hurt you."

In the kitchen the white-enameled pot stood mute and unused, the lone cup of tea on the table forgotten and untouched.

Later when they both got up, Mei Oi started to sob, very softly.

XXI

One day several weeks later, Chong Loo, after making his customary rounds collecting rents, stopped by the Wah Que Barber Shop on Mott Street. This time he was in need of a haircut. At other times he would come to collect rent or just drop in to "fire" his *big gun*.

"You sonovabitch," greeted Ah Mow, the proprietor. "So hot you have to wear a jacket?"

Chong Loo dropped down on one of the waiting chairs, with his ever-present brief case beside him. He was almost out of breath. "I want a haircut. The last time I got a haircut here, you didn't do such a good job."

"Blame it on your hair," said Ah Sing, the second barber. "Your hair looks more like a brush than hair on someone's head. What is the latest news?"

"Wow your mother, how should I know?" Chong Loo lit a cigarette and the oscillating fan on the opposite wall blew his smoke away.

"That which does not concern me," he added nonchalantly, "does not worry me." He got up and walked toward the first barber's chair.

"Wow your mother," said Ah Mow. "Take off your coat."

"Ha, ha. I let you be the judge," said Chong Loo, turning to remove his coat. When he returned to the chair he asked pointedly, "Ah Mow, why don't you get your *rice cooker* over here and . . ."

"That which does not concern me, does not worry me," Ah Mow began quoting him.

"Wow your mother."

"I'm just repeating what you said a moment ago."

"You sonovabitch, I'm telling you for your own good," replied Chong Loo. "If you have your old woman here, everything would be better for you. If you get sick . . ."

"What's the use of getting her over here?" said Ah Mow. "She's already many times ten."

"It's better than getting a young wife in this country," continued Chong Loo. "Hey, cut it a little shorter here." Chong Loo's hand went up and pointed to a spot of hair.

"You crazy man," said Ah Sing. "Which would you want? Sleep with an old woman or a young one?"

"That's just the trouble," said Chong Loo. "Everyone wants to sleep with a young one. Nobody wants to sleep with an old one. She's all yours, and you're safe. Heh, heh, that's what's good about it."

"Wow your mother. You go to hell."

"Look out. Don't cut my ear!"

"Wang Wah Gay's daughter-in-law." Ah Sing was making idle talk. "She's been here almost a year now. She has no big belly yet. I wonder why."

"Do you know what I've heard?" asked Chong Loo excitedly. "That son of his . . . he . . . when he was younger, he got mixed up with the wrong people."

"I thought his father sent him to . . ."

"Yes, Wang Wah Gay sent him to a small town to work so as to keep him from the evils of the big city. Ha, ha, he sent him to work in Stanton." Chong Loo smiled at himself in the wall mirror.

"Ben Loy's a good boy," said Ah Mow. "He don't gamble. His father was more worried about his son becoming a gambler than anything else."

"What he didn't know was that the son used to come into New York several times a week for women," laughed Ah Sing. "Didn't you tell us that, Uncle Loo?"

"The boy ruined his health," Chong Loo said sadly. "They say that thing can't come up any more."

"People talk too much," said Ah Mow. "Maybe there's no truth to it."

"He's had all sorts of diseases, from gonorrhea to syphilis," continued Chong Loo. "If that is not the case, why hadn't his wife been pregnant now? Why hasn't she been with child?"

101

"Wow your mother," said Ah Sing. "Maybe they don't want any baby. Many young couples don't want babies right away."

"We Chinese are different," said Chong Loo. "The old heads would see to it that the young ones produce. Anyway, I think Wah Gay's son is *no can do*. Heh, heh, just like me."

Ah Mow flipped off the white cloth apron from Chong Loo's neck and the rent collector stepped off the chair. He walked up to the mirror and examined himself, turning his head this way and that way. "Me? I look like a sixteen-year-old," he announced.

"Wow your mother," said Ah Sing. "You'll be sixteen in the next world."

XXII

Mei Oi's affair with Ah Song was the sort of thing that a country girl would never dream could happen to her. Once it happened it was not within the easy-going personality of Mei Oi to halt it. Things might have been different if Ben Loy had gone back to Stanton to work; but to please his wife, he remained in New York. In his own words, he wanted his wife to feel more at home, close to Chinatown. He felt Mei Oi would be too unaccustomed to the living conditions in a small town like Stanton. Chin Yuen had recommended him for a job at the New Toishan at 53rd Street. He had decided to stay.

The seasons came and went. Ben Loy continued working at the New Toishan.

When Mei Oi got up one morning in April, she complained of feeling ill. She put her hand to her forehead and it felt warm, warmer than usual. "I think I have a little fever," she said.

Ben Loy put his palm to her forehead. "Yes, it feels warm."

"I feel a little dizzy too," added Mei Oi. What alarmed her most was that the day before she had eaten very little. There was a general lack of appetite. "I wish you wouldn't go to work today," she said.

Ben Loy immediately called the boss of the New Toishan Restaurant and told him he could not come in to work. Then he accompanied Mei Oi to the doctor's.

At the doctor's small crowded office, they took seats and began reading the scrolls hanging on the walls of the waiting room. Next they watched the old fish swim in the glass tank by the window. When they got tired of watching the fish, they looked up at the clock on the wall, whose sweeping second hand seemed not to move fast enough. Every fifteen minutes or so Dr. Long

103

would open his inner office door and someone among those waiting would get up and walk in.

When Mei Oi's turn came, the doctor greeted her with a perfunctory "hello."

"Name?" the doctor sat down at his desk.

"Wang. Wang Mei Oi."

"Have you been here before?"

"No, this is the first time," said Mei Oi.

The doctor led her into the examination room. "What seems to be the trouble?" he asked. "Open your mouth." The doctor stuck a thermometer into her mouth.

"Sit down," Dr. Long pointed to the stool. "Roll up your sleeves." He brought out the instrument for measuring blood pressure.

When that was done, the doctor announced, "I have to take a blood test."

"A blood test? What's the matter, doctor? What's wrong? How much blood are you going to take?" asked Mei Oi, timidly.

"Oh, not much," said the doctor. "About half a gallon. Ha, ha. Is that too much?"

The outer door could be heard opening and closing. Then footsteps. More people were coming in.

The doctor gave Mei Oi a little bottle to bring back the next day. "Don't forget," he reminded. "It's the morning sample that I want."

A week later Dr. Long called Mei Oi to inform her that she was pregnant.

The news jolted her like a bolt of lightning. She sighed and clasped her hands tightly. Of course, she never had been pregnant before and had no idea how it felt to be with child. She wished her mother were here to tell her what to do. She wanted to tell the whole world she was pregnant. She was going to have a baby after all! She found herself saying "I'm pregnant . . . I'm pregnant!" Everybody who gets married has a baby, sooner or later. Now her turn had come. She hurried to the mirror to stare at the soon-to-be-mother. She liked the way she looked. She dashed to the phone.

"Will you please call Ben Loy to the phone?" She waited.

"Hello, Loy *Gaw*?"

"What's the matter? Speak fast. I'm busy right now."

"The doctor just called. He said I'm going to have a baby!"

"Did you have to call me to tell me about it now? Is that all? I have six tables to wait on." He hung up.

Her husband's cool reception to the news did not dampen her own enthusiasm. Even her meetings with Ah Song did not hold any significant meaning for her in the light of her pregnancy.

XXIII

When Wang Wing Sim's wife heard from her husband that Ben Loy's wife was pregnant, she hurried from Stanton to New York to visit her. She wanted to comfort Mei Oi in her first pregnancy. Originally the suggestion had come from Wang Chuck Ting, who had telephoned his son from New York: "Ben Loy's wife is going to have a baby. See when daughter-in-law can come out and tell her what to do. The other one is too young to know anything."

"Number Two Aunt," said Mei Oi when Wing Sim's wife paid her a surprise visit, "you are very kind to come. For the last few days I've been feeling sleepy and dizzy. My appetite is no good."

"Those are normal signs of pregnancy," cautioned Aunt Wing Sim, a mother of three. "The first is always the hardest. But when you get to be like me," she chuckled, "after you have had a few, it comes very easy."

"I'm so ignorant of everything," said Mei Oi.

"Everybody is the same way," Number Two Aunt hastened to say. "When I was pregnant for the first time, I didn't know anything either. But I was in the village at that time and my mother-in-law had to teach me everything."

"I wish I had my mother-in-law here," sighed Mei Oi. "She could be such a help."

From a large shopping bag Aunt Wing Sim extracted a brown paper bag of ox tails, a whole chicken, and some Chinese herbs.

"Oh, you shouldn't have brought all these things," exclaimed Mei Oi. "There's no need to spend so much money."

"This is of no consequence," said Eng Shee. She asked Mei Oi where the big pot was. When she got it down from the shelf, she rinsed it, put the already cut ox tails and herbs into the pot, and added water to them. "Let it boil with a small fire for at

106

least two hours," she instructed. "Now you lie down and rest. I'm going to buy a bottle of Ng Gar Pai." She walked quickly to the door, paused, and called back. "Nowadays you can't get the real Ng Gar Pai."

"Oh, please don't bother," said Mei Oi. "You have done enough already."

Number Two Aunt ignored her request and closed the door behind her. Actually she was Number One; but because her husband's brother, the first-born, had died when he was two years old, Eng Shee became known as Aunt Number Two.

Mei Oi called Ben Loy to tell him that Aunt Number Two had come in from Stanton with the ox tails and chicken and herbs, and that she was now going to buy a bottle of Ng Gar Pai.

"She has a kind heart," said Ben Loy. "When she comes back, be sure to ask her to stay for dinner."

When Number Two Aunt returned with the Ng Gar Pai, Mei Oi was already preparing dinner. She sliced the flank steak into small pieces to be cooked with bok toy. She cut part of the chicken into small pieces to be steamed with chung toy and mushrooms, adding a teaspoon of soy sauce.

"You don't know how happy I am to be pregnant," confided Mei Oi. "You know how people talk. So and so is married so long and no sign of a baby yet."

During dinner, Number Two insisted that Mei Oi drink a large bowl of soup brewed from the ox tails and herbs and Ng Gar Pai. "It's good for your back and good for your dizziness," she said, refusing to have some herself. "Tell Loy Gaw to go out and buy these things so you can cook and eat them regularly."

Mei Oi thought Number Two Aunt was a wonderful person. With three children of her own, she took time to come and visit her on her first pregnancy. That's more than Ben Loy would do for her during this first experience. From Number Two Aunt she learned that it was quite natural for her to want to eat something sour during the first days of pregnancy. When she had mentioned this peculiar desire to Ben Loy earlier, he thought it was just an upset stomach. There were many things she had liked to eat before she became pregnant—things which she now only looked at. When she spoke of this, Number Two

Aunt assured her that it was normal for one to be choosy about food during the first days with child. Now she recalled with a chuckle how the older women in the village used to talk about the younger ones: Number Three over on Lane Two is getting too choosy about what she eats.

In spite of her discomfort in this new experience, Mei Oi considered herself lucky. Number Two Aunt told her that when she was carrying her Number One Son Ah Ming, she had terrible headaches all the time. She had to go to the fields to gather the taros and potatoes; for it was harvest time and there was no one else to help her mother-in-law. Whenever there was meat on the table, she, as the daughter-in-law, would not dare direct her chop sticks to the meat dish unless her mother-in-law first partook of some. But Wing Sim's mother was the type who would deny herself the meat so that there would be more for her son. And Eng Shee would find herself picking little bits of salt fish and bok toy.

She also remembered for Mei Oi's benefit that, when she was pregnant, her mother-in-law cooked a whole pig's knuckle with peanuts and vinegar for her. And the old lady would say to Number Two Aunt: Ah Sow, the vinegar is good for you. Drink plenty of it. After the birth of the little cow-sitter, you will have plenty of milk for the little one. Vinegar produces milk like nothing else can. Vinegar chases away the wind and dampness in the human system...

"But here," continued Number Two, "they have babies in the hospital. In China you would be lucky if you could get a day off to give birth to the baby. When my first boy was born, I went to Sands Market and there was this midwife Lew Hing Tong . . . she was supposed to be one of the best in the area. She charges fifty dollars, I remember. And she prescribed for me Ovaltine."

For the many weeks that followed, Mei Oi had a steady diet of chicken and herbs and Ng Gar Pai brewed for several hours, to help give her strength for the new baby.

As soon as Wah Gay had heard the good news, he, too, started bringing foods for the mother-to-be. The foods were of the same variety: chicken, pig's feet, herbs. Sometimes whiskey was sub-

108

stituted for Ng Gar Pai. Mei Oi's range was kept busy from one meal to the next. Something was always brewing on it. If it was not pig's feet, it was chicken, and if it was not chicken, it was goat's meat. On one of his trips to the apartment with the food, Wah Gay cautioned his daughter-in-law, "Ah Sow, you must take it easy. Don't do any heavy work. If the windows need cleaning, have Ben Loy do it."

Mei Oi was pleased with all this attention and thoughtfulness. From the doctor had come this advice: Do as little traveling as possible. If traveling by bus or subway, be extra careful in getting on and off.

After a moment of long reflection upon her new glory, Mei Oi continued with her goat's meat.

XXIV

All the chairs were occupied when the rent collector hobbled into the Wah Que Barber Shop one afternoon the following month. The oscillating fans were going. But Chong Loo, as expected, was wearing his jacket. His brief case was by his side. After the usual *What's the matter with you wearing a jacket on such a hot day and where the hell is your sweater?* beginning, Ah Mow continued rather casually, "Uncle Loo, what is the latest news?"

"Wow your mother," said Chong Loo curtly. "What do you think I am? A newspaper reporter? Why are you always asking me for the latest news?"

"I just thought perhaps you have the latest news," replied Ah Mow. "You don't have to be talking so loud."

"Go sell your ass, what do you think I am?" Chong Loo removed his coat. "Whew, what a hot day for May!" He let himself into the barber's chair which a customer had just vacated. "Cut it short, little brother. Too hot, you know."

"You want to cut it like a monk's?"

Another customer walked in and took a seat. He opened the China Evening NEWS and began to read. Something caught his eye. He folded the paper neatly to facilitate handling. "Listen to this," he announced to no one in particular. He was a man in his early sixties with very little hair. "Nowadays women are not trustworthy. Here's another case where the husband is advertising for the whereabouts of his wife. Ha, ha. Married only two years. There's a reward for information leading to the whereabouts of his wife . . ."

"Today's school girls are like that," put in Chong Loo with relish. "But everybody wants to marry a school girl. So everybody's daughter becomes a school girl, even if she has to go in one entrance and out the other."

110

"Uncle Loo," taunted Ah Sing, "that which does not concern me, does not worry me."

"Aw, go sell your ass, you barbering jackass."

"I'm only quoting you."

Chong Loo was putting on his coat now. "Don't let what I have to say out of these walls," he whispered. "Let it dissolve and evaporate right here." He lit a cigarette and took a long puff. He lowered his voice. "Last week I was coming downstairs from the third floor of a building . . ."

"What were you doing there, Uncle Loo?" interrupted Ah Sing, who had edged closer toward him.

"Wow your mother, I was there collecting rent. I heard the door of apartment three opening on the second floor. I stopped short and did not move. After the door opened, there was a moment of quiet. Then footsteps. I tiptoed down the stairs to see who it was. Who do you think it was? Who do you think came out of apartment three? That's the apartment where Wang Wah Gay's daughter-in-law lives. Do you know who it was that came out? It was that three-ply smoothie boy, Ah Song!"

"Wow your mother, what does that prove?" asked Ah Mow. "Maybe Ah Song was on an errand for Wah Gay."

"Maybe so," shot back Chong Loo heatedly, "but not after that dead boy Ah Song pinned some flowers on his daughter-in-law at the wedding banquet. Since then Wah Gay had not much use for him. And that's why I don't think Ah Song was on an errand for the old man."

"If what they say about Ben Loy is correct," said Ah Sing, "then his wife . . . well, can you blame her for having something to do with another man? What could a girl do with a guy who is like a wooden block?"

"I'm positive what they say is true," said Chong Loo. "Ben Loy . . . this young man has ruined his health. Too many girls and too much. Too careless. Gonorrhea, syphilis. He's had them all."

"Too bad, but it's too late now," Ah Mow shook his head. "He's got a beautiful wife . . . to look at. What a stinky dead snake."

"A wife with such a husband has got to go out and hook

somebody else," said Ah Sing.

"Today's women are no good," said the customer who had started it all. He put away his paper and was now listening attentively.

"Uncle Loo," Ah Mow teased him, "maybe you are eligible for the competition."

"Go sell your ass, you stinky dead snake," Chong Loo tore into the barber furiously. "Don't say anything like that! If you want to make laughs, talk about something else, you trouble-maker. You many-mouthed bird. You want to get me into trouble?"

"Nobody said you go after someone's daughter-in-law. I merely said . . ."

"I don't want your ass. Go sell it somewhere else, you sonova-bitch!" Chong Loo grabbed his brief case and stormed out of the barber shop. The others laughed at his abrupt exit.

"He has a bad temper," explained Ah Mow, "but he means no harm. He's just many-mouthed."

The door swung open and in stalked Chong Loo. "Here's your money!" He handed a dollar to the proprietor, turned, and stormed out again.

XXV

Chinatown is a closely knit community where everybody knows almost everybody else. If somebody does not know you, there are others who do; though you may have no idea what a celebrity you are in your own community. Ben Loy was such a celebrity. Aside from his own family and the people with whom he worked and the cousins from his home village, Ben Loy could say that he knew hardly anybody else. Even at his own wedding party, he had scarcely known a fraction of the invited guests. They had come at the invitation of the father. But many people knew him because he was Wang Wah Gay's son. Those who did not know him, had heard of him; for his father belonged to many organizations: The Chinese Masons, the Kuomingtang, the Chinese Elks, Ping On Tong, and the Wang Association.

In a homogeneous community like Chinatown, people spent most of their free time in the shops, sipping tea or coffee, just talking with their friends. Each had his own favorite spot. The coffee shop. The corner candy store. The barber shop. The steps in front of the Chinese School. With rent collector Chong Loo, it was the Wah Que Barber Shop and Money Come.

"Hey, do you know that Wah Gay's daughter-in-law has a big belly?" Chong Loo announced the next time he showed up at the Wah Que Barber Shop. He eased himself into the first chair.

"You dead man, don't be making up stories now," admonished Ah Mow, his hands temporarily stilled. After a moment, as if by habit, his right hand began manipulating the scissors again, though they were not touching Chong Loo's hair. "Wow your mother," he continued, "don't go around pulling off your big gun or I'll clip off your ear."

"Wow *your* mother," retorted Chong Loo. "Go ahead and try if you want to die. Cut it off and see how many pennies per four *liang* you would make." The scissors kept clipping at the air, close to Chong Loo's ear. "You sonovabitch, what do *you* know what's going on? All day long you stay here and work on your scissors . . . *chop* . . . *chop* . . . *chop*. If what I say is not the truth, do you think I would tell it? Last week I saw her with my own eyes. She was coming out of the grocer's on East Broadway . . ." He paused to peer at himself on the wall mirror. "She looked to me like she has a big belly."

"Wow your mother, maybe she's getting fat," Ah Sing laughed. "But I thought you said the husband is no can do."

"You go sell your ass. When someone talks about a hammer, you talk about a chisel."

"Drop dead, you old bastard," said Ah Sing.

"I told you the last time that . . ." Chong Loo's eyes surveyed the four walls and then lowered his voice. "I told you the last time that Ah Song . . . I saw him coming out of Wah Gay's daughter-in-law's apartment. He didn't go there just to pin a flower on her dress this time either."

"Rumors," Ah Mow rebuked him. "Nothing but rumors."

"Wow your mother. You wait and see."

XXVI

Wang Wah Gay walked around these days with an air of a man who is about to pass out a boxful of cigars to his friends in celebration of something or other. He had a gleam in his eyes and a ready smile when he stopped to talk with his friends. He was a man with a happy secret. He was to become a grand-father. Even when his mah-jong game was going against him, he was light-hearted enough to laugh and joke with his cronies. Formerly when he had lost, his face would tighten and there would be fire in his eyes. He would remain silent. But all that had been changed lately.

One night he stayed up late after the mah-jong game to write a letter to his wife Lau Shee.

Dearly beloved wife, Lau Shee:

I'm writing to you as if we were together and talking face to face. The years passed like the mere closing and opening of the eye. Another spring has passed. I know I should pack my belongings and return home for a reunion with you, my kind and beloved wife. But there is always my business which has kept me here. Someday soon I will leave America and come back to you. In the meantime I'm forwarding two hundred American dollars to Sang Chong Bakery for your household expenses. When you have received this money, let me know by return mail. Both of us are getting on in years and especially you at home should not be too austere in your eating habits. Buy some good food and no one will say you are a woman who likes to spend money a great deal.

Our little son and Ah Sow are going to have a baby. Boy or girl we shall love and cherish it just the same. The baby is expected in a few months. Later on I'm going to send you the necessary funds to use in the setting of several tables for the celebration of the first born of our son. I will do the same here. I will advise you by airmail when the baby is born . . ."

The next day Wah Gay, carrying a bulging bag of groceries and beaming, pushed the doorbell to Mei Oi's apartment. The door opened slowly. "Heh, heh, Ah Sow, how are you?" The father-in-law smiled broadly.

"Lao Yair," the startled Mei Oi bowed slightly. "You come in." She noticed the brown paper bag. "You have bought so many things. There's no need for all this." She turned and Wah Gay followed her in. "Yes, come in and sit down," she invited belatedly. When they reached the kitchen, she added, "You have a kind heart."

"I wanted to come up last week," said the father-in-law, putting the groceries down on the table. "But something came up to prevent me."

"Yes, I know. I know you're very busy." Mei Oi remained standing. She began putting the food in the refrigerator. There were a whole chicken, some pork chops, a bottle of Ng Gar Pai, *Ong gay* roots, herbs, and some shelled peanuts. While she was putting away the groceries, she kept looking at her watch. With the passing of each minute, she got more nervous. Wah Gay was without his usual cigar, an obvious concession to the presence of his daughter-in-law. Mei Oi began stealing glances at the kitchen clock. Five minutes to two. She could almost hear it tick. She wanted to ask her father-in-law to stay for a cup of tea but she didn't dare. Yet to turn one's father-in-law away without offering a cup of tea was unforgivably rude. Mei Oi stared at the watch again. Should she ask him to stay? Maybe she'd better not. There wasn't much time. Two o'clock . . .

Suddenly Mei Oi grimaced and placed her palm on her forehead.

"What's the matter, Ah Sow?" asked Wah Gay, alarmed. "Are you all right? Is everything all right?"

"I . . . I was going to lie down for a moment. I have a terrible headache. I . . . I was going to lie down when you rang the

116

door bell. I have been this way for the last few days."

"Go to your room and lie down and rest," said Wah Gay. "Is there anything I can do before I leave?"

"Are you leaving so soon?" asked Mei Oi weakly from another room.

"Yes, I'm leaving. Try and get a little sleep."

Nearing the corner of Catherine and East Broadway, Wah Gay saw Ah Song crossing the street, coming toward him. "You sonovabitch, where do you think you're going?" he asked.

"I . . . I'm going to look up a carpenter to fix my door," said Ah Song. "My door is no good."

"I didn't know you get up this early," said Wah Gay and continued down the street.

When Ah Song saw his mah-jong crony continue toward Chatham Square, he felt relieved. He stood and watched Wah Gay cross over to Mott Street. Then he turned and headed for Mei Oi's apartment.

XXVII

When Ben Loy first learned that his wife was pregnant, he was not impressed. In fact he was a little irritated because Mei Oi had called him when he was busy at the restaurant.

Upon further reflection, however, he became elated over the news. He remembered the encounters he had had with friends: Is Auntie going to have a baby? Is there any good news? Heh, heh, what are you waiting for? And from his father: How is Ah Sow these days? Is she well? The old man did not come right out and ask it, but Ben Loy knew what he meant. Wing Sim's wife was no exception: When are you going to invite us to the happy banquet? From his mother Lau Shee, writing to his father: Ben Loy and Lee Shee have been married more than a year. I should think it's time that they have a little one.

Only a week earlier he had seen no way out of his predicament. He had reconciled himself to remaining childless, and he would defend himself with: We don't want children. He consoled himself that in America many couples are childless. But being Chinese, he supposed that his parents would insist, sooner or later, that he and Mei Oi adopt a little boy to carry on the ancestral name, so that someone will cry at his and her funerals. In China, if the children were all girls, the parents would eventually adopt a boy. They want to keep the family name in the tablet house forever, and only a boy could make that possible. A daughter would merely become somebody else's wife.

Ben Loy told himself that, if the baby was a girl, he would not go looking for a boy to adopt. Boy or girl, what's the difference? In America, girls are looked upon with more love and affection than boys anyway.

He was happy because it was the most natural thing for a married couple to do, to have a baby.

When he thought of his youthful foolishness, he despised

118

himself. He felt guilty for speaking sharply to Mei Oi when she called to tell him about the baby. But he would have been more courteous if it had not been so unexpected.

Mixed with this glad tiding, the father-to-be experienced an emotional shock. He had not believed that he was capable of becoming a father. The many months that it took for his wife to become pregnant certainly did not add to his manly pride. With some exceptions, during his year and a half of marriage to Mei Oi, he had been sexually incompetent. He knew he had not been a successful husband. He had left his wife unrewarded.

He kept trying to ignore questions in his own mind. Where did the baby come from? Could it be his? If not his, whose? At first, Ben Loy scoffed at the idea of confiding his problem to another. Nevertheless, he considered as a possible confidant his old roommate, Chin Yuen. Chin Yuen had been a school teacher in China. But how could Ben Loy bring up the subject without embarrassment to himself? Say, my wife is going to have a baby and I think it's someone else's? That would be enough to start the laughter rolling. Where would he hide his face then? He certainly could not mention the matter to his father. No doubt a non-Chinese son would take such a matter up with his father. Only last week Ben Loy had overheard in the restaurant a son calling his father George and his mother Beatrice. From his agonized predicament he envied and admired the outspoken American. On second thought, however, he dismissed this out-spokenness as animal behaviorism. A Chinese would never confide to his own father that he suspected his wife of infidelity.

"Hey, waiter!" called out the man in booth four. "We ordered subgum chow mein." He lifted the lid off. "This is shrimp chow mein." He replaced the metal lid quickly and looked up at Ben Loy, who meekly took the dish away.

In the same evening two other customers complained: I ordered barbecue spareribs. Is this barbecue spareribs? One customer ordered egg rolls and Ben Loy brought him an order of roast pork.

A boy about six wanted vanilla ice cream and Ben Loy made the mistake of bringing him chocolate. The parents could not persuade the little boy to change his mind. When Ben Loy finally arrived with a dish of vanilla, the mother said: "He's just being disagreeable. Lots of times at home he eats chocolate ice cream. You can't tell me he doesn't like chocolate ice cream!"

That was no solace to Ben Loy. Because of his confused mind, he decided to see Dr. Long on his next day off. "I'm nervous, doctor," he said. "I kept making mistakes in the orders."

The doctor prescribed some pills for his nerves and told him to take a few days off from work. On the way out of the doctor's office, Ben Loy, sounding as casual as he could, asked: "Say, Doc, could a fellow who has trouble in getting an erection become a father?"

"Sure, why not?" replied the doctor.

That was enough for Ben Loy. His face glowed as he walked home.

When he got home, he called his friend Chin Yuen. "Work a few days for me, will you?" Ben Loy asked.

"What's the matter, sick or something?"

"Yes, sick," he replied. "Nothing much, just a little sick."

XXVIII

When Ben Loy left the Chinese Theater the next day, he intended to get a haircut. But when he peered through the plate glass of a nearby barbershop and saw there were others waiting and only one barber in attendance, he did not go in. He swung into Mott Street.

As he descended the stairs of the Wah Que Barber Shop, strands of Cantonese opera music floated from inside the shop. Blocks and cymbals. A shrill voice called out. A heightened cadence of the drums. Excited dialogue which he did not make out. As he neared the door, the music became louder. Some more dialogue. It was Gim Peng Moy, a well-known Chinese classic, a story about a housewife married to the older of two brothers. When the Second Uncle returned from the wars, she impetuously fell in love with him and subsequently, through wiles and trickery, seduced him. Ben Loy purposely slowed his steps and listened intently. He immediately compared Mei Oi to Gim Peng Moy. Are they the same type of woman? But I have no brother, he consoled himself.

Next he found himself seated in the barber's chair. "What's the name of the record that's playing now?" he inquired.

"That's Gim Peng Moy. A good record." The barber wrapped a towel around Ben Loy's neck.

"Oh, is that a popular record?" pursued Ben Loy.

"Yes, I guess so," said the barber, now flipping an apron on the customer. "I guess people like it because of the sexy story. Everybody likes sex, you know."

Ah Mow knew who Ben Loy was, but he refrained from revealing this knowledge in his conversation. Very often he would come up from his shop and stand at the top of the stairs and watch people go by. He didn't know his name was Ben Loy, but he knew he was Wang Wah Gay's son.

Expertly guiding the clippers around the edges, the barber looked for strands of grey on Ben Loy's head, but he could find none. Looking for grey hair on a customer's head was a sort of hobby with him. He allowed himself the observation that many young folks, men and women, get grey prematurely.

"You're still very young," he finally remarked. "Not a strand of grey hair on you."

"Yeah?" replied Ben Loy unenthusiastically.

"Some people get grey pretty young. Even in their early twenties."

The record player continued with Gim Peng Moy. Second Uncle was about to be seduced by his brother's wife. The crashing of cymbals and blocks testified to the urgency of the action. Even the barber stopped his barbering momentarily to concentrate on the climax of this opera. Ben Loy was listening attentively too; but it was obvious that he was not enjoying it as much as he should.

"Many years ago when they had the opera house right here on the Bowery," volunteered Ah Mow, "whenever they played Gim Peng Moy, they played to standing room only."

"Everybody is interested in sex," cut in Ah Sing, who had kept quiet up to now.

"Everybody but you, you dead boy. You're dead," said Ah Mow pleasantly to his employee. Then the cymbals and blocks became so loud that talk was impossible and they waited for the music to subside. "Some girls nowadays aren't worth a copper penny," he resumed expectantly. "Just like Gim Peng Moy." He watched for any change of expression on Ben Loy's face. His eyes almost touched the customer's face, who seemed to wince. The proprietor waited for him to say something. Then he saw the lips slowly part. But Ben Loy opened them only to compress them. He began to hate himself for having come into this hole of a basement. He should have waited at the other barber shop, he told himself. But how could they be talking about him? They don't even know him. They certainly don't know Mei Oi.

He closed his eyes tightly and tried to relax, pretending to listen intently to the long playing record. But his thoughts took him back to the conversation at hand. He could hear the . . .

chop . . . chop . . . of the scissors. . . . Girls nowadays aren't worth a copper penny. Just like Gim Peng Moy . . .

Is Mei Oi like Gim Peng Moy? Is she? No, she can't be!

When he got home he told his wife he was tired and wanted to lie down and rest.

"Yes, you must be tired," said his wife tenderly. "You'll feel much better after a rest." Immediately she was sorry she had said it. She wished she had asked him to go out to buy something for her so she could call Ah Song. She would ask him yet. She got up and tiptoed to the bedroom and gently pushed open the door. Her husband was curled up in bed in street clothes, minus his shoes, apparently already asleep. Let him sleep. With another wifely glance at Ben Loy, she walked brusquely back to the living room and put away the knitting needles. She must hurry. Ah Song had no set date to drop in to see her. All he knew was that Wednesday was Ben Loy's day off. What if he should show up today, Thursday? As noiselessly as she could, she dialed Ah Song's number. The silence between rings seemed endless, like the Pacific Ocean. The moments ticked away like a whole lifetime until finally someone answered the phone.

"Hello?"

"Uncle Song?" Mei Oi whispered. Her heart pounded hard and fast, and she began to perspire. "This is Mei Oi. Ben Loy is home. Yes, he's taking a few days off. Don't come up to the house until you hear from me. No, I can't talk to you anymore. Bye." She hung up. She was frightened. It was the first time she had ever called Ah Song. The mere thought of it made her feel ashamed. She gently pushed open the bedroom door. Ben Loy was still asleep. Seeing him there, sound asleep, she felt safe and undiscovered.

For many weeks Ah Song had been bringing Mei Oi chickens, pork chops, herbs and Ng Gar Pai, all deemed nutritious for the expectant mother. There was always a pot or two boiling on the range in Mei Oi's apartment. When Ben Loy came home at night, he would walk over to the range, lift up the lid, and sniff at the concoction.

"That's pig's tail," Mei Oi would call out. "It's good for my back."

He never asked her where she got the pig's tail; he assumed she bought it herself. Ben Loy himself had gone out once and bought a pullet when Mei Oi complained of dizziness. Chicken and herbs and whiskey, brewed in a double boiler, would be very beneficial to her. Not being a drinking woman, a few drops would make her face like Quon Gung's, the red-faced hero of the Three Kingdoms. Even sipping the soup brewed with whiskey made her face red. But she liked these things. She liked even more the attentions that came with them. She enjoyed being sick and eating these liquid foods. And it made her especially happy when Ah Song came with all these things.

As she resumed her knitting in the living room, her heart continued to throb rapidly. The great pleasures she got from her indiscretions were worth the risk, she assured herself. Later when she walked into the bedroom, Ben Loy stirred.

"What's the matter, can't you sleep?" Mei Oi asked softly.

"No, I can't sleep," he replied drowsily. Slowly he brought himself up to a sitting position, with his feet dangling from the edge of the bed. "I think I'll go and see a movie."

"But you have just come back from one," Mei Oi protested.

"I'm going uptown to see an American movie."

"Eat something before you go. I'm going to cook now."

"I'm not hungry." With that he walked out of the room.

Once out on the street, instead of going uptown, he turned north on East Broadway and headed for the Chinese Theater. He purchased a ticket without bothering to find out what was playing. After an hour or so in the theater, he couldn't keep his mind on the screen. He didn't know what was playing and he didn't care. The ghost of Gim Peng Moy kept hammering at his consciousness. Is Mei Oi the same type of woman as Gim Peng Moy? Does she belong to the "nowadays women are no good" brand of human beings? What is she doing at this very moment?

On the screen, the leading man was singing a love song.

Ben Loy got up abruptly and bolted out of the theater. He sped home as fast as his legs could carry him. As he inserted his key to the apartment door, he was full of violence and suspicion. The next minute he was calm, sheepish, and full of good will. Mei Oi was on the couch, knitting, just as he had left her.

124

XXIX

The next day, during the lull between lunch and dinner, Chin Yuen called from the restaurant to find out how his old friend, Ben Loy, was getting along. Mei Oi answered the phone.

"Hello, is Ben Loy home?" asked Chin Yuen.

"No, he is not home. Who is this?"

"This is Chin Yuen," he announced. The voice at the other end sounded soothing and exciting to the former school master.

"Oh, Mr. Chin, you're working for Ben Loy."

"Yes, I'm calling to find out how he is."

"He's much better. Thank you. You need not worry."

"I hope he'll be able to come back to work soon." Chin Yuen made his voice as pleasant as he possibly could.

"He's all right now," assured Mei Oi. "There's nothing the matter with him. You have a very kind heart to call."

"Kind of you to say that," said Chin Yuen, delighted at her sweet voice. He smiled into the receiver.

"You have a kind heart. Thank you." A gleam appeared in Chin Yuen's eyes as he hung up. "Please come and visit us." He wondered if Ben Loy's wife still remembered him from the brief meeting when he had dropped in to welcome them on their arrival in New York. Ben Loy had introduced him to his wife as an old friend. He had been asked to stay for dinner, but had found it necessary to decline. Ever since then Chin Yuen had regretted his inability to accept this dinner engagement. For, if he had stayed for dinner, he would have had the opportunity to become more familiar with Mei Oi. He hoped for another such invitation, but none had come. Perhaps an invitation to dinner was too big a face to expect; so he began to entertain the thought that some day his old friend might invite him to his home for tea. He supposed that, after all, there was much work involved in the preparation of a dinner. But tea . . . was different.

Chin Yuen went to an empty booth in the rear of the dining room and sat down. A few moments later another waiter joined him.

"How is Ben Loy today?" asked the waiter.

"I just called his home. His wife said he is much better."

"His wife? Did you talk to his wife?"

"Sure. What's wrong with that?"

"Nothing, except . . . except that . . . that people say his wife is seeing another man. Oop—I shouldn't have talked."

Chin Yuen shook his head in disbelief, startled at the disclosure. To him Ben Loy seemed a little boy, lost in the wilderness, not knowing which way to turn. That first night with Ben Loy at the Hotel Lansing flashed back to him. The night of the big snow. Ben Loy then was a naive, likable lad. He hadn't changed much. . . . But who could this other fellow be? Chin Yuen thought he was the only one, aside from Ben Loy's father and father-in-law, to have set foot inside his apartment. There was a scintilla of jealousy on the part of Chin Yuen, who admitted to himself that he might have been the other man in the love theft if it had not been for his friendship for the husband. Now, with the revelation of Mei Oi's infidelity, he felt a personal challenge in the situation.

XXX

Inadvertently one Sunday, Lee Gong overheard snatches of conversation drifting from a nearby table while sipping coffee at The Coffee Cup on Bayard Street. The stools at the counter were all taken. Lee Gong was at the end stool, and the five tables were occupied. The gossipers were three men sitting at a table next to the end of the counter.

"Did you know that Wang Wah Gay's son is wearing a *green hat* and he doesn't even know it?" said the thin man whose back was turned to Lee Gong. While his hand, now a little shaky, brought the cup's brim to his mouth, Lee Gong did not drink it. His ears strained for the conversation at the table.

"Nowadays girls are no damned good," said the second man.

"Yeah," said the third, "a stinky fish matched with a stinky shrimp."

Lee Gong toyed with his coffee. When he replaced the cup on the saucer he drew out a cigarette, but his shaking hands made lighting it difficult.

"They say this guy goes up to her apartment when her husband is at work."

A steady stream of customers kept pressing through the door, coming and going. Finally, with one gulp, Lee Gong finished his coffee and left hurriedly. He was afraid of meeting someone he knew who might have heard the conversation. The very thought made his face darken. The veins stood out around the temples.

Outside the coffee shop, the fresh air was a welcome relief. Slowly he walked on Mott Street, with bowed head. . . . These sonovabitches are liars . . . I like to cut open their bellies . . . Mei Oi would do no such things . . . trouble makers . . . these people are trouble makers . . . the name of the man involved was not mentioned . . . Liars. . . . Could this happen to me, Lee Gong? . . . A good thing it had not been Wah Gay who was sitting there . . . listening . . . for he patronized the place several times a day . . .

Someone called "Uncle Gong" to him on the street but he did not hear him and continued walking toward his apartment. He climbed the stairs slowly, sighing heavily with each step . . . Mei Oi . . . why did you do this to me? . . . to your mother? . . .

He fumbled for the key and finally he stuck the wrong one in the key hole. He cursed furiously. Once inside he sank down on his single folding bed and buried his head in the pillow . . . If Ben Loy were a bad boy . . . a husband who goes after other women . . . it might be excusable . . . but Ben Loy is a good boy . . . a good husband . . . a good provider . . . a conscientious worker . . . he's the kind of son-in-law anyone would pick . . . no vice of any kind . . .

He flopped over and lay on his back. He was breathing heavily, like a physically wounded man. It was strange to find himself in his room at this time of day. He should be at Wah Gay's club house playing mah-jong, which was what he had planned to do after his cup of coffee. He stared absently at the coal stove with its blackened chimney sticking into the wall.

He had lived in this room for more than twenty years. Twenty years is a long time. Maybe this room is unlucky. . . . Look what happened to his old roommate Lee Sam . . . still at the hospital somewhere on Long Island. . . .

Sam was working in a laundry when one night two men came in to beat and rob him . . . after that he was never the same . . . he kept saying that someone was after him . . . someone was looking through the plate glass at him with a butcher knife . . . finally they had to come and take him away . . . maybe this room brings bad luck. . . . Sooner or later the scandal about Mei Oi will get back to the village . . . the whole village will hear about it . . . Lee Gong's daughter . . . hardly two years in America . . . look what has happened to her . . . I don't care for myself because I'm here in New York . . . just feel sorry for the old female rice cooker in the village . . . she has no place to hide . . . no place to go . . . in New York it is different . . . maybe . . . maybe all this talk is nonsense . . . still why should people make up such a story? . . .

128

After a long while he got up and walked over to the window facing Mott Street. Directly across from him was the Congregational Church. Lee Gong had never gone inside that church except to try his luck on the dice tables when the church ran a bazaar. He stared down at the church for a full minute, picturing himself going to church for any other reason than to play dice. This thought almost brought a suppressed chuckle. . . . Had she been a little older, she would have been in a better position to judge things for herself . . . she was like a child lost in thick forest . . . perhaps it would have been better if she had been permitted to marry a school teacher instead of marrying Ben Loy and coming to New York. . . .

But like all fathers in the village, Lee Gong had wanted to do the right thing, marry his daughter off to a *gimshunhock*. And in Wang Ben Loy, he thought he had found the most eligible bachelor. He knew Ben Loy was a good boy and a conscientious worker. A handsome lad without vice. What more could a prospective father-in-law want in a son-in-law? Ben Loy was the embodiment of the perfect son-in-law. Who could have forecast what was going to happen in less than two short years? In another two years maybe Lee Gong himself would be dead and buried, dead of a heartache. But even his death would not prevent people from talking: Lee Gong's daughter knitted a nice green hat for her husband to wear and it fitted him perfectly.

Slowly Lee Gong rose from his bed again. It was his usual time to eat but he was not hungry. He didn't think he would feel like eating for many days to come. He could never sleep tonight if he didn't hear from the lips of Mei Oi what had happened.

He walked across the converging traffic at Chatham Square without noticing the lights or the traffic and a north-bound car on Park Row screeched to a stop. The driver shouted "Hey, why don't you watch where you're goin'!" But Lee Gong continued on to the sidewalk without so much as turning his head.

He became confused as to which street to turn to for Mei Oi's apartment. He seldom had been on this side of Chatham Square. The last time was when he visited Mei Oi upon her arrival in New York. It was only when he came upon the school

129

building that he knew that Mei Oi's apartment was close by. He remembered the little candy store on the ground floor. Satisfied that he was at the right place, he wearily climbed the stairs. His feet dragged. He mounted the steps as if he were carrying a hundred pounds of rice on his back. He had to grab at the railing to pull himself up.

Although there was a button for the bell, he knocked on the glass panel of the door and called out hoarsely, "Mei Oi, Mei Oi!" Through the glass panel he could see the lights come on in the apartment. Then he could hear the shuffling of feet.

"Who are you?" a woman's voice called from inside.

"Mei Oi, open the door. This is your Papa." The voice sounded urgent in the darkened hallway.

The door swung open. "Papa, come in," invited Mei Oi in a surprised tone.

Lee Gong walked in without saying anything. Mei Oi led him into the living room, where he sank down on the big arm chair. "Mei Oi," the father began accusingly, "why did you do this to me?"

"Do what?" asked Mei Oi. "What are you talking about, Papa?"

"Today when I was having a cup of coffee at the Coffee Cup, I overheard three people talking about Wah Gay's daughter-in-law. *You* are Wang Wah Gay's daughter-in-law, aren't you?" Lee Gong stared fiercely at his daughter. "They said this Wang Wah Gay's daughter-in-law knitted a *green hat* for her husband to wear!" he roared.

"Where did you get such a story?" demanded Mei Oi, shaken by the accusation.

"I just told you where I got it from. Are you deaf?"

"Propaganda," said Mei Oi. "Rumors. Just many-mouthed birds spreading rumors." She was terrified of her father.

"If it's not true, why should people talk like that about you?" retorted Lee Gong.

"I don't know," Mei Oi searched frantically for an appropriate answer, trying to pull her thoughts together, fearing that her father might be enraged enough to strike her. Her mind was a blank. She couldn't think. After a long time, she added uneasily, "I have no control over their mouths."

130

"Such talks will ruin me. Ruin you. Ruin Ben Loy and Wah Gay," said Lee Gong, his face flushed. He waved a menacing finger at Mei Oi. "Have you no shame?"

"Papa, I did nothing wrong," she sobbed. She had never seen her father this angry before. "Don't listen to what others say."

He had no proof of Mei Oi's infidelity. As a father, Lee Gong was already experiencing a mixture of bitterness and pity. He was bitter because he felt his own daughter had brought disgrace upon himself. He was condescendingly compassionate because Mei Oi was so young, so naive and ignorant of life-things.

"If you didn't do anything wrong, why do people talk this way?" growled the father.

"I told you I don't know." Mei Oi's heart sank and she was full of shame.

"If you did do anything wrong, consider yourself no longer my daughter," said Lee Gong. "I have no such daughter."

"Please don't be angry, father," said Mei Oi. "I'll make you some coffee." She got up to go to the kitchen.

"Don't bother," said the father. "I just had a cup before I came up."

"Maybe you'll stay for dinner then," said the daughter, trying frantically to change the subject. How could she confess such a face-less thing to her own father? It might have been easier if she had known him all her life.

"No. I'm leaving!" Lee Gong jumped up and without saying another word, stalked out of the apartment.

"Don't worry, Papa," Mei Oi called after him. "You don't have to worry about anything." Then she burst into tears.

XXXI

Mei Oi's vehement denial left Lee Gong unconvinced of his daughter's innocence. He kept asking himself: If it isn't true, why do people say such things about my daughter? Why did they mention Wang Wah Gay's daughter-in-law and not someone else's? He wondered how many people had heard of this face-losing affair of Mei Oi. What hurt the old man most was that Mei Oi was an only child, a son and daughter rolled into one. In a family of many children, one should expect some bad ones, but an only child such as Mei Oi—she is her parents' whole world. A father with many children could take solace in the soundness of the good ones. But Lee Gong had no other children to turn to. At a time when he needed the comfort and sympathy of his wife most, she was many thousands of li away. His whole body shook with anguish. Who is this scoundrel who had wronged his daughter? He wanted to pump his body full of bullets. Then he could die peacefully.

Lee Gong grabbed the bottle of Ng Gar Pai from the table next to the bed and poured himself a full glass. He downed it quickly. He kept it there for mild insomnia. When he tossed in bed and found it impossible to sleep, he would reach for the bottle and pour himself a drink. Then he would sleep like a child. But never before had he felt the urge to resort to the bottle during the day. Even when he drank at night, it was done in moderation. He never downed a full glass in one gulp.

An hour later, the bottle was empty. He decided to write a note to Ah Song; for he had concluded that Ah Song was the number one suspect . . . Mei Oi had been in New York less than two years. . . . During that period, who could have had the chance to know her well enough to bring on the scandal? . . . Ben Loy had been a good boy, above reproach. . . . If Mei Oi had married an old man, as some girls do, it might have been excusable for her to seek a young lover. . . . But Ben Loy and Mei Oi were the same age and they had every reason to be happily married. . . .

He poured some thick black ink into the dried inkwell, which held a piece of black-stained cotton. He used the writing brush only when he wrote to his wife Jung Shee. But now he wanted to impress Ah Song with his business-like determination, and he thought a writing brush and black ink would convey his feelings with added dignity. He began to write with strong, steady strokes, quickly and without hesitation.

Ah Song, you dead boy: In accordance with our Chinese culture, you have committed an unpardonable sin. Kung-fu-tze had said "male and female are not to mix socially." You have brought shame and dishonor to an otherwise honorable family. If you do not stop seeing this housewife immediately, you will have an unfortunate ending. You will not be warned again. You know what I mean. If you value your life, leave this woman alone! From one who fights injustice.

He paused and reread the message before inserting it in an envelope and addressing it. Unsteadily he made his way downstairs to mail the letter. After he dropped the letter into the mail box at the corner of Mott and Bayard Streets, he felt a sense of great accomplishment. He would now sit back and watch for the results of his missive.

As he walked back to his lonely room on the top floor, Lee Gong's shoulders sagged noticeably. Dusk was fast descending upon Chinatown, and a sudden, sharp wind twirled in the sky. Lee Gong grabbed at his left shoulder with his right hand and then banged his fist against it several times, futilely. Damned rheumatism! He looked up at the threatening sky. He breathed deeply, defiantly, the rain-filled air. Yes, he said to himself, it will rain tonight.

XXXII

The president of the Wang Association glanced at his watch and it was only a quarter to one. He would wait until one o'clock and then call Wah Gay. His cousin was not one to get up early, Wang Chuck Ting thought to himself.

His mind flashed back to the day of the Grand Opening of the Wang Association Building in 1934. The chair and desk set where he now sat was a gift from the Ping On Tong on that auspicious occasion. Back in the thirties he had been president of Ping On Tong, and during those years he had appointed Wah Gay a member of the deliberating committee. Now after so many active years in Tong politics, he enjoyed the status of an elder statesman. No longer a candidate for any Tong office, he was a friend of everybody. He had a reputation for fair dealing and everybody respected him for this. His China Pagoda in Stanton served as a semi-retirement hangout for him. He was perennially elected president of the Wangs, although he himself had declared he did not want the job.

In another moment he was angry. Angry that his cousin Wah Gay should have the misfortune to be involved in a scandal. It wasn't his cousin's fault, of course, but the good name of the family was at stake. Not only Wah Gay's family, but all the Wangs would lose face if some means could not be found to hush this whispering campaign that was finding its way into attentive and eager ears in the shops and rooms of Chinatown. He consulted his watch again and deftly picked up the receiver and dialed a number.

"Hello? Elder brother Wah Gay? This is Chuck Ting."

"How are you, Chuck Ting *gaw*?" answered Wah Gay gleefully. "What is it now?"

"There is a small matter I'd like to talk to you about," he said.

"Where are you now?"

"I'm at the social club."

"Okay. I'll come up in a few minutes."

Wah Gay had no idea what the president wanted him for. As he walked toward the five-story Wang Association Building on Mott Street, he wondered if his cousin might want him to act as co-signer for some cousin who wanted to borrow money. Two months ago Chuck Ting had called him for just such a purpose. Why can't he get someone else for a co-signer this time?

The Social Club was filled with smoke and people when Wah Gay opened the door to what was formerly apartments two and three. Their common wall had been torn down to convert them into a social gathering place for the Wangs and their friends in New York. He heard the clack of mah-jongs even before the door was opened. The mah-jong table was in the center of the room. Several elbow-rubbers sat watching and kibitzing. Ah Ton was preparing dinner in the tiny alcove to the right. A heavy blue apron hung loosely on his person.

"Ah Ton gaw, cooking rice so early?" asked Wah Gay when he saw Ah Ton with a dipper in his hand.

"Not early, brother. Not early," replied Ah Ton. He was a dark and lanky man in his early sixties.

"Want to play a game?" someone invited Wah Gay.

"Come here and take my place," enticed another.

"No, thank you," said Wah Gay, raising his hand in mild protest. "I'm busy. I'm here to see the president."

"He's in there," said someone, pointing to an inner office.

Without knocking, Wah Gay pushed open the door. He backed out quickly when he saw the president was engaged in conversation with someone else. He turned to while away the time by joining the kibitzers and putting his nose close to the mah-jong table. He lit a cigar and contributed to the smoke floating about the room.

"Wow your mother, I should have won this hand!"

"You illegitimate boy, consider yourself lucky."

"You guys would rather talk than play."

Smoke clouds filled the room and the aroma of cigars and cigarettes vied with the odors of Ah Ton's cooking.

The door to the inner office opened and a man stepped out,

followed by Chuck Ting. The latter motioned for Wah Gay to enter.

He indicated a chair for him. "I have a little bad news for you," began Chuck Ting painfully. He interlocked his fingers and twirled his thumbs. He swung on the swivel chair and came face to face with his visitor. "It concerns your daughter-in-law."

"*My* daughter-in-law?" asked Wah Gay, startled. He tried not to look alarmed. "What about her?" He was more curious than shocked.

"I got my story from my boy, and he got it from his wife," continued Chuck Ting. "He came out here and told me about it the other day. Said something about his wife hearing about it in a beauty salon on Mulberry Street last Sunday. . . ."

Wah Gay sat numbed and speechless. His earlier nonchalance was gone. But, as serious as the matter sounded, he was confident that there was nothing to it. What could his daughter-in-law do wrong? After all, she had been in New York only a year and a half. What could be so terribly bad about her? And Ben Loy was a good boy too. . . .

"I'm talking to you as a brother. As an elder brother, not as president of the Association. There's nothing official about this. . . ." He paused to light a cigar and began puffing on it until it glowed. Then, as if he had committed an unpardonable sin, he hurriedly pulled another cigar out of his inside pocket and apologetically offered it to Wah Gay, who accepted it with thanks. "I hope this matter will never be taken up by the association," continued Chuck Ting. "It would be too much of a disgrace. Maybe a little talk will smooth out this whole thing. But it has to be confidential."

Wah Gay did not interrupt. He waited for his cousin to continue.

"Nowadays the young are not like what they used to be," resumed Chuck Ting. "They have no respect for their elders. They are all out for a good time. They don't know right from wrong."

He paused to throw out a stream of smoke from his cigar. His face tensed and a pained expression appeared. The easy flow of language was no longer there. "That sonovabitch Ah Song is absolutely useless!" he roared. Only the fear that someone outside the office might hear him made him lower his voice. "He has a history of being a stinky dead snake. Everybody knows that. It has gotten out that your daughter-in-law and Ah Song are seeing each other. Now you see how this thing has gotten around. Even in Connecticut people have heard about it. You can see how far this thing has gone."

"Ah Song?" Wah Gay refused to believe it. "Ah Song and my daughter-in-law?" He was stunned. "If someone else were to tell me this, I would not believe it. We all know he's a rascal but I would never have thought he would do this to me. I have known him for more than twenty years. Every day he plays mah-jong in my basement. . . ."

"There are all sorts of people," said Chuck Ting. "The bad will always be bad. A person like Ah Song would gouge out his father's eyes."

"I'm going to wrench his head off," said Wah Gay angrily.

"His type you should no longer allow in your basement," said Chuck Ting. "Don't even let him set foot inside your threshold."

"I wish we had some proof. Some proof that he is seeing this good-for-nothing daughter-in-law of mine!"

"Women cannot be trusted," said Chuck Ting. "I've always told my boy to run his family with a firm hand."

"And we always say that *jook sing* girls are no good," sighed Wah Gay. "That's why everybody goes back to China to get married. A village girl will make a good wife, they say. She will not run around. She can tell right from wrong. She will stay home and cook rice for you."

After the initial outburst against Ah Song, the crimson on the president's face had disappeared and he was now calmer. "No one can foretell everything," he said, once more swinging on his chair. "We'll have to keep this quiet. At least as quiet as we can."

"I have no face to meet my friends," said Wah Gay sadly.

"I don't think you should say anything to Lee Gong about it yet. What has happened, has happened. As soon as I heard of this thing, I thought I would let you know first. I don't want you to be the last one to find out."

137

"You have always been a good brother," said Wah Gay. "And I know you will always do the right thing."

"You can go back now." Chuck Ting got up and stretched his arms. "Keep everything quiet."

On his way out, Wah Gay waved goodbye perfunctorily to those gathered at the table. The moment he stepped out of sight, voices began talking all at once in hushed tones.

"I'll bet he was talking about his daughter-in-law," whispered someone at the table.

"He always said what a fine boy his son was," said another.

"What's the boy got to do with it?" demanded another. "It's the girl, the wife."

"Yeah, it's that good-for-nothing bitch!"

"Someone should make an example of that Ah Song or whatever his name is," said the third man.

"We ought to hang him."

"No, it would be better to cut his throat."

Just then the president emerged from his office, and an unusual silence fell. He stuck his hands in his pants pockets and started to make light talk. "Who's winning? Who is going to buy coffee?"

"Hey, Uncle Ton," said the man who had the most chips in front of him, "go and get some coffee, will you?" He toyed with the chips and then dug into his pocket and pulled out two singles. "Here, get us some coffee and pastry."

"Wow your mother," said the man opposite him. "We're going to eat soon. Why do we have to get coffee now? They say a cup of coffee spoils a bowl of rice."

"Wow his mother. He's jealous because someone is spending a couple of dollars."

Without saying a word, Ah Ton came over and, hurriedly wiping clean his hands on the apron, grabbed the two dollars that were extended to him.

Over coffee the cousins continued to discuss the case of the *green hat*, after one of them had broken the ice by cautiously saying, "By the way, Chairman, did you hear about a recent scandal involving one of our own members?"

But Chuck Ting cautioned his cousins not to discuss the matter with outsiders, adding, "Family shame is not for the outsider."

XXXIII

Shortly after his return to work, Ben Loy received a call from his father, asking him to come to see him on his day off. Ben Loy had asked his father to talk over the phone, but the elder Wang replied that the matter could not be discussed over the telephone.

The following Wednesday Ben Loy steeled himself for the ordeal of meeting his father. He had always dreaded talking to the old man; for there existed a stern relationship between a Chinese father and his son. The prevailing practice is for neither to speak to the other unless he has to. As he walked toward the Money Come Club, the thought foremost on his mind was to get out of his father's place as soon as possible. Perhaps his father had another one of those letters from his mother. What could a letter from Lau Shee contain? The usual things: "Need more money, send more home." Or: "What is Ben Loy and Lee Shee waiting for? I'm getting old. I want a grandchild before I close my eyes . . ."

When he tried the door, it was locked. He took a quarter from his pocket and knocked on the glass panel. Tap . . . tap . . . tap. There was no movement within. Then he put his nose against the glass, and he could see the silhouette of his father in the darkened interior hurrying to open the door.

"Come in," the elder Wang greeted.

"Did I wake you up?" Ben Loy stepped inside.

"No, I woke up a long time ago. I didn't bother to get up. I was reading the papers in bed." The father fiddled with the belt of his bathrobe. "Sit down. I'll be with you in a moment."

Even with the 100-watt bulb burning in the middle of the room directly above the mah-jong table, the room looked dingy. To Ben Loy, having just come in from the sunlight, the room was like a dimly-lit tunnel. As the minutes ticked by, he began to discern the various objects in the room. He felt a dampness coursing through his body. This he attributed to his unfamiliarity with the place. This was really the first time he had sat in the room. Previously he had been in and out, like a mailman. He wrinkled his nose. "It's like a dungeon," he said to himself. Only an old man like his father could stand a shut-in dingy place like this. It seemed a long time before Wah Gay came out.

"Ben Loy," he began slowly, taking a seat almost opposite from his son. "I've heard some very distressing news. Do you have any idea what it is?"

"No," he replied sulkily.

"I've heard from reliable sources that Ah Sow is running around with another man. Is that true?" His voice was stern but his manner was not unpleasant. He placed his palms on his lap and leaned forward. "I want to listen to the truth."

The question exploded on Ben Loy like ten thousand fire-crackers. It took him several seconds to recover from the shock. "This is the first time I've heard of it," he said nervously but defiantly. He pursed his lips. His first reaction was to dash out of the place, but he changed his mind and waited.

"It is your business to find out!" Wah Gay raised his voice, jumping to his feet. "She's *your* wife, not mine." He gestured vigorously with his hands. "It's a disgrace. Maybe you feel no shame, but I do!" He started pacing the floor. He whirled and faced his son. "People will say Wang Wah Gay's daughter-in-law is running around. They don't say *your* wife is running around!"

"Where did you get the news from?" demanded Ben Loy, not knowing what else to say. "It's all a lie," he added weakly.

"I hope it is," Wah Gay growled. "I hope it is. But when people talk like that, it's my business to find out!"

"People can say anything they want," retorted the son.

"But why should people say such a thing if it's not true?" the father demanded impatiently, clenching his fists. "Can you tell me that?"

"How should I know?" Ben Loy shot back. "I have no control over other people's mouths."

"No, but you can find out if it's true or not." Wah Gay shook a finger at his son. "People just don't talk for nothing. There must be a reason." He paused for an answer, but there was none. "Some people are stupid, but they are stupid only to a degree," continued the exasperated father. "Not like you. Unless your wife is no good, people don't say she's no good!"

Ben Loy stormed out of the club house and slammed the door behind him.

"Wow your mother," Wah Gay shouted after him, his face red and his veins bulging with anger. "You think because you can open and shut your eye lids, you're a human being? You dead boy!" He rushed up to the door and flipped the latch on the lock. "Sonavabitch!" His whole body shook with rage. Foolish. How foolish it was to get this no good dead son to this country in the first place! Should have left him in the village to work the fields . . .

The end of the world came crashing down upon the shoulders of Wah Gay. He saw in his son a renegade. A no good loafer. A stupid, useless youth. A son who would disgrace his own father. He had lost his one and only son. He and his wife had lived for the boy. The hopes of grandparenthood were just emerging over the horizon and they could see in their future many grandchildren. Wah Gay had enjoyed thoroughly the pleasant task of writing to his wife Lau Shee, informing her that Ah Sow was at last with child. This, he assumed, had only been the first of such missives. For indeed, in America, with the best possible nutrition, babies would come as regularly as the harvest. Lau Shee would announce proudly to their cousins in the village: Our Ben Loy has another son. And then there would be celebrations. There would be thanksgiving at the temples for Mei Oi's mother. Tiny feet and tiny voices would come in to see Grandpa . . .

But this beautiful picture was only a dream, a dream mirrored in the subconscious fantasy of the man. A mirror shattered by the alleged scandal of Ben Loy's wife. A mirror shattered and irreparable. The destruction of a beautiful picture. Wah Gay sighed an agonizing sigh, alone and to himself. What was there for him to do? Ben Loy had denied any wrong-doing by his wife. If Ben Loy did not care, why should the old man care?

The private meeting with Chuck Ting flooded his mind. But how could *he* stop it? He had just tried . . . with Ben Loy. What about Lee Shee? Could he talk to her? No. That would be out of the question. She is much closer to her husband than to her father-in-law. But the old man would be the first to feel the brunt of scandal-talk. Once this hushed whispering burst into lively coffee shop topics, where could an old-timer like Wah Gay hide? Get out of town? He would have to! The father-in-law gets out of town because the daughter-in-law misbehaves. What a farce that would make. One would think the father-in-law was a party to this misconduct.

If he hadn't sunk such deep roots in New York, Wah Gay would find it easier to pull up his stakes and disappear. After more than forty years in the community, a sudden uprooting would be bound to have repercussions. If he were to go else-where, say Boston or Washington, D.C., he had many friends there too. How could he face them? Through his membership in the Ping On Tong, he had made many contacts with out-of-town delegates when they came to New York for their conven-tions. Frequently these friends had come in and played mah-jong at his club house. They had sipped coffee together. Now when he needed to get out of town, the choice of site for his exile be-came agonizingly difficult. What would he say to his friends if they should ask him: Why did you leave New York after so many years? His type of business demanded a large enough city to have a number of mah-jong players. True, he could always go back to the restaurant business, but he was not yet ready for such a drastic move. At his age he would consider that only as a last resort. The prospect of returning to manual labor made the old man shake his head, more in shame than in self-pity. He had worked hard and long to leave the drudgery of the restaurant business for the semi-retirement of the mah-jong game. Return-ing to it now would be humiliating.

To write to his wife, Lau Shee, informing her of what had happened to her daughter-in-law, would be an insurmountable task. What words could he compose that would not bring tears and heartache to the recipient? That his own son is the wearer of a *green hat?* The mere words *green hat* would strike terror

142

and shame to anyone capable of human emotions. Like typhoid or polio.

His head spun with pains. Big pains. As big as a boulder. Now this boulder came tumbling out of the sky, like an exhausted satellite, and crash-landed on Wah Gay's head. The basement club house suddenly was dark and empty.

XXXIV

When Ben Loy bolted out of his father's club house that afternoon, he was fuming. Although he had long feared the possibility of an erring wife, he had not expected to hear of it from the lips of his own father. First he was shocked, then angry. He was all the more enraged because he had been told by the old man. This made it somehow official.

Anything that is officially reported must be acted upon. If it had been just a rumor, he might have been able to turn the other way, pretending he was deaf. But to be informed by one's own father of his wife's infidelity, that was the end of all pretense. How could he deny the allegations when he himself had no basis for this denial? He had planned to take Mei Oi to a movie uptown after his visit to his father, but now he did not feel like taking her to anything. In his mind he tried to formulate something concrete, something sensible to say to her. If his wife had to go to bed with another man, why did she have to be discovered! The discovery of an act is even more humiliating than the act itself. Impotency, when it is confined to the bedroom, may be condoned; but when it becomes public gossip, it is mortifying. Ben Loy was most concerned about any publicity over the cause of his wife's infidelity. Try as he would to dismiss the subject-matter as inconsequential, the humiliation and jealousy that raged within him could not be tamed.

When Ben Loy arrived home, Mei Oi was getting dressed to go out with her husband. She had on one of her long Chinese gowns, which she had grown fond of wearing lately. As he rushed into the bedroom, she was applying make-up to her face and neck.

"You don't have to doll up so much now," he jeered sarcastically.

The startled Mei Oi turned to meet his eyes. At first she

144

hoped he was joking. After one look at him, she knew he was not. "Loy Gaw," she said uncertainly, "I don't understand. Are you angry?"

"You want me to draw a picture for you?" he retorted.

"Not a picture," she said, "but at least tell me what's troubling you." She moved toward him to throw her arms around him, but Ben Loy pushed her away.

"Keep away from me!" he shouted. "You dirty my hands."

"Whatever it is, please tell me," pleaded Mei Oi. "I hope my husband is not an insane man."

"Insane?" Ben Loy rushed up and stared fiercely at her, showing his teeth. "Is that what you call it, insane?" Shaking with anger, he clenched his fists.

"I was merely saying I hope you're not insane because of the way you act."

"The way I act! If a man objects to his wife sleeping with another man, is that insane? Tell me! Is that insane?"

"I . . . I don't know what you're talking about . . ."

"You knitted a nice green hat for me, that's what."

"It's not true."

"You're lying!"

"I'm not! You're the one who's lying."

"You lying sonovabitch!" He slapped her across the face.

She bowed her head and started to whimper, first softly, then loudly, then uncontrollably.

"You wife-beater, that's the only thing you know how. What kind of a husband have you been? Why don't you ask yourself that? Why don't you . . ."

"Who was it? Tell me who was the sonovabitch who slept with you. Are you trying to protect him? Sooner or later I'll find out, and when I do, I'll kill him! You just wait and see. I'll kill him!"

"I didn't do anything wrong . . . I didn't do anything wrong . . . I thought I've married a young man . . . but it turns out that I've married an old man . . . an old man who's too old to make love to me . . ."

"Shut up, you useless woman!" Ben Loy backed out of the room. "If it were not for your pregnancy, I would have beaten you to death. Just remember that."

She continued to sob uncontrollably, with her head buried in her arms, lying on the bed. Ben Loy wished he could make her tell him who the guilty man was. He would put a hole through his body. He would. The invasion of his privacy was unbearable. He felt that the violation of something as sacred as his marriage, if permitted to go unchallenged, would make his the greenest and biggest hat of them all.

Still fuming, he returned to the bedroom.

"That baby you've got there, it's not mine! Whose is it?"

There was no answer. Mei Oi was lying on her side, facing away from the doorway, sobbing. The slits on her long dress exposed her thighs.

"That baby! Whose is it?" Ben Loy roared. Anger took reign within him. He rushed up to the bed and picked up his leather slipper from the floor. His hand must have come down at least half a dozen times. Then, perspiring, spent and dazed, he walked out of the apartment, leaving behind the wailing and terrified Mei Oi.

XXXV

The following Wednesday, on his day off, Ben Loy went to the social club of the Wang Association, as requested by Uncle Chuck Ting. He sat down to wait. A table model TV was suspended at one nook of the room. Ben Loy watched television along with the others, whose upturned faces followed the story on the TV screen intently. A few moments later, when Chuck Ting entered, Ben Loy got up to greet him.

The Association President extended his hand, almost exuberantly. "How are you, little nephew?" he asked. "You are not busy today?"

"No, I'm off today."

"Come in." Ben Loy followed him into his office. "Sit down." He indicated a chair.

Wang Chuck Ting was the elder statesman of the Wang Association, although there were others older than he, because of his office as president of the family association. In matters of mediation, in which he played a prominent role, people would give him face to make his job easier. For a great many years, he had been called upon to mediate various disputes and grievances. Sometimes it would be between cousins. At other times, it would be between a cousin and an outsider. Seldom had he been called upon to deal in a matter of stolen love.

Once before, almost twenty years ago, a young man from the Wang family had made a habit of visiting a married woman at her home on his days off. The husband's family elders had complained to Wang Chuck Ting about the young man's off-day activities. Chuck Ting had called in this young man and ordered him to discontinue his visits to this married woman at once. The young man had categorically denied he had ever visited this woman. When Chuck Ting had not heard further from the husband's side, he assumed that the matter was closed. He ob-

147

served now with a chuckle how much more difficult it was to achieve a satisfactory solution in a love case, for the man involved invariably vehemently denied the charges. He attributed to good luck the peaceful solution of his first case of love theft.

Ben Loy was more than just another member of the family association. Wang Chuck Ting and Ben Loy's father had come from the same village, attended the same schools together. Their families had worshipped at the same tablet house. The two regarded each other as brothers, and Ben Loy was no less than Wang Chuck Ting's own nephew. If one were disgraced and lost face, the other would be similarly affected. The scandal had broken upon one, as it had upon the other. Chuck Ting had always prided himself on being a good fixer. He believed anything could be done if one went about it in the right way. If the problem of Ben Loy's personal affairs could have been brought out into the open, he would have consulted some of his associates on all possible solutions. As it was, the less said, the better.

The Association President had not seen Ben Loy since the wedding banquet at the Grand China Restaurant shortly after he and Mei Oi arrived in New York. He had announced at the gathering that a year hence, they would drink again, this time to the new addition of the family. Recalling this event, Chuck Ting was moved to inquire, "How is Ah Sow?"

"Hao," replied Ben Loy, wondering what the old man was up to. The slowness of the unfolding made him nervous and irritable, but he assumed an outward calm.

"How is business at the restaurant?" Chuck Ting asked casually. He lit a cigarette, puffed on it, and tilting his head, blew smoke into the air.

"Fair," Ben Loy said flatly. He had always seen him smoking cigars.

"Are you making a little money where you are now?" Uncle Chuck Ting smiled broadly. His casualness was disarming.

"Some," replied Ben Loy, a little annoyed at such a personal question. Then he added, "But not enough to get rich on."

"No matter what you do in this world," said Chuck Ting, "it is not easy to do. A lot of things sound easy but when you come

148

to do it, it's not easy as it seems. Do you agree with me?" His voice was fatherly.

"Yes."

They could still hear the blaring of the TV and the voices of the mah-jong players from the outer room.

"How is Ah Sow?" he asked again.

"She is fine," replied Ben Loy impatiently. "You have a kind heart."

"Does she like New York? I guess she has been here for almost two years now."

"She likes New York very much." But to himself: He certainly didn't ask me here to ask me this!

Chuck Ting stretched his legs and took another puff on his cigarette, and slowly blew out the smoke, turning his head away from Ben Loy. Then he faced him again. There was a moment of hesitation, of a thoughtful pause. He crunched his cigarette on the ash tray. He returned to the nephew with renewed enthusiasm. He looked directly into Ben Loy's eyes.

"Nephew, your uncle is in trouble. Big trouble."

"What trouble?" Ben Loy was taken aback by the remark. He felt that he, Ben Loy, would be the last person Chuck Ting would come to for help. It had always been the other way around. People went to Chuck Ting for help. He anxiously waited for an explanation.

"Labor trouble." He leaned forward, a little closer to his nephew. "As you know, nowadays it is very hard to get people to work for you. The China Pagoda in Stanton is in need of someone to work." He shook his head sadly, then continued. "If your Uncle were a few years younger, he would go right back to work. But your uncle is getting on in years." He looked at Ben Loy with a twinkle in his eyes. "Do you know how old your uncle is? Heh, heh, take a guess. Go ahead, take a guess."

"It's hard to guess sometimes," Ben Loy said uncertainly. He examined the elderly man's face briefly for tell-tale deeply-lined furrows, but there were none. "Well, I would say you're between sixty-five and seventy."

"More than that," Chuck Ting chuckled. "Time flies, especially in America. Days go by like the blinking of your eyes. My dear nephew, your uncle is seventy-four this year."

"I didn't think you were that old," said Ben Loy shyly. "And you're so strong-looking. Nobody would guess you're seventy-four."

"I'm almost ten years older than your father," he confided. "I stopped working only four years ago. As I said before, if I were a few years younger, I would go back to work today, this very minute. Ben Loy, your uncle needs a waiter for the China Pagoda." His voice took on a pleading tone. "I want you to help uncle out. You will not only help out uncle, but you will be helping out the whole family, my little boy, his wife, and everybody else."

"It's a lot of trouble traveling back and forth."

"Live there, my boy," said Chuck Ting, almost gleefully. "Move out there with your family. It would be a hardship for you to travel back and forth every day."

"If I were single, I could just pack my bag and that's all there is to it. Having a family is a different thing."

"I see, you want to talk to Ah Sow first," said Chuck Ting. "That's good. I think you should talk to her first before you decide. But if you could go out and help my boy, all of us would be grateful to you."

"Let me talk to my woman first and see what she has to say," replied Ben Loy.

"That's very good," said the uncle, extending his hand to Ben Loy. "I know I can depend upon you." The two men arose. "How is your mother?" asked Uncle Chuck Ting, pushing open the door.

"She's fine. I got a letter from her two weeks earlier."

"That's good. I'm glad to hear that."

When the door opened, a jumble of voices rushed at them. The room was filled with smoke. Ben Loy did not even look at the TV screen to see if the same show was on. He walked brusquely out of the room.

Inside his private office, Chuck Ting beamed. He was confident he had persuaded Ben Loy and his wife to move out of town.

XXXVI

Lee Gong let go a typhoon-sized sigh of relief when he learned that his daughter and son-in-law were moving to Stanton. Mei Oi had called to tell him that she and Ben Loy were moving, that the China Pagoda needed Ben Loy to work out there because help was so hard to get, and that Uncle Chuck Ting had implored Ben Loy to make the trip. Mei Oi herself felt deeply, since her earlier talk with her father, the need for a change. When Ben Loy had come home that evening from his meeting with Uncle Chuck Ting and told her what he wanted him to do, she readily agreed, to herself, that getting away from New York would be good for both of them. It afforded a plausible excuse to get away from the big city and its gossipy community, she thought. It would be like starting life anew, changing a soiled blouse for a new one.

While her heart had jumped at the chance to move, she saw no point in acquiescing so readily. The proposal had come from her husband, and she was still mindful of his violent behavior of the previous week when he had returned home from seeing his father. Her face and posterior were still smarting from the slaps he had administered. When Ben Loy sounded her out, she had protested mildly.

"Moving is so much trouble," she had said. "It seems we have just settled down." But she had added sympathetically, "But if you want to go, it's all right with me."

Ben Loy had hoped that distance itself would release a curtain of inaccessibility to Mei Oi's admirer, whoever he might be. When he was not in anger, he blamed himself for whatever indiscretion had cast a shadow over his young and pretty wife. He did not even want to discuss the subject with her at all. Privately he hoped that his wife's misbehavior could somehow be pushed back into the dark recess of his mind, to be buried

151

and forgotten.

Nevertheless, he found it exceedingly difficult to assume the role of the wearer of the *green hat*. Like any wronged husband he cried out for revenge for the scoundrel who had enticed the confidence of Mei Oi. Somewhere in the back of his mind he told himself that there would come a time when the identity of his rival would be disclosed. He vowed vengeance but had not decided on a definite course of action. In spite of Mei Oi's vehement denial, he had no doubt that what his father had told him was true. He embraced the philosophy that you need not draw the intestines in a picture to know they are there. So it was with the picture of his family life.

He sadly conceded himself to be the incompatible husband. What more was there to be said? If his wife were going to have a baby, what was so terrible about that? Is it strange for a married woman to have a baby? For one thing, the birth of the baby would put a stop to inquisitive people. *They are married for two years and they are still barren.*

A small town like Stanton, with no Chinese community to speak of, would be ideal for a self-exiled couple. If Ben Loy could have his way, he would lose himself in a far-off place not even listed on the map. But you can't just pack up and go without any thought of survival. For the present, Stanton beckoned to him like another golden mountain just over the horizon. The years away had blotted from his memory the monotony of small town living, so that now he was actually anxious to return to it.

If only he hadn't met Chin Yuen . . . things might have been different! But how could you blame someone else for your own stupid mistakes? If there had been no Chin Yuen, there would have been someone else. Chin Yuen was a good and loyal friend.

So when Chin Yuen called Ben Loy at the China Pagoda shortly after he and Mei Oi had moved to Stanton, and practically invited himself out for a visit, the latter exclaimed that it would be just fine. Anyway, Chin Yuen hadn't been in Stanton for many years. He would want to visit the old place where he used to work.

152

The door bell of Ben Loy's apartment rang about mid-afternoon the following day. They hadn't had any callers at their new home. Not even Wing Sim's wife had dropped in, a visit which both Mei Oi and Ben Loy felt they were entitled to as a matter of courtesy.

Ben Loy opened the door.

"Ah Loy, how are you?" beamed his old roommate Chin Yuen, with a wide grin on his face.

"Ah, Yuen *Gaw*, it's you!" Ben Loy grabbed his hand. "Please come in. You are a kind friend to come all the way from New York to visit us. Such a long distance."

Mei Oi met them in the living room. "Mr. Chin, you have just arrived from New York?"

"Yes. I hope I'm not disturbing you."

"Oh, no, not at all," said Mei Oi. "You are very kind to come."

"Let's not stand on formality," said Ben Loy, taking the visitor's hat.

"I don't know how to stand on ceremony," chuckled Chin Yuen. He rubbed his palms together.

"Let me boil you some tea," said Mei Oi and disappeared into the kitchen.

Chin Yuen looked over the apartment carefully, noting the wallpaper design, the rug on the floor, the high ceiling, and the chandelier type of lighting for the living room.

"It's all furnished," volunteered Ben Loy by way of explanation. "We didn't buy a thing. Maybe later on we will buy what we still need."

"We've just moved here," said Mei Oi, putting down the tray on the small round table in front of the sofa. "I'm afraid everything is rather disorganized." Of course she didn't mean it, but she said it anyway because she thought that was the right thing to say.

"Ben Loy and I are old friends," explained Chin Yuen, lifting his cup of tea and sipping it. "We should not stand on ceremony. In fact we used to room together, right across the street from the China Pagoda." He turned to Ben Loy. "Isn't that right, Loy?"

"When we got off work, all we needed to do was walk across the street and we were home," answered Ben Loy. "It's very convenient, especially in bad weather." At the mention of bad weather, he recalled the time it snowed and the Pagoda closed early because there simply was no customer bold enough to venture out of the house to come in to eat. That was the night he and Chin Yuen had gone to New York to spend the night at the Hotel Lansing. Ben Loy winced inwardly as he remembered that night.

"Remember that time we had the big snow?" asked Chin Yuen, grinning as if he were mind-reading. "It snowed so hard we had to close early. Remember that night, Loy?"

"Why don't you have some more cookies?" said Ben Loy, not anxious to speak of that particular night. He picked up the plate of cookies and handed it to Chin Yuen.

"Please do have some more cookies," echoed Mei Oi. "I hope the tea is not getting cold." She put her own cup to her lips.

Chin Yuen's eyes followed the smooth, delicate hand as Mei Oi lifted the cup. She was sitting directly across from him. Aside from the obvious bigness of her pregnancy, Chin Yuen thought her face was more full and rounded-out than when he had met her for the first time when she arrived in New York. He detected a velvety smoothness of the skin now, compared to what had seemed to him at first the rural beauty of a country girl, dark-skinned and almost devoid of make-up. Now, even under the inadequate lighting of the living room, he saw in Mei Oi maturing womanhood. A softer, smoother, whiter skin. A more fully developed body. There was an impressive improvement in her make-up technique.

"The tea is just right," he said, smiling at his hostess. "The cookies are good too. I think I'll have another one."

"Please do." Mei Oi quickly picked up the plate and offered it to him. She did not think her maternity dress revealed too much of her big stomach. She knew that Chin Yuen was watching her every movement, and she enjoyed his glances as if each of them was a compliment. "You have always been in New York, Mr. Chin?"

"Oh, yes," replied the guest. His eyes fell upon her bracelet, made of seven five-dollar gold pieces. "That's a pretty bracelet," he remarked. He noted that the hostess's fingers were rather long and pointed as compared to his own fat stubby fingers. The stubbiness of his fingers had caused the village conjurer to remark that he, Chin Yuen, would lead a life of manual labor.

"Do you like it?" she asked pleasantly, extending her hand to him for a closer inspection of the bracelet. Chin Yuen grasped the hand gently and immediately felt a softness the like of which he had never known before. It made his heart throb erratically.

"You don't see many bracelets like these anymore," he remarked. His right hand fondled the bracelet while his left held her hand. "H'mn, very nice." Then, turning to Ben Loy, who at the moment was munching quietly on a cooky, he complimented, "You're lucky to have such a lovely wife."

"Yeah," said Ben Loy noncommitally. He did not like the idea of Mei Oi wearing a bracelet. He supposed it would be all right for a woman to wear jewelry to a party, but not at home, particularly when the guest was an old friend like Chin Yuen. There is no need for such ostentatious behavior, he told himself. He always found it difficult to understand why women wear jewelry at all; for you cannot eat it, and it does not keep you warm on a cold day.

A twinge of jealousy came over him when he saw his old friend still holding Mei Oi's hand. But because he was such an old and close friend, he dismissed it. When Chin Yuen finally let go of her hand, Ben Loy felt a surge of pride coursing through his veins, for he could see very plainly that his wife was being admired and he was being envied. But what could you expect from an old bachelor like Chin Yuen? He probably hadn't seen a woman for weeks. . . .

"I'm very fortunate in having Mei Oi for a wife," Ben Loy continued.

"He's teasing me," said Mei Oi, her eyes fixed on Chin Yuen. "My husband . . . he's just like a little boy." She threw a glance at Ben Loy. And they all laughed.

Chin Yuen felt his face flush as Mei Oi stared at him; but he enjoyed this special consideration.

He remembered the rumors about Ben Loy and Mei Oi. Just the other day he had run into an acquaintance in Chinatown. Over won ton at the Sun Key this friend had asked bluntly if

Chin Yuen had heard anything of the scandal, explaining that he asked only because the latter was such a close friend of Ben Loy. Chin Yuen had answered negatively.

As he reflected on the chance meeting now, he concluded that he had given him the right answer; for his desire to protect Ben Loy was stronger than ever before. He was saddened by all the ugly-to-listen-to stories about Ben Loy and Mei Oi. Certainly Ben Loy never mentioned his own marital problems to Chin Yuen. Yet because of his closeness to him, Chin Yuen felt a personal sharing of his tragedy. Sure, he had taken him to the uptown hotel where he probably got his first taste of woman. But he had no idea he was such a fool. When he looked at Ben Loy now, he thought his face seemed to be drained of blood.

"How do you like Heightstown?" Ben Loy deliberately changed the subject. Chin Yuen was presently working in New Jersey.

"Not bad," said Chin Yuen. "Business is good, but the summer is better. I'm working there just this week."

"Do you live there too?" asked Mei Oi.

"Yes," replied Chin Yuen. "They have a little bungalow where the employees sleep, about four blocks from the restaurant." He appreciated Mei Oi's interest in asking such a question. "Otherwise, nobody would go that far to work."

"You're more free to travel," said Ben Loy with just a trace of envy. "A bachelor can move about more easily. Just pack a few things and that's all there is to it. But me . . . we're here for more than two weeks now and we're still not straightened out yet."

When they had finished their tea, Chin Yuen offered to help Mei Oi clear the table. He carried the platter of cookies and his own tea cup into the kitchen. For a brief moment he and Mei Oi were alone in the kitchen. Having carefully placed the dishes in the sink, Mei Oi turned and found Chin Yuen directly behind her. Their eyes met and they smiled at each other. They stood still, silently, staring at each other. It seemed a long time before Mei Oi spoke. "Let's go back to the living room."

156

Again he let Mei Oi precede him. The fragrance of her perfume tickled his nostrils, sending an appreciative ripple of light-heartedness through him, making him feel like flying through the clouds. Her closeness electrified his whole body, charged him with a gaiety that knew no bounds. He wanted to warble a song, written and set to music especially for her. But Chin Yuen was no singer. He could not even read music.

Back in the parlor Ben Loy was impatient. "You want to go over to the restaurant and say hello to your old boss?" he asked Chin Yuen.

Before Chin Yuen had an opportunity to answer, Mei Oi spoke up. "He just got here. He can visit the restaurant any time." She threw an inquiring glance at her guest.

"Maybe we can visit the restaurant later," acquiesced Chin Yuen. "Is that all right with you, Loy?"

"I just thought you wanted to see your old friends at the restaurant, that's all," said Ben Loy. A sheepish grin slowly formed on his face. "Don't misunderstand me, I'm not trying to chase you out of the house."

"As the old saying goes," began Mei Oi. Then she paused, uncertain of the quotation. "I'm not very good at quoting these clever sayings . . . *The first time raw, the second time well-done.* This reminds me. I must go and rinse some rice."

Chin Yuen was quick to object. No need to stand on ceremony, he said. He was not hungry. After what seemed like a whole day of pleasant insistence that the guest stay for dinner, and his equally eloquent non-acceptance, it was finally agreed that Mei Oi would go and wash some rice.

Ben Loy suggested that he and Chin Yuen drop in to see Wing Sim now and the latter readily agreed.

Mei Oi was glad the two men had left. It gave her a chance to plan her cooking without interference. She hurriedly checked herself in the mirror and, in a moment, she was at the supermarket, four doors away, shopping for additional things for her dinner.

When the two men returned almost two hours later, they sat down to a meal of watercress soup, fried chicken, and a dish of string beans with beef, cooked in a brown bean sauce; and, of course, rice.

During the dinner, Chin Yuen praised the culinary art of his hostess, who accepted the compliments with great modesty, saying she had had no experience in cooking. Ben Loy was proud of his wife, too, for having cooked such a splendid dinner on such short notice. His ego swelled at the thought that his dutiful wife had just proven herself to be an exceedingly versatile and courteous hostess.

"Is the landlord giving you any trouble?" asked Ben Loy after dinner. It was to Chin Yuen that they had entrusted their New York apartment.

"No, not yet," he replied. Ben Loy had made it plain to the landlord that he still owned the apartment.

When the time came for the guest to leave, Mei Oi walked Chin Yuen to the door. "Don't forget to come and visit us again soon, Mr. Chin," she said.

On the train home, Mei Oi's parting words kept crowding into Chin Yuen's mind. Was it just a casual, ordinary way of saying good-bye? Or was it something special? For an answer he reached back to scrutinize the smile she had given him in the kitchen. Her general demeanor while he was there came in for a minute analysis. He flattered himself with the thought that Mei Oi liked him. He was very pleased with this notion, though the indulgence carried him away on a floating carpet. In her moments of frustration, he deduced, she was willing to let her eyes fall upon an older man. By comparison with Ben Loy, Chin Yuen was anything but handsome. Ben Loy was a good-looking man and much younger. But, floating on his carpet, Chin Yuen elevated himself to becoming Mei Oi's ardent lover. . . . If Mei Oi was going to have a baby . . . and he thought of her as Mei Oi and not Ah Sow for the first time . . . someone other than Ben Loy could be responsible. *Fatty water should not be allowed to flow into another's rice paddy.* Why should a stranger be permitted to ravish the beauty of Mei Oi? Mei Oi . . . Beautiful Love. Her father must have named her for her beauty. If he could in some way take Mei Oi's affection away from this outsider, he would be doing Ben Loy a favor.

158

As the train neared New York, the memory of the delicious dinner and the fragrance of Mei Oi's perfume drifted back to the dozing Chin Yuen. He had leaned back on his chair, stretched out his legs and closed his eyes. A more rewarding day he had not had in a long time.

XXXVII

Ben Loy's cousin Wing Sim and Eng Shee had been married for ten years now. They had been married in the same village as had been Ben Loy and Mei Oi. Eng Shee was from the village of the Wooded Ridge. When her mother had heard that the prosperous Wang Chuck Ting's son, Wing Sim, was coming home from the golden mountain to take a bride, she quickly fetched Fat Three, a reliable matchmaker from the Lai Village. People said she was reliable, reliable to the extent that she would not lie unless there was something to lie about. She would not tell little lies, a normal procedure followed by all the lesser matchmakers. If Fat Three thought she could get away with a lie, she would tell it. But before telling it she would explore all the risks involved. She would have all explanations ready, just in case. That was the way she operated. Because of her thoroughness in telling a lie, Fat Three had come to enjoy quite a reputation as a matchmaker. When she arrived at Eng Shee's house early that morning, the future mother-in-law had been waiting breathlessly for her.

"Chuck Ting's son is coming home next week!" Eng Shee's mother confided excitedly to Fat Three. He's the richest man in the whole village, did you know that? His son is about twenty-two or twenty-three. Our Sue Ling is eighteen. I want you to take Sue Ling's *Year of Birth* to his mother now."

"What a splendid match!" exclaimed Fat Three. "Eighteen and twenty-three. That's a wonderful combination. The girl is eighteen. The boy twenty-three. My dear, I feel so happy for you!"

And so it had come to pass Wang Wing Sim and Eng Sue Ling were married in the village within a few weeks of the *gimshunhock's* arrival at his native home.

"I think you ought to go over and visit Ben Loy's wife," said Wing Sim to his wife the second week after their cousins' arrival in Stanton.

"If you want to visit that useless woman," snapped his wife, "you go ahead and go. I'm staying here."

"I don't want to go by myself," said Wing Sim. "If it were a matter of seeing Ben Loy, I would go. But it's his wife. That's your responsibility."

"I have no use for her kind. If I had known she got pregnant by another man, I wouldn't have taken those ox tails to her. I would have given her cow's dung." Eng Shee clenched her teeth. "Even that's too good for her!"

"I just don't want you two to be fighting," said Wing Sim firmly. "After all, we're cousins. We come from the same ancestor."

"The next time I see her, I'm going to spit in her face!" roared Eng Shee.

"Do you think you're in China now?" the husband shook his head in disgust.

"No matter where," his wife shot back at him, her face taut in indignation, "it makes no difference. When a woman commits a bad thing, it is not right, no matter where it takes place."

"But she's our cousin," Wing Sim implored. "We should try and help her when she's in trouble."

"After what she has done, no one can help her!" pouted his wife.

"We can help her by continuing to be her relative," continued Wing Sim icily. "In spite of everything she is still our cousin, good or bad. We don't want to claim her for a relation when she is good and be ready to disown her when she is bad." He paused pensively, collecting his thoughts. "Our children —— can we say they will grow up to be good? What if one or all of them turn out to be good-for-nothings? Are we ready to abandon them? Disown them? Because they are not what we want them to be?"

"Our children are different," countered Eng Shee. "They are our own flesh. They are ours. And nothing can change that."

"You've made up your mind she is no good. I can't tell you

161

anything," said Wing Sim dejectedly.

Her mouth twisted into a sneer, "If I were like her, would you want me to stay under the same roof with you? Do you? Would you say, good or bad, she is my wife?"

"Let's not talk nonsense," said Wing Sim. "That has nothing to do with it. You can do what you like. If you don't want to go and see Ben Loy's wife, all right. Have it your way."

He put his hand to his chin and scratched, as he often did when puzzled. "Remember this, Ben Loy came out to work only because he has the loyalty of a true cousin. You know how hard it is to get people to work for you nowadays. He didn't have to come out. He quit his own job to come out to help us." There was a small quiver in his voice. "We don't want to regard him as an outsider, that's all."

Wing Sim had long considered his wife a rural girl with a limited knowledge of everything, possessing a narrow point of view. He did not want to see Ben Loy hurt by Eng Shee's misguided snobbishness. Of course he and Ben Loy had never been too close. But this was a rule rather than an exception as far as Chinese cousins go. They maintain a rigid, formal sort of relationship, doing only what is expected of them: To be present for the baby's first haircut, for a wedding, or for a birthday banquet. Frequently that would be the only time they saw each other. They were never close enough to spend the day at the beach together or an evening at home. Yet they would be willing and ready to help in an emergency. But in the case of Ben Loy and Mei Oi, there was no ready helping hand from Wing Sim's wife.

"How would you like it when people start saying 'Wing Sim's cousin Mei Oi is a bad woman?' Where would you hide your face then? Tell me that!" Eng Shee growled at her husband. "Don't worry about the restaurant. If Ben Loy quits, I'll come out and wash dishes for you."

Her offer to wash dishes only aggravated Wing Sim more, for Ben Loy was not a dishwasher.

That evening about ten o'clock Wing Sim received a call from his father in New York. Earlier he had called to inform his father of the difficulty he had with his wife. He now turned to Eng Shee. "It's Papa. He wants to talk to you."

"Me?" said the surprised Eng Sue Ling. Never before had the father-in-law called and asked to talk to her. It was always Wing Sim. "Hello, *Lao Yair*," she said nervously.

"Ah Sow mah?"

"Yes, how are you, *Lao Yair*?"

"Ah Sow," Wang Chuck Ting began soothingly. "There is a little matter on which I need your cooperation and help. You know Ben Loy's father and I have been good friends and cousins for many a ten-years. Ben Loy's mother and your mother-in-law are on very good terms. . . . Now when one of the younger folks gets into trouble, and we extend a helping hand to her, it is not for the one at fault that we show this kindness, but to those whom we dearly love . . . the relations of the guilty one. If we look kindly upon Lee Shee, and we all know that she deserves no consideration whatever . . . but when we say a kind word on her behalf . . . we are being kind and considerate to the parents, Ben Loy's father and mother. We owe it to them not to cast aside this young woman. It is. . . ."

"Yes, *Lao Yair*. I understand. . . ."

The following afternoon she and her children made a courtesy call on Mei Oi.

"*Dai Dair*," said Eng Shee stiffly, using the formal term for Number One Aunt, when Lee Shee opened the door. "We are not busy today and we come over for a short visit."

"Come in, come in," said the surprised Mei Oi.

"I hope we are not intruding."

"Oh, no. You are very kind to come."

"Ah Ming," Eng Shee turned to the oldest of her three children. "Say hello to Number One Aunt." But the boy ignored the request, looking shyly at his shoes.

Mei Oi closed the door. The visit was totally unexpected. She had begun to think that Eng Shee would not come to see her. She was certain that the bad rumors about her had reached Eng Shee. This quiet town would be no refuge for her. She and Ben Loy would have to move to some place else. But the presence of Eng Shee and her brood now changed her feelings about moving. It reassured her that she still belonged to the Wang

163

clan.

"You are so kind," she repeated. She noted that it was three thirty by her watch. "I see they have gotten out of school just now." She patted one of them on the head.

"Yes, they usually get home from school around three o'clock," explained the mother. "Today when they came home, I said we should come over to visit you."

"Please don't stand on ceremony," said Mei Oi. She hadn't seen the little niece and nephews for a long time. "Oh, how they have grown!" she exclaimed. "Do all of them go to school now?" Then she proceeded to ask each of them what grade he was in. To each tiny, hesitant voice that answered, she repeated, "Oh, is that so? Soon you will be graduating. You'll be able to help your father and mother."

"Yes, they help their father and mother all right—to eat," chuckled the mother. For the first time she seemed relaxed. "They always ask: 'Mommy, when are we going to visit Number One Aunt?' And I always say: 'Give her and Uncle Loy time to settle down.' Ha, ha, and here we are. I hope we are not disturbing you."

"Oh, no. Not at all," answered Mei Oi. "As a matter of fact I had been hoping you would drop by. You should come and see us often when you have the time." She looked at the children again, who were now seated by the sofa. A little too quiet for children, she thought. "I'm going to get them some cookies and candy," she said and disappeared into the kitchen.

When she returned with the cookies and candy she noticed that the oranges which Eng Shee had brought were still in the brown paper bag, standing on the lamp table, momentarily forgotten and unwanted. Fearing that Eng Shee might feel her gesture of bringing the oranges unappreciated, Mei Oi added quickly, "We'll have some oranges later. But you shouldn't have brought them."

Her eyes took a fleeting glance at Eng Shee from top to bottom and she almost giggled to herself. The tan suit Eng Shee had on was at least one size too small for her. It reminded Mei Oi of a tightly-wrapped *May Festival Sweet Rice Cake*. She did not want to comment that Eng Shee had gotten fat, for such a reference would point enviously to her life of ease and good eating. She changed the subject. "How is business at the restaurant?"

"About the same," she said uncertainly. She really didn't know how to answer that; for she never bothered to ask her husband how business was at the restaurant. She thought such a question odd, coming from Mei Oi. "Nothing changes much," she continued. "Out here it is not like in New York. In the big cities, it is different. But in our little town, business is always the same. Not much tourist trade." She thought she was really clever in adding the last remark. Having come from a country where women seldom ventured into the business world, it was an admirable feat for her to make such an intelligent reference to the restaurant trade. She glowed inwardly. She had heard her husband say almost the identical thing, word for word: Not much tourist trade. What pleased her particularly was to be able to repeat these words now in front of Mei Oi, who was supposed to be a school girl and had knowledge of many things. The type who wear long-robed gowns instead of the more common two-piece suits. In her mind, Eng Shee firmly believed that Mei Oi had never so much as put her shoulders to a bamboo pole and that she herself might be looked down upon by the much more educated Mei Oi. School girls, she often sneered, all they know is how to chase after men. Yes, Mei Oi is good at that. Mei Oi—Beautiful Love. But she now asked, "How is your *Lao Yair?*"

"Oh, he is fine," said Mei Oi. "You have a kind heart." She offered them some more cookies.

When Eng Shee thought she and her children had stayed long enough, she perked up and said: "Did you read in the Chinese GAZETTE last week where a husband is advertising for information leading to the whereabouts of his bride of three months?" She paused long enough to throw an inquisitive glance at Mei Oi. "This generation of girls, I tell you, is no good." Wing Sim had told her of having read the article.

"No, I didn't read that," conceded Mei Oi, burning inwardly at the bringing up of such a subject.

"They say she ran away with a fellow she had met while they

were attending middle school in Canton. I wonder what the husband will do to her when he catches up with her."

"What could he do?" Mei Oi retorted icily, feeling sharply Eng Shee's obvious delight in the nature of the conversation. "He might make the other fellow pay for his wife's fare to this country. He can't force her to stay with him if she doesn't want to," she added succinctly.

"I think you're wrong, *Dai Dair*," replied Eng Shee, her voice charged with indignation. "Some of the younger generation are getting away with almost anything. They think they can marry a husband one day and the next day, if they don't like him, just pack up and leave. And in most of the cases, some boy is there waiting for her. There should be a stop to all that."

Mei Oi swallowed hard. She turned to the children. Ah Ming was chasing his little brother around the room. "Ah Ming!" Mei Oi called. The boy stopped short and looked in the general direction of his mother and Number One Aunt. Number One Aunt spoke up. "Do you want some more milk?"

He shook his head and resumed playing. Mei Oi had hoped he would say "yes" so she could escape momentarily the unpleasant presence of the mother by going to the kitchen to fetch the milk. From what she knew of her cousin, she was certain Eng Shee had intended to embarrass her. She was naturally angry. But she must not show it. She wanted to throw her out of the house. But wouldn't such a demand be tantamount to admission of guilt? If the general discussion of one unfaithful wife does not concern you, why should you be so touchy on the subject? Why the self-conscious revulsion? No, she must not show any antagonism toward Eng Shee. She turned to the mother and managed a weak smile. "Does any of the children care for more milk?" she asked.

"No," replied Eng Shee. "That's all they drink all day at home. We get five quarts of milk a day and all day long they drink and drink. Too much milk is not good for you, it makes your system too cool."

Mei Oi did not want to be disagreeable with her visitor about the benefits of milk. She considered anyone who would talk like that to be unlearned and holding fast to beliefs of the old.

166

Such show of ignorance only breeds contempt for the young mother. She thought to herself: *You ignorant pig . . . what do you know about anything?* She knew that if she talked back to her, one word would lead to another and soon there would be a fight on her hands. Perhaps sooner or later she would have to have it out with Eng Shee, but today was certainly not the time for it. After the remarks about runaway wives she was sure she could not like Eng Shee. She would be civil and cordial to her but only at a distance.

"Who would think that there are so many wild women in our generation?" Eng Shee resumed her little talk. "If I didn't see it with my own two eyes, I wouldn't have believed it."

Mei Oi forced a grin. *Go ahead you stinky old female . . . you go ahead and say what you like. No matter how good I am, you would find something bad to say about me. It is not in your nature to be kind to anybody.* The forced smile widened and she said half-heartedly, "Yes." Then she added dryly, "Times change. Not what it used to be."

"Over here," continued Eng Shee, showing obvious delight, "some women would think nothing of having an illegitimate child." She looked squarely at Mei Oi, looking for a tell tale reaction, which failed to come. Her high cheek bones seemed higher to Mei Oi, and her dark complexion looked more like the color of mahogany. "And some husbands don't care either," she added scornfully. "I mean they don't care whether the baby is his or not. I think a woman who has such a husband and doesn't go out and have a baby by another man is just crazy, don't you think? Wouldn't you say so?"

"It all depends," said Mei Oi, not knowing what to say. If there had been any doubt about the target of Eng Shee's well-placed words, it now disappeared completely. At first Mei Oi was irritated and angered by her oblique technique of attack. But the anger turned into a slow burn when she realized she must not tip her hand. She could just picture Sue Ling breezily blabbing to gossipy women about the episode: *She got so mad because I said something about illegitimate children. Now I ask you . . . if one is not guilty of such conduct, why should one feel so indignant about such a remark?* No, Mei Oi would not give

167

her the satisfaction of seeing her lose her temper at these remarks. "There are two sides to any argument," she continued. "Sometimes the husband is in error too."

"Ha, husbands are different," Eng Shee almost laughed aloud. "They can go out and sleep with another woman and we women folks can't do anything about it. It's different with a woman. She gets talked about . . . if she goes out too often at night."

Except for the pandemonium of the children from the kitchen, there was a temporary quiet. "Some women," said Mei Oi deliberately, "would like to have a baby by another man but they don't get the opportunity because no one else would have them." Mei Oi was quite pleased with this observation, and after she had said it, she wondered why she hadn't thought of it before. She was positive it displeased and distressed Eng Sue Ling greatly. That was what she wanted to do. She went on, "Some would stay home and just dream of a *pretty boy* whom she could never have. That's very true, isn't it?"

Little Georgie came running out from the kitchen. He was crying. "He took my cooky. Ah Ming took my cooky, Mommy. He took my cooky."

"You dead boy, what are you crying about?" She grabbed little Georgie by the arm and shook him vigorously. "You dead boy, you wouldn't cry like this if your mother dies." She turned to Mei Oi. "He is always like that. For no reason at all, he's got his mouth wide open. You two dead ones are no good either," she waved a menacing finger at Ah Ming and his sister, who stood mutely at a distance from their mother.

"Children are like that," said Mei Oi. "All children are like that." She walked over and wiped the tears off little Georgie's face and went into the kitchen to get him another cooky. She disapproved of the way Eng Shee had called her children: *Dead boy this and dead boy that.* But there was nothing she could do. In the villages one would expect children to be called *dead boy bitches* or *dead girl bitches* by their aroused parents. But in America one would think that a parent, be it father or mother, would feel more affectionate toward his offspring. . . .

She began thinking of her own child in its fifth month of life. Soon it would be born. She would never call her offspring a *dead girl bitch* or a *dead boy bitch.* She would shower upon it all the love she could. She would cherish it. The birth of the child would make her very happy. She would be like other women when they go to banquets and parties. She would have *her* child along too. A married woman without a little one feels naked at social gatherings. These gossipy women, young and old, are alike: *Ben Loy's wife has been married two years now and still without child. I don't know what's the matter with her.* A woman's fertility is not something of everlasting quality and she had begun to dread the time when she and Ben Loy would have to *take* a son. She would not like to *take* a son if she could help it.

It was all Ben Loy's fault for marrying her in his physical condition. But a marriage is a marriage. That's the way *her* life was fated. She did not wish to have it changed. When she thought again about how Eng Shee was trying to destroy her verbally, she became furious and wanted to bite her and bite her hard. She wished she would go home. Eng Shee was the type who has a good mouth but a wicked heart. She would entice you to death with her tongue.

Toward six o'clock, when Eng Shee at last decided she was ready to leave, she said that she had to return home and cook dinner, that there was still a lot of work to do at home. Mei Oi thought it odd for her to say she was going home to cook dinner, for Ben Loy had told her that Wing Sim usually had something prepared at the restaurant to take home to his wife and kids. And Wing Sim had mentioned to Ben Loy in casual conversation that for lunch the children usually had bread and something else. This indicated to Mei Oi that many of the chores which the average housewife encounters every day had been eliminated for Eng Shee. But when she said she was going home to cook dinner, Mei Oi was only too happy to see her leave.

Eng Shee's pointed question had come close to unnerving Mei Oi. She wasn't afraid of her. Nothing like that. It was just that she did not like Eng Shee's sinister insinuations. Before the rumors of scandal got around, Eng Shee had been, at least on the surface, civil and pleasant. The oxtails and whiskey she had brought Mei Oi when the latter was still living in New York only made the present poorly camouflaged bitterness harder to take. Your friend one minute and your enemy the next. She had seen women like that at New Peace Village. They would shout at the top of their voice and call each other names in the public square. Trouble makers.

Try as she would, Mei Oi found it increasingly difficult to rid Ah Song from her mind. He had promised to call *some* evening. So many days had gone by and still there was no call. Many an evening she just sat and waited for the phone to ring. Sometimes when it did ring she jumped to answer it, full of anticipation and exuberance, with her heart throbbing faster and her cheeks flushed. When it turned out to be a wrong number, her heart sank. It required an effort on her part to mumble in her newly acquired English: *I am sorry. You have the wrong number.* After the initial shock of disappointment came anger and hatred. Hatred for herself, hatred for Ah Song. Why? Why doesn't he call? Could a man be so uselessly fickle? So forgetful? And so ungrateful? Men are no good. They are all alike. She remembered his words very distinctly: *I will call you. I will call you in a few days.*

Almost in tears she went to the writing desk in one corner of the bedroom and hurriedly scribbled:

Uncle Song: The few days I have not seen you passed like so many springs. I will have much to tell you when I see you. You know as well as I do, youth is but a momentary dream, and once flown away, it will never return again. I can write a thousand pages and yet I will not be able to tell you all my feelings concerning you. Please telephone me any evening except Wednesday. I love you. . . .   One Who Loves You

The following day, when Ben Loy came home from work, he told his wife that Eng Shee had come to the restaurant earlier that afternoon. Following the example of her children she always called him "Uncle Loy," for he was from the same generation as Wing Sim.

"Uncle Loy," she had said with a big smile when she spotted him sitting at one of the booths in the rear of the dining room. Ben Loy had noticed her coming in and was about to get up to greet her. "Number One Aunt is going to have a baby real soon," she said pleasantly.

"Not right away," replied Ben Loy awkwardly.

"We are all so happy for you," continued Eng Shee, her eyes gleaming with mischief. "Other folks have babies and you will have one too." She glanced at Ben Loy briefly before resuming. "It does not matter how you get one, as long as you get it."

At the time he had thought it odd for Wing Sim's wife to make such a remark. But he had shrugged it off as one of the funny things that women say sometimes. He now related this incident to Mei Oi.

"That woman is absolutely no good!" exploded Mei Oi. She could feel her anger rising within her. "If she can't even be civil, why should we stay here and take these insults from her?"

"Wing Sim is not at all like her," grumbled Ben Loy. He recalled how the woman always did the talking, while her husband kept his mouth shut. "Wing Sim is no troublemaker, not like his female."

"It's you who let her get away with such remarks," Mei Oi raised her voice. In her emotional state she saw in her husband a little of Wing Sim. Not at all aggressive . . . someone who would permit others to push him around.

"What can I do?" replied Ben Loy resentfully. "Do you want me to slap her?"

"You slapped me when . . ."

"You're my wife. Eng Shee is Wing Sim's wife."

"There's one thing you *can* do," retorted Mei Oi. "You can pack your things and go back to New York! Since we came here, all we hear are insults." She pulled out a handkerchief and pressed it to her eyes. Then she resumed slowly, more reflectively, "The best she could ever do for Wing Sim was to bear him children. Outside of that, show me one thing that she has accomplished. She just talk and talk and talk . . . about other people!"

"Some people are like that," shrugged Ben Loy.

"Tell Wing Sim you're going back to New York," demanded Mei Oi. The very thought of being so close to this woman, Eng Shee, was sickening to her. A continuation of this nearness would bring nothing but additional aggravation to all concerned;

although she had no animosity toward the husband.

But there was another reason why Mei Oi did not like to remain in Stanton—a more compelling reason. It was Ah Song, her lover. The mere reference to the word *lover* made her shudder. She had never dreamed that she would ever apply the term *lover* to herself. Right or wrong, justified or not, she was only human in wanting to be a woman. In Chinese weekly magazines, as well as in the newspapers, she had frequently come across the word *lover*, spread across the pages in large letters. These stories had seemed so distant and out of reach.

In her own village, she remembered there was Aunt Six's daughter, Spring Love. She was only sixteen when she and that good-for-nothing Lung Ying, the son of Wide-mouthed Doon, became lovers on a dark and moonless night out in her mother's straw shack by the edge of the stream. When signs of her pregnancy began to appear, her family had quietly made arrangements for her to leave the village, never to return again. Up to this date nobody knew where she had gone. It was presumed that she had gone to the big city to keep her shame to herself. Public pressure was enough to force the girl's family to get rid of her. There was no official ostracism. But not so with Lung Ying. He was expelled from the village for a period of five years. At the time of Mei Oi's marriage and subsequent departure for America, he had not yet returned to the village. He was sent to some big market town where nobody knew where he had come from.

But where can one escape from a big city like New York? It would not be New York City *she* would be running away from, but New York's Chinatown. She could move from one Chinatown to another. She, too, would be leaving on her own initiative, although as a result of public pressure. No official action would be necessary. But she hadn't come to that point yet! She was not going to start running from the very beginning.

"Yes, let's move back to New York," she almost sobbed. "Living in this small town . . . you see more woods than people."

"We can't move back to New York right away," said Ben Loy, stunned at his wife's abrupt request. "We can't move back just because you want to. We have to give them a chance to get someone to work."

"Well, go ahead and tell them," said Mei Oi resolutely. "It makes me sick just looking at Eng Shee. She's got her eyes up on her forehead."

"You just have your mouth," said Ben Loy. "All you do is talk, like the rest of them." He paced the floor, for his agitation was too great for him to stand still. He turned to face his wife. "What about Chin Yuen? I have to give him time to move out of our apartment. When we needed him to stay there, the guy was good enough to oblige. Now you want to move right back in it!"

At the mention of Chin Yuen the sternness on Mei Oi's face disappeared, replaced by a glowing tenderness. She had almost forgotten about this old friend. It pleased her to remember all the little attentions he had given her when he visited their apartment. Her intuition told her that Chin Yuen had a warm heart for her, in a friendly way. As long as men are men, they will always like to look at a pretty girl. A pretty girl? Does she consider herself a pretty girl? Yes, she could pass for a pretty girl. She could apply make-up much more expertly than the average rural Chinese girl. Some do such a bad job of applying powder to their face that they look better without make-up. It looks so much like a bad plastering job.

"Well, give him a notice to move out," said Mei Oi after some reflection. Inwardly she was hoping that when she moved back to New York, Chin Yuen would come to see her.

She privately entertained the fantasy that he, Chin Yuen, might eventually seek some sort of relationship with her. Ah Song had proven himself very unreliable in his failure to call her. She had looked forward to a rendezvous with Ah Song with great anticipation; for in a new town, such a meeting would be free from the prying eyes of neighbors. What did her neighbors know of her? How would they know Ah Song was not her brother, or her cousin?

After many days had passed without a word from her lover, Mei Oi was resigned to the fate of the discarded mistress. This infuriated her. Knowing Ah Song as she did, she supposed he would have a ready excuse for not having gotten in touch with her. He might not even wait to be asked why. He would offer a convincing alibi.

Perhaps he was just plain scared of her father-in-law. After all, the two men were good friends. He played mah-jong at the club house almost every night. Any number of things could have been the cause. Maybe he was tired of her. Mei Oi refused to believe this . . . still, maybe he loved somebody else.

Alone in her apartment when her husband was at work, she felt many a lonely moment. She would sit back in the upholstered chair in the living room and dream about her erstwhile lover. In her need for escape, she convinced herself she must return to New York to continue her search for happiness. She would harass her husband until they would eventually move back to Catherine Street.

There were instances when she had the urge to call Ah Song but dared not. Not from Stanton, she cautioned herself. She would not hesitate to call if she were in New York. Once she had picked up the phone and was about to dial for the operator when she lost her nerve and replaced the receiver. She had become thoroughly disgusted with herself.

Only a few days before, she had sat by the kitchen table with a writing pad in front of her and a pen poised. She started to scribble rapidly on the upper right hand corner of the paper: *Dearly beloved*. She read that aloud to herself. She studied the penmanship. She considered the calligraphy fair. Strong, sturdy strokes. At first glance one would think the writing was in a man's hand. Should she put down *dearly beloved*? Her hand reached for the bottom left hand corner of the sheet and yanked it off the pad. *Uncle Song* the second sheet began. Yes, this was better than *dearly beloved*. Why should she be overly tender to him? He did not bother to call or write. She picked up the pen again and this time alternately poised it and waved it back and forth about a quarter of an inch above the paper before the next thought came to her: *By the flip of the eyelids it has been many weeks since we parted. Here in this wilderness I feel the loneliness of those who have cherished their loved one but now the opportunity of being together is gone. I am in a constant mood of worry. I am worried about the one I love. I don't know what is happening to him because he does not write to me or call me.*

174

I am always thinking of him. I long to be with him.

Should she sign it with her own name? Mei Oi? Yes, why not? What is there to be afraid of? But when she picked up her pen again she meekly signed it *Moi Moi*, little sister.

She reread her letter and examined her penmanship. She was immodestly proud of her writing. Not many men could write as well as this, she assured herself. Slowly and carefully she reread the letter. Suddenly her fingers tightened and she tore the letter to shreds. I will *not* write to him again, she whispered determinedly through compressed lips.

XXXVIII

When Wah Gay heard that his son and daughter-in-law were moving back to New York he was disturbed because he felt Ben Loy was letting Chuck Ting down. He knew that Chuck Ting had asked Ben Loy to go to Stanton to help him out. Upon hearing of their impending return, he had gone to his elder cousin and said: "Can you get someone else to work for you? Because if you can't I'm going to see that my boy stays there until you do."

When Chuck Ting assured him that he had already hired a replacement for Ben Loy, Wah Gay felt better. If, in a crisis, one cannot depend on a cousin, who else could one depend on?

"Ben Loy is a good boy," Chuck Ting hastened to the defense of his nephew, at the same time wanting to lessen the father's anxiety over the boy's behavior. "He had assured Wing Sim he would not leave the restaurant until someone else came to work in his place. What more could anybody ask?"

No one knew better than Chuck Ting that, if it had not been for his asking him, Ben Loy would not have gone to Stanton. It was a personal victory for him and he considered it as such. He hoped that it had accomplished its purpose. At this point, he felt that Ben Loy was not obligated to do more than give him a chance to get a replacement before he left. This had already been done.

Chuck Ting saw in this action a retainment of some phase of Chinese culture on the part of Ben Loy: To be obedient when practice and tradition demand it. A *jook sing* would have most likely taken this attitude: To hell with you. Why should I go to Stanton to work for you? If you have a problem, that's your business, not mine. So when Wah Gay called to denounce his son, Chuck Ting happily informed the father that Ben Loy was a good boy.

176

Wah Gay was reassured for the moment. But for the next few days he gloomily reflected on the danger of further scandal because of his son and daughter-in-law's return to New York.

Fat man, the head cook, usually came to the club house on his day off, Thursday. Fat man's sole recreation on his day off, in his own words, was to go to the Chinese movies when he thought they were worth seeing. After that he would stop by one of the smaller restaurants in Chinatown and have a plate of rice, sometimes with beef and tomatoes, or scrambled eggs with diced ham. This would cost him 65¢. He would leave a 10¢ tip if he felt he had not been treated too poorly by the waiter. If he had to wait too long to be served, he would forego the tipping. Or if the cooking was too salty or greasy, he would not tip the waiter.

This Thursday, when he showed up at the club house around eight o'clock in the evening, he was greeted like a long lost friend. When he was not within hearing distance, he was always referred to as the Fat Man. But in his presence they good-naturedly called him *The Great Kitchen Master.*

"Come on," the mah-jong players invited him. "You're just in time."

"How come you're so late today?" asked another.

"I didn't think you got off today," said Wah Gay.

"I went to see *Ten thousand Li In Search of a Husband*," replied the Kitchen Master.

"Good show?"

"*Ma ma foo foo*," said the Fat Man, a broad grin on his face. "After the show I stopped by the Sun Moon Restaurant and ate a little 65¢'s worth of rice with beef and tomatoes."

"And 10¢ tip," someone laughed, and the others joined him.

"You cheapskate," said Ah Song, keeping his eyes on the tiny tiles in front of him.

"Haven't seen you sonovabitch for a long time," the Fat Man turned his full attention to Ah Song. "What do you mean I'm a cheapskate?" he demanded. "You sonovabitch, if every time you push a plate of rice under somebody's nose and get a dime for that, you'd be mighty wealthy, you bastard." He nodded to the others. "Am I right? You tell me."

"You're a kitchen master," said Ah Song sarcastically, still not looking up from his mah-jongs. "I believe that's the title you go by here. Boy, that title alone will get you anywhere. Whatever you say, goes . . . with that title of yours." He drew a deep breath and continued, "If we don't want to be polite, we would call you Fat Boy, you fat pig!"

"Wow your mother, you dead boy. Hasn't anyone taught you not to talk to your father like that?"

"You want to be *my* father?" sneered Ah Song. "Go ahead and be my father. He is dead. My father is dead, six feet under the ground. And you want to be my father!"

"Wow your mother!" cut in Wah Gay angrily. "Go ahead and play and stop talking. If you don't want to play, get the hell out of here!" The proprietor's face was red like a cherry. He had been burning slowly at Ah Song.

"You're no longer welcome!" snarled Lee Gong, pounding his palm on the edge of the table. "We don't want you here!"

The others were too stunned to say anything.

Ah Song calmly consulted his watch. "I have another appointment anyway," he said. He got up and turned to the Kitchen Master. "Here, Fat Boy, the game is yours, chips and all." He nonchalantly put on his coat and walked out.

The game resumed under a strained silence until Chong Loo walked in shortly after nine.

"You're just in time," Wah Gay told him. "Play a few hands for me. I'll be back in half an hour."

"Where are you going?" asked Lee Gong concernedly.

"I want to drop in to see Chuck Ting for a while," said Wah Gay.

"Don't stay away too long," said Chong Loo, easing himself into Wah Gay's chair. "I was just going to stay for a short while and then go home to sleep."

"What's the latest news?" asked the Kitchen Master. It seemed that everywhere Chong Loo went he was asked *what's the latest news?* So, when he was asked *what's the latest news?* now, his ire was aroused.

"Wow your mother," he replied curtly, "how should I know

178

what the latest news is? Are you trying to get me into trouble?" His hands came up to the table and helped shuffle the white ivory tiles. He was hoping Lee Gong would say something; but, when he failed to open his mouth, Chong Loo felt compelled to speak. When someone ignored him, as in the case of Lee Gong, he felt he was being discriminated against. "Your daughter has returned to New York, I heard," he said pleasantly to Lee Gong, trying to be friendly.

"Yeah," replied Lee Gong sullenly. Wah Gay had already gone out the door. He hated Chong Loo for bringing up the subject of his daughter. Anything from this many-mouthed bird's mouth was suspect to Lee Gong but, irritated and embarrassed though he was, he felt the need for a diplomatic calm in order to avoid any mistaken impression. Wanting to change the topic, he turned to Fat Man, "What was the show about?" he asked.

But Chong Loo cut in. "It is better in New York, isn't it?" His hands were still busy stacking up the tiles in front of him. "It is not good for a young girl to be living out in the woods. As they say, lots of trees and very few people, ha ha. There is so much more company in New York, ha ha."

"You sonovabitch, pay attention to what you're doing," admonished the Kitchen Master.

"When one is many-mouthed, one's got to open it often," said another. "But there's one way to shut him up." He threw a knowing glance at Chong Loo and then continued, "Just stick your hot dog into his mouth, that ought to shut him up."

Everybody laughed but Lee Gong.

Wah Gay had gone across the street to the Sweet Smell Coffee Shop for a cup of coffee. He took his time. The counterman asked him why he was not playing mah-jong at the club house. Wang replied briefly that he had some business to attend to and had asked someone to sit in for him. He was in no mood for talking, but he was not impolite to the counterman.

In his many years in the restaurant business and in the operation of his club house, Wah Gay had learned to get along with people. He seldom lost his temper. Wrapped in his own thoughts, he had failed to instruct the counterman for black coffee. He thought of asking for another cup of coffee, a cup of black coffee, but didn't. He kept his frustrations to himself and sipped the cup's contents slowly. Then he left quietly.

He walked south on Mott Street toward Chatham Square. He stuck his right hand into his coat pocket and felt something cold and hard. A chill went up his spine. Slowly he released his grip, with a grimace of satisfaction.

Neon signs blinked up and down the length of three blocks that comprised Chinatown. For the moment there was hardly any traffic. The few pedestrians hurried on, minding their own business. Wah Gay reflected that, at this very moment in his own native village many thousands of miles away, all human activities would have ceased with the fall of night. Here in New York, life seemed to go on endlessly regardless of the time of day, regardless of the weather. Instinctively he looked skyward. A clear, unclouded galaxy of stars and heaven. Surely it would not rain tonight.

XXXIX

Catherine Street was dimly lit. The lights were farther apart than some of the other nearby streets. There were a few stores along the block where Ben Loy lived. A variety store on the corner of Catherine and Henry Streets. A one-chair shoe repair shop. Further down the street, a grocery, then a barbershop. At the next corner, an outdoor soda fountain with a newsstand beside it. Across the street, an oblong empty lot. Next to it a condemned building with a big sign in front: Will Build To Suit. In the middle of the block, on the odd-number side, was 45 Catherine Street. The candy store on the ground floor was now closed. So were the other small establishments on the street. Occupying the second store in the same building with the candy store, was the chiropractor, the first Chinese ever to practice this profession in New York.

Now all the stores were closed for the night. Their windows were dark. As Wah Gay made his way toward 45 Catherine Street, he was glad of the dimness of the lights, for it afforded him protection against being recognized. He stopped in front of number 45 and darted into the vestibule. He hoped he would not be seen by the housekeeper, whom he had encountered once on an earlier visit, rolling a garbage can in the hallway.

If the super should stop and ask him what he was doing, he could tell him he was looking for his son, Ben Loy, and that would be the end· of the inquiry. *It's no crime to visit one's son.* But there was no one in the hallway now, and he climbed the stairs furtively. He had heard Ben Loy mention once that the super's wife often came out of her apartment on the second floor when she heard footsteps, to see who was coming up the stairs during the early morning hours.

The stairway was empty and desolate tonight. Well, maybe it was still too early for the super's wife to be on the prowl for

181

strangers. Wah Gay glanced at his wrist watch: 10:20.

When he got to the landing he suddenly felt trapped. The hallway was too small. The distance from the landing to Ben Loy's apartment door was only about ten feet. He wanted to back down to the vestibule. Perhaps he could stay downstairs. If someone should come into the hallway from the street side, he could start looking at the names on the mail box, pretending to be looking for someone in the building. Yes, that was what he would do.

As he turned to go down, his eyes fell on two doors facing the stairway. These must be the toilets, he told himself. A childish elation swept over him. Upon closer scrutiny he saw that the two doors were unlocked. He was in luck. He chose the one closer to Ben Loy's apartment and gently opened the door. Stealthily he stepped inside.

The tiny room had a dank and chilly smell. Water dripped ceaselessly from the plumbing into the wooden water tank. A strange foreboding plagued him in his self-imposed prison cubicle.

He kept looking at his watch. Of course, Ben Loy would not be home yet. He would not get home until after midnight. His right hand felt for the cold, hard object in his pocket. He pursed his lips. His hand nervously gripped and loosened the object in his pocket. It seemed as if eternity had stepped into the room and was standing with him. He tilted his head and blew his breath into the air, letting out a big sigh.

At last a half hour had passed. To Wah Gay it had been like a night stretch in the water-jail. *To hell with him. He will never come.* He cocked his ear to the door crack and listened. All was quiet. Too quiet. Nobody out in the hall. No one coming up the stairs. He unhooked the door and stepped out. Immediately he felt the freedom of the hallway.

Through the upper frosted glass panel of the door to Mei Oi's apartment, he detected a glow of light. Suddenly it occurred to him: Why not go into the apartment? He could inquire how she was. After all he had not dropped in to see either Ben Loy or his daughter-in-law since they moved back from Stanton. Tonight was just as good a night as any to make the

182

call. In two quick steps he was at the top of the stairs, with only a short distance separating him from Mei Oi's apartment. Then he heard the latch on the apartment door click. He whirled and fled down the stairs. He could hear footsteps coming toward the landing.

But by the time the footsteps reached the landing on the second floor, Wah Gay was safely hidden underneath the staircase. He tensed and listened for the tread. His heart pounded inside him. Thump . . . thump . . . thump.

The footsteps started coming down the stairs, walking rapidly but softly, as if tiptoeing. He felt an exultant shock.

The back of a man appeared down the hall after having stepped off the stairs. The figure started walking quickly toward the door, hands in his pocket, without a backward glance. There was an arrogant rocking of the shoulders.

At that moment, a fury of hell racked Wah Gay. With the swiftness of a tiger, his hand shot into the pocket and pulled out a razor-sharp knife. He rushed after the man. Hearing footsteps behind him, the man whirled. Wah Gay was almost upon him. In another second, Wah Gay's hand flashed up and then came down, quickly, unerringly.

Ah Song's left ear dropped to the floor.

"You sonovabitch, I'm going to kill you! . . . You bastard . . . you sonovabitch . . . you good-for-nothing . . ." Wah Gay was incoherent in his rage.

Ah Song dashed out into the street, holding the spot where his left ear had been with a handkerchief. Wah Gay was hot in pursuit. The elderly Wang was puffing and a few doors down the street he was almost out of breath. Ah Song was already nearing East Broadway and was pulling away from his pursuer. Wah Gay saw his back disappear up Catherine Street under a circle of light from the street lamp, and soon his view was cut off by a truck. He slowed down. He would never catch the sonovabitch. For the first time he realized he still had the knife in his hand. The blade was smeared with blood. He crossed the street. At the corner a silver-painted sanitary basket stood invitingly in the night. Scanning the street quickly, he threw the knife into the basket. No one was astir. No one was

183

even near him. Even if someone had seen him, the streets were so poorly lit that no one could positively identify him. He passed P. S. 1 on Henry Street. The block was deserted. He slowed to a casual walk. The night air was crisp and clean, full of life. It was good to be able to breathe.

The shadows on the sidewalks afforded him temporary refuge from his flight. Flight from what? From whom? Only a moment earlier he had been intent solely on vengeance. To catch the man responsible for having brought him disgrace.

Suddenly he began to worry about the police. He nervously surveyed the street. No one was in sight. Should he return to Money Come? Where did that sonovabitch Ah Song run to? Did he go to the police? Did he go home? Did he rush to a doctor? That bastard . . . he ought to let himself bleed to death . . . Ah Song the dead boy deserves to die . . . but I am too good to him . . . I only cut off his ear. Ha ha, let that be a lesson to him! Let someone else kill him. Some day someone will kill him if he doesn't mend his ways.

He stood at the beginning of St. James Street, where it meets the circle of traffic that is Chatham Square, and scanned the scene beyond. He let out a sigh, more from the satisfaction of one who had accomplished what he set out to do than from physical exhaustion. The breathlessness from running was replaced by the shudder of a man whose emotions had long been held in check, and only now released. He had done what he wanted to do. He had cut off the ear of the man who was responsible for giving his daughter-in-law a bad name. Yes, some day someone will chop off his head. I am too good to him . . . I only cut off his ear.

He considered whether the police would come for him. Would Ah Song dare go to the police? What could he tell them? They would ask him: What happened to you? Who cut off your ear? What could he say to that? Could he say someone's father-in-law cut off his ear because he was running around with the daughter-in-law? Ha ha. Just let him go to the police. He wouldn't dare.

In retrospect Wah Gay decided there was no point in taking chances. Why go back to the club house and have the cops come and pick him up. Or perhaps they were waiting for him now. No, he would not go back.

The neons blinked across Chatham Square on the Mott Street side, punctuated by the red and green of the city's traffic bureau. Head lights and tail lights whizzed by and stopped and resumed and turned in the merging traffic pattern of a busy thoroughfare. Wah Gay stood at the curb and stared for several long minutes. He had seldom been on this side of Chatham Square. An El train rumbled past on the uptown side. Often he had wished he could bring his wife over just so he could show her the beauty that is New York.

He crossed St. James Street and went into the Cafeteria. He sat down at the counter and ordered coffee. Then he checked himself and asked for black coffee. He took two sips and got up. He went to the telephone booth and dialed a number.

Lee Gong answered the phone.

"I'm too busy to make conversation now," he said firmly after having ascertained that it was Lee Gong at the other end of the line. "I will not be back tonight. When you finish playing, turn off the lights and lock the door."

XL

Wah Gay could have asked Lee Gong on the phone if he could spend the night with him, but he did not want to impose on his in-law. He trusted Lee Gong with the responsibility of locking the door of the club house because Lee Gong, aside from being a relative, was a reliable man. But he would hesitate to spend the night with him in the same room, for the chilliness of formality between relatives would make them as uncommunicative as strangers.

After he called Lee Gong, Wah Gay called an old friend in Newark, New Jersey, and asked if he could come over and spend the night with him. He was an old school mate whom Wah Gay had not seen since their school days. Mee Kee and Wah Gay were roommates when both were students at the Poy Ying Middle School in Sunwei City. They had roomed together for two years until Mee Kee quit school to come to America. They had been buddies at school, frequently visiting whorehouses together on Cow's Dung Road. But when they came to America, each had gone his separate way. Mee Kee had been in the cafe-type of restaurant business in the mid-west somewhere before coming East. He had mentioned the name of the town to Wah Gay but, during the intervening years, he had forgotten it. They had run into each other on Mott Street by chance some years ago. Mee Kee had jotted down his own address and telephone number for his former roommate and asked that he call on him when in New Jersey. At that time, Wah Gay never dreamed that some day he would want to spend the night in his laundry. But, when pressed for a good friend, Mee Kee's was the first name that came to him. Here was someone he could trust; and, if he remembered correctly, Mee Kee was not the talkative kind.

Arriving late that night at Mee Kee's small laundry on Court

Street in Newark, Wah Gay poured out the whole story to his former schoolmate.

"That's the way it is with the world," said Mee Kee quietly. "Such an occurrence could happen to anyone. You should not be too concerned over it."

"I am many times ten," said Wah Gay wearily. "What is there to worry about? I will pass away the remaining years in obscurity."

"This Ah Song you were talking about . . . what is his family name?"

"Jo. His last name is Jo."

"H'mn, why didn't you kill him?" chuckled Mee Kee. "No one would ever miss him. I don't think you can find another Jo in New York."

"I'm no murderer," replied Wah Gay. Mee Kee poured him a cup of tea. "I'm not that kind of man. I just wanted to teach him a lesson. Now, everywhere he goes, people will know that he lost his ear because of some wrong-doing."

"That is good," said Mee Kee. He was slight of build and at least three inches shorter than Wah Gay, weighing about fifty pounds less. His chin was pointed and his mouth, when closed, gave the impression of a straight line across. When it opened, it reminded one of a frog's mouth. "I approve of what you have done," he continued. "It will teach him a lesson." His mouth opened wide and he laughed. "In this world one's fate is pre-destined. Take myself for example . . . I asked the old rice-cooker to come to America many years ago . . . and what do you think she said? The unlucky one said she didn't want to come to America. She is content to remain in the village, where she could watch over the rice paddies . . . and where the idols and spirits could watch over her . . . and me . . ." He chuckled again.

The two old schoolmates reminisced and laughed as they had never laughed since the days they roomed together, and Ah Song's lost ear was temporarily forgotten.

At one point of the conversation, Mee Kee understandingly shook his head. "We can talk and we can scold the young ones," he said. "Remember when we were young? Do you still remember what we used to do in those days? Remember that *chicken house* on Cow's Dung Road? Remember your favorite girl . . . what was her name? . . . Tsuey Far? Yes, it was Tsuey Far. Ha ha."

Wah Gay knitted his brows and studied the movements of Mee Kee's mouth. He recalled that Mee Kee, in the old days, was not as talkative. Maybe it was because they had not seen each other for so long and they had so much to talk about.

"When we got to the whorehouse, you always asked the lady boss for Tsuey Far. Remember? When told she was not around, you went to all the rooms looking for her. Life is like that. You cannot hope to change the world in just our one generation." He eyed Wah Gay compassionately. "Don't be too harsh on the young man," he continued. "You went to the whorehouses and when your boy got old enough to go, he went too. The only difference, I suppose, was that you knew when to quit and he didn't."

"The useless dead boy," Wah Gay fumed. "He should die from mere stupidity."

"The past is behind you now," said Mee Kee. "Don't worry your heart over it. Look at me. I have a wife but I'm living the life of a widower. She said she didn't want to come to America. Can you imagine that? Others would sell their homes and rice paddies to be able to come." Mee Kee went to the back of the room and fetched a towel for Wah Gay. "Go wash up a bit and get some of the dust off you," he said, pointing to the tiny washroom. Wah Gay accepted the towel and headed for the washroom. So crammed were the quarters in the laundry that the small washroom was only an arm's reach from where the two had been sitting. Wah Gay left the door open, and Mee Kee continued talking. "One's life in this world is but many times ten. It is like a short dream. We just sit down by the roadside and watch the show go by."

"How right you are, old friend," Wah Gay stood by the doorway, wiping his face with the towel. "I shouldn't be worrying about the young ones any more. A grown son belongs to the world. I have done my duty. I had seen to it that Ben Loy got married."

"We have been here too long," chuckled Mee Kee. "But we still retain a little of the Chinese culture. Otherwise we wouldn't consider marrying off the young ones. I think you have done as much as any father can do for his boy . . ."

"You know what kind of a man I am . . .I am a man with a red face. I cannot take my daughter-in-law's running around with another man without trying to do something about it. This will ruin my name. But under the circumstances I could do no less." He came out of the washroom. "I don't think there is much to this ear chopping . . . I mean as far as getting put in jail is concerned. If I am unlucky, I might get six months or a suspended sentence."

"Don't worry about it," said Mee Kee. "Maybe the police will never catch you. If they don't know whom to look for, they don't know where to look for him."

"If Ping On Tong takes up the fight for me there is a good chance I will go free. Unless I can remain free, there is no point in trying to hide from the authorities. You can hide today but you cannot hide tomorrow. My stay here is only temporary. I will not get you into trouble."

"What trouble can there be?" Mee Kee mildly rebuked him. He was indignant that his old friend should even remotely imply that he, Mee Kee, was afraid of a little trouble. "I am many times ten in years. What serious harm can come to a man in my years? If we cannot help a friend in need, what is the purpose of friendship?"

A surge of gratefulness slowly expanded within Wah Gay. Mee Kee had been no showoff during his school days. He was a rather quiet, non-aggressive boy. But he had principle and he could be very serious about it. One could count on Mee Kee to remain a loyal friend, but he could bend with the wind too. Wah Gay thought that his friend, though so puny in looks and having survived a bullet wound, would outlive him. Mee Kee was shot seven years ago when a holdup man came into his laundry and demanded money. Although weighing less than one hundred and ten pounds, Mee Kee prided himself on having trained in his youth in the village tablet house as a pugilist. What he lacked in weight he made up in alertness and

189

steadiness of nerves. In a daring gamble he had tried to disarm the gunman, but the gunman was no sluggard. The bullet missed his heart by a quarter of an inch. Mee Kee was taken to the Presbyterian Hospital. Wah Gay had gotten someone to take care of the laundry for Mee Kee and had visited him at the hospital.

Mee Kee was not one who would forget a kindness. "That's what friends are for," he continued, recalling how his old schoolmate has responded to his call for help.

After having talked throughout part of the morning, the two friends dozed off to sleep.

XLI

Detective Percy B. Nolan of the Fifth Precinct went around
to familiar spots in Chinatown, dropping hints that he was
looking for Wang Wah Gay. Several times he had been to the
Money Come Club House, trying the door. It was locked. He
waited on the corner of Mott and Canal Streets, where he had
a commanding view of the stairs leading down to the basement.
At length he spied a figure at the stairs of the club. He strolled
over to meet him.

"Where is Wang Wah Gay?" the detective demanded.

Lee Gong was startled. He turned his palms up and shrugged
his shoulders. "I don't know. I come to look for him too."

"What is your name? Where do you live?"

Lee Gong reluctantly told him, and he was permitted to go,
after a warning by the detective to report at once to the Fifth
Precinct on Elizabeth Street if Wang returned to the store.

Lee Gong went directly to the Wang Association building to
look for Chuck Ting. He tried the Social Club. If he were to
be found, he would be at the Social Club on the second floor;
for the Association headquarters were on the top floor and
seldom used except for business meetings. Lee Gong was lucky.
Chuck Ting was in his second floor office.

"Mr. Chuck Ting," began Lee Gong the moment the door was
closed behind him. "There was a detective looking for Wah
Gay. Wah Gay and I are in-laws . . ."

"Oh, you're Mr. Lee Gong," said Chuck Ting amiably. He
lit a cigar. "I've heard of you but have never had the opportunity to meet you until now."

"We met once before but I don't suppose you would remember that," said Lee Gong. "I remember meeting you at the wedding banquet almost two years ago at the Grand China Restaurant."

191

"Oh, yes. You're right. I'm sorry. I owe you an apology."

"Please don't talk like that. I don't consider you a stranger." Lee Gong's eyes studied the man who had been president of the Wangs for more years than any previous president, and had been national president of the Ping On Tong. "Of course I know you and Wah Gay are like brothers, and in a way, we are all related. I am a little worried because my in-law failed to open his club house today. Another thing that bothers me is this detective who was looking for him. At first I thought he was from Immigration. You know how those Immigration people work. They hang around out in the streets and all of a sudden they would walk up to you and ask you for your papers. So I thought at first he was an inspector from Immigration."

"Of course this is the first I've heard of the matter," said Chuck Ting pensively. "I was in Stanton yesterday and I just came back to New York today. Did the detective say what he wanted him for?"

"No," said Lee Gong, feeling stupid for not having asked the detective what he wanted Wah Gay for. He supposed that, even if he had asked him, he wouldn't have told him anyway. "You know how those detectives are. Their mouths are big and yours is small. The less you say to them, the better."

"Yes, I suppose you're right," Chuck Ting agreed. "I would have stayed in Stanton and helped out in the restaurant if it had not been for my rheumatism. Maybe I can find out why the detective was looking for Wah Gay." He took a puff on his cigar and looked at Lee Gong reassuringly. "If I can find out anything about this, I will get in touch with you. In the meantime, don't worry. Everything will be all right."

He was going to add that he hoped Wah Gay had not done anything foolish, such as shooting the man who was responsible for breaking up his son's marriage. Then he checked himself. He realized he was talking to the father of the girl. He remembered vividly how he had called Wah Gay into this very room only a few weeks before, to discuss the impending scandal. As he thought of the matter, the more he was convinced that Wah Gay had gotten into trouble because of his daughter-in-law. But how could he tell Lee Gong that? Instead, he repeated, "If I find out anything, I'll let you know."

Lee Gong scribbled a telephone number on a piece of paper and left it with Chuck Ting. "If you find out anything, call me at this number." Then he turned to leave. "What about Ben Loy?" he asked anxiously. "Will you notify him?"

"Ben Loy? We'd better not bother him with anything until we find out definitely what the police want his father for. If you tell him the police are looking for his father and nothing more than that, he would be unnecessarily worried. There's nothing he could do. We will tell him and his wife when the time comes."

As soon as Lee Gong had gone, Chuck Ting picked up the phone and dialed a number.

"Hello? George? This is Chuck Ting. Will you take a short walk for me? Will you go over to the 5th Precinct and find out why they are looking for Wang Wah Gay? That's right. Okay, George. I'll be at this telephone number . . ."

Although Chuck Ting was no longer active in Tong politics, he was nevertheless a much respected elder statesman in matters affecting the Tong. Whatever he set out to do or say was treated with much face. He knew that when he picked up the phone to *harass* George a little, a word he was fond of using when he wanted someone to do a little favor for him, the English Secretary of Ping On Tong had no choice but to do what was asked of him. George D. Dong was known as a nice fellow. He had been reelected English Secretary for the third straight year, while the president and the other officers were newly elected. George was the choice of both factions. He was always out to do somebody a favor.

When Chuck Ting called him, he was baby-sitting at home while his wife was out visiting. But he called her right away and said, "Honey, something happened and you'll have to come home for a while. Why? I can't explain it over the phone. Come home for about half an hour and then you can go back and finish your visit."

The 5th Precinct was just a short walk from where George lived with his wife and baby girl. Fifteen minutes later, he arrived at the Elizabeth Street Police Station. The desk sergeant sent him upstairs to see Captain Wilbur King, in charge of detectives. In answer to George's inquiry the captain said: "A man by the name of Ah Song complained that Wang Wah Gay, of 87 Mott Street, assaulted him with a knife on the night of September 9th in the hallway of 45 Catherine Street. We are now looking for this Wang Wah Gay. If you know of this man's whereabouts, let us know. If you're a friend of his, you'd better have him come in and surrender himself."

"What's the charge, captain?" asked George.

"Assault and battery, with intent to kill."

"Okay, captain, thanks." George left the station house.

The Wang Association Building was only a block from the 5th Precinct. Instead of returning home and calling Chuck Ting, George walked rapidly toward the Association Building. At the tiny office of the president, George Dong matter-of-factly told Chuck Ting that Ah Song had made the complaint against Wah Gay and that Captain King wanted Wang Wah Gay to surrender.

George added, "But between you and me, Chairman, that Ah Song deserves more than just being assaulted."

"Someone like Ah Song will never learn," said Chuck Ting. He wanted to say more but did not want to discuss Wah Gay's daughter-in-law for fear of causing embarrassment to his cousin. And inasmuch as Wah Gay was like a brother to him, he would be only courting shame for himself at the same time.

"Wah Gay's daughter-in-law must be involved in this too," commented George cryptically. "Otherwise, what reason would he have in attacking Ah Song with a knife? Only last week I heard people say: 'If Ah Song is not playing mah-jong at Wah Gay's, he's playing with the proprietor's daughter-in-law.'"

"Listen, George," broke in Chuck Ting sternly. "I want you to keep this whole thing confidential. Give me a little time. I have to think this one out. I'll call you later if I can locate Wah Gay. For the present I have no idea where he is. His place is still closed. In the past, when I wanted him, all I needed to do was to pick up the phone and call the basement club house. Maybe he will try to get in touch with me. That's our only hope."

After George left, he considered calling Ben Loy. He didn't even know where Ben Loy worked. He would have to call his home.

194

"Hello? Ah Sow? This is Uncle Chuck Ting." This was the first time he ever talked to her on the phone and he thought she had a pleasant voice.

"Oh, Uncle Chuck Ting, how are you?" Mei Oi's soft girlish voice came over the wire. "What have you to teach me today?"

Chuck Ting could not help but chuckle over this remark. "Ah Sow. I'm afraid I don't have anything to teach you today. You are too polite, and you need not be."

"I'm always eager to listen to your advice and teaching," she said.

"Heh heh, I'm many times ten. If there is any teaching to be done, I think the young should teach the old." They both laughed. "Nothing serious. I just want to have a word with Ben Loy. Where is he working now?"

"Oh, I hope nothing is wrong . . ."

"No, nothing like that. Please give me his telephone number."

"His telephone number is . . ." There was a brief pause and then the voice continued, a little more anxious than before. "Is there anything the matter?"

"Ah Sow, kindly allow your heart to be free from worry," assured Uncle Chuck Ting. "I am many times ten. What could I possibly gain by lying to you? I just want to have a word with my nephew."

She gave him the number.

"Okay, thank you, Ah Sow. Now there's nothing to worry about. I just want to talk to him. I haven't spoken with him since you people moved back to New York."

"Maybe Ben is busy now. Call him a little later."

"Yes, I will call him later. Did your Lao Yair call you?" He tried to make the last query sound inconsequential.

"No," said Mei Oi. "Is there something wrong? My Lao Yair seldom calls."

"No need to worry," Uncle Chuck Ting reassured her. "Don't be alarmed." His voice had a ring of sincerity and strength. "But just in case he calls, you tell him to call me. I want to talk to him too."

Mei Oi hung up, thinking it odd that Uncle Chuck Ting should call her to try to locate her father-in-law.

Chuck Ting dialed the number Mei Oi had just given him. As he waited for Ben Loy to come to the phone, he gathered that he must be busy. He could picture his nephew rushing back and forth with a tray on the palm of his hand between the dining room and the kitchen. Maybe Ah Sow was right in cautioning him to wait a little while before calling. He was about to hang up and try again later when there was a *hello* on the line.

"Loy, are you very busy? This is Uncle Chuck Ting."

"I was, but it's all right now," said Ben Loy. "You know how it is . . . they all get hungry at the same time."

"Loy, did your father call you?"

"My father call me? No. What's the matter?" asked the puzzled Ben Loy. "He didn't call me. Why should he call me? He knows I'm back in New York."

Chuck Ting thought it better not to mention anything about the father's disappearance. "Oh, nothing. I thought he might have called you. I can't get him at the club house."

"Maybe he got arrested for playing mah-jong," said Ben Loy lightly. "You know they do that once in a while."

"No, your father is not arrested," said Chuck Ting. "I know that much."

"If he's not at the club house, I don't know where he can be." Ben Loy sounded bewildered.

"Don't worry," said Chuck Ting soothingly. "Everything will be all right. I will let you know if your father calls me. If he calls you, you let me know too, won't you?"

From Lee Gong, Chuck Ting learned that Wah Gay had not called him either. There was nothing to do but wait. Chuck Ting whirled around in his chair, pressing his fingers together. He closed his eyes. During his many terms as president of the New York chapter of Ping On Tong, and more recently as its national president, he had been maneuvered into many decisions that were not always popular or easy to make. He had fought many legal battles with the authorities.

Wang Chuck Ting drummed his fingers on the desk and blew smoke rings into the air from his cigar. Although for the moment he was concerned with Wah Gay's whereabouts, he was not seriously worried that any harm would come to him. The fact

196

that both Wah Gay and Ah Song belonged to Ping On Tong simplified his job as a possible mediator in the matter. In spite of the fact that Chuck Ting held no office in the organization now, he nevertheless exuded authority. The present officers of the Tong always sought his opinion on matters of general importance. And his advice was always followed. When the occasion was a matter of factional disputes or preference, he would say to both sides: *I'm keeping my hands off this thing. You young people must decide for yourselves. I am impartial to both.*

Wang Chuck Ting felt it would be a matter of days or even weeks before his cousin would show up. According to his own thinking, Wah Gay must have gone into hiding after the attack on Ah Song. It was as simple as that. Cutting off Ah Song's ear was nothing. No corpse, no case. In his mind, he began formulating a defense for his cousin. To begin with, Ah Song's reputation in New York's Chinatown and other Chinese communities was well known concerning his behavior with women. The family name of Ah Song, Jo, was so insignificantly few in number that, when Chuck Ting tried to recall if, during his many years associated with Tong activities, he had ever come across another Jo, he could not. When the show-down came, in addition to being on the side of righteousness, Wah Gay would be on the side of numerical superiority too, because the Wangs had many cousins in New York. Even if the matter was referred to the Chinese Benevolent Association, there would be enough voices raised on behalf of Wang Wah Gay that any voice heard on behalf of Ah Song would be Ah Song's own voice. Chuck Ting was quite satisfied with the preliminary outlook of a possible defense for Wah Gay.

A wide grin now broke out on his face. Wah Gay's business was *his* business, he told himself. He would call up this year's president of the Tong, Ho Soon, and ask him to get in touch with Ah Song. He would explain indignantly to the president that Ah Song was morally wrong in breaking up the home of Ben Loy and Mei Oi. That Wang Wah Gay was justified in his attack on Ah Song for having destroyed an otherwise happy family. He could then add something about setting an example for others like Ah Song to think twice before embarking upon a career

197

of love thievery. If an example was not made of him, he would argue, it might be an encouragement to others to follow in his ways. This would be purely an internal problem, since both men were members of the Tong. There would not be need for outside interference, the police included.

The phone at the little office began to ring. Before the first ring ended, Chuck Ting anxiously grabbed the receiver. "Hello," he barked.

"Mr. Chuck Ting? This is Lee Gong."

"Yes, yes!" exclaimed the usually calm Chuck Ting. "What news do you have for me? Did Wah Gay call you?"

"Yes, he just called me. I've already told him the police are looking for him."

"What did he have to say to that?"

"He told me to let you know. He said he will be back in a day or two. I asked him what was the matter but he didn't say anything. He told me nothing."

"Did he leave you a telephone number?"

"No," replied Lee Gong.

"I don't see why he has to be so mysterious about the whole thing," said Chuck Ting. "I can tell you this much: He is in hiding because of that daughter of yours. The police are looking for him because he slashed Ah Song's ear when he caught him coming out of your daughter's apartment while Ben Loy was at work. Why didn't you bring her up right!"

"That dead girl is absolutely no use." Lee Gong could hear the click at the other end. "Hello? Hello?" But there was no answer.

As soon as he had said these things to Lee Gong, Chuck Ting was sorry he had said them. Certainly he had not intended to be so rude.

Until Wah Gay returned, nothing could be done. Why did he call Lee Gong and not me? That guy didn't have the spleen of a bat. That Lee Gong . . . what a friend . . . what a father he turned out to be! . . . what a relation!

Chuck Ting had tried several times to call the president of Ping On Tong. At first he had tried the Kwongtung Inn, where Ho Soon was boss, but he was told to try Tong headquarters.

Headquarters told him to try the restaurant. He dialed the number of a club house on Mulberry Street but Ho Soon was not there either. He called George Dong, who gave him a couple of numbers to call and he got the president on the second try.

"I've got a little matter which requires your assistance," he began in a smooth, pleasant voice. Briefly he unfolded the story to the president, who said he would look into the matter as soon as he contacted George. As an afterthought, Chuck Ting added that it might be a good idea to send George down to Beekman Hospital to talk to Ah Song.

XLII

The twenty-four hours just passed had seemed like two long years to Wah Gay. The tiny laundry of his former schoolmate was too confining to suit him.

"Who would think that some day I would end up in jail?" Wah Gay shook his head sadly and assumed the pose of a philosopher. "Maybe my birth date is not the right one." He was trying hard to be flippant but, deep inside, he was worried. Flashes of his wife Lau Shee going to the fields in the early dawn, passing and meeting with fellow-villagers, came to him. After Lau Shee had passed, the others would say: Have you heard? Ben Loy's father is sitting down in jail in the golden mountain!

And in New York people would say: Wah Gay is in jail for cutting off Ah Song's ear! He might as well go to jail for killing him. The mere thought of going to jail tortured him. He would have done society a favor if he had killed Ah Song.

The skin on his face was getting thicker by the minute. He was not sorry for what he had done. He was shamed by the underlying reasons that had forced him to take action. He had found himself in an impossible position where, for a man of his temperament, he had no choice but to resort to violence. And after having resorted to violence, thereby inadvertently parting the curtain that had shielded the ugly behavior of his daughter-in-law, he could no longer bear to lift his head before his many friends in New York. He thought of calling Ben Loy to give him an ultimatum concerning his wife. Several times he had been on the verge of picking up the phone, but each time he changed his mind. What could he say? Could he say to Ben Loy *I have just slashed your wife's lover? That one of Ah Sow's friends met with an accident? Your wife is no good, go get yourself another one? I have cut off Ah Song's ear because you refused to*

do it yourself? . . . If you had just a little ember of fire in you,
you would have killed him!

Kill him? Why didn't *you* kill the scoundrel? Why did you only slash his ear? Yes, why didn't you kill him? . . . That no good dead boy, he would still say his wife is innocent. He must be a slave to that female. What could I say to him? He is not even on my side. He is on *her* side. He is on Ah Song's side. That sonovabitch! I'll kill him yet . . . what have I got to lose?

Should he call Chuck Ting? He could picture him roaring at him: You stupid hot dog! Why did you bungle the thing? Why didn't you say a word to me about it?

He decided to call Lee Gong again.

Lee Gong was waiting for the call in his apartment. He had no place to go now that the club house was closed. When the phone rang, he rushed to answer it.

"Hello?"

"Wah Gay. I'm all right. I . . ."

"Where are you calling from?"

"I can't tell you now."

"Mr. Chuck Ting wants to talk to you."

"Tell him I'm all right."

"The police are still looking for you. Yesterday . . ."

"Tell Chuck Ting that. He'll know what to do."

Hardly had he hung up when an idea flashed to his mind. Why not get Lee Gong to operate the club house for him? He abruptly left the stool by the pile of soiled clothes and turned to the startled Mee Kee. "I'm going to make another call. I want Lee Gong to come over and pick up the key for the basement."

Once again Lee Gong rushed to the phone. "This is Wah Gay again. Get a piece of paper and pencil and take this address down carefully. I want you to come over to this address right away and don't tell anyone."

After he hung up, Lee Gong stood reflecting by the phone for a long time. Then he picked up the phone and dialed: "Hello, Mr. Chuck Ting . . ."

XLIII

That night when Ben Loy got home, Mei Oi was waiting up
for him. Normally she would be in bed and asleep when he returned home. She was by the sofa, reading a Hong Kong movie
fan magazine when the latch on the door clicked. From where
she sat, if she listened for it, she could hear the insertion of the
key into the key hole, then the turning of the door knob. The
night was quiet and she was listening.

Ben Loy was surprised to find his wife not yet asleep. "Still
up?" he asked perfunctorily, removing his coat.

And from the sitting room came Mei Oi's voice. "Loy Gaw,
you're home?" She did not get up but remained seated. "You
are early." She always said that as a form of greeting, regardless
of the time. When she said it, she never even bothered to consult her watch. The truth of the matter was that Ben Loy was
not home early, and he was not late. He was home about the
usual time. As she often did, she now asked him: "How was
business today?" Meaning, of course, how did it go in the tips
department?

"A couple of long tables. Made four in one and five in the
other. The others were *fried chop sueys*," he said.

She put down the magazine and walked over to him as he
came into the living room. "Did you get enough to eat for supper
tonight?" she asked with wifely interest, throwing her arms
around him and kissing him.

He accepted the kiss without much enthusiasm. Except for
the early part of their marriage, such display of affection had
been non-existent in their daily life. To Mei Oi's interest in his
appetite, he replied that those who work in restaurants gener-
ally lose their appetites, and that the cook who fixes supper for
the employees at night is not interested in making something
palatable but just stirs the stuff a few times in the cauldron and

202

dishes it out.

This reminded Mei Oi of the anecdote Ben Loy had once told her. Ben Loy used to work with a cook named Chow who was nicknamed Prince Chow because there was a prince by that name thousands of years ago. One night Prince Chow was cooking supper for the employees when accidentally the bandage around his middle finger came off and got mixed up with the vegetables and meat he was cooking in the cauldron. When one of the waiters tried to chew on it, it soon became apparent that whatever he was chewing defied mastication. He extracted it from his mouth and it was then that he came to realize he had been chewing on Prince Chow's bandage.

Tonight Mei Oi cuddled next to her husband on the sofa and teased him with: "You didn't chew any bandages tonight?" And they both laughed. That was what Mei Oi wanted Ben Loy to do . . . to laugh. She wanted him to be in a good mood. What if her husband should suspect that Ah Song had been to see her last night?

"Did you hear of any special news tonight?" she giggled and nudged closer to her husband.

"News? What news?" asked the startled Ben Loy. His wife had never asked him such questions before. Then he recalled having received a phone call from Uncle Chuck Ting. "Oh, yes. Uncle Chuck Ting called me. Said the old man is not at his basement club house."

"Not at his basement club house?" exclaimed Mei Oi. "Where could he be? He is always there." She assumed a pensive pose. "Oh, maybe he went off to visit some friend."

"He had never gone visiting before," said Ben Loy sullenly.

"What else did Chuck Ting say?" pursued Mei Oi anxiously. "I hope nothing has happened to Lao Yair." A rash of night muggings had broken out on the lower East Side recently, not far from Catherine Street, and this was the first thought that came to her. But she did not mention these not-good-to-listen-to things for fear that speaking of them now might bring on bad luck. She recalled hearing a commotion on the stairs right after Ah Song had left her apartment. Maybe Ah Song was the victim of such an attack—she winced at the thought. If such an attack did occur, would the entire Chinatown hear about it? Would they put it in the Chinese newspapers? "That's why I always say," resumed Mei Oi, "when you come home at night, be especially careful."

"Such matters are not up to one's being careful," said Ben Loy. "Sometimes when you are afraid of stepping on dung, fate will have you step on dung!"

"What did you tell Uncle Chuck Ting?"

"Nothing. What was there for me to tell him? I don't know anything."

Apprehension slowly threw a tightening grip around her whole body. Last night was the first time she had seen her lover in many weeks. Now that she was back in New York, it was their first meeting. Why had she risked disgrace to have an affair? But Ben Loy was no good as a husband. Ah Song was so tender and understanding. The important thing was that she had become pregnant. She had always wanted to be a mother. Now that the baby was coming, no one could say she was incapable of bearing a child . . . Still, she was worried about her father-in-law's disappearance.

"Please go out and see if you can get some information about Lao Yair," she said.

XLIV

Ben Loy first went to the social club. Not finding Chuck Ting there, he entered one of the coffee shops and ordered a cup of coffee, sipping it slowly. Without turning, he recognized the gossiping voices of Chong Loo, the rent collector, and Ah Sing, the barber, from a nearby table.

"Not even Wang Chuck Ting knows where his little brother is."

"Atta boy, Uncle Loo, you're not bad as a reporter."

Ah Sing encouraged him. "Go ahead and tell me. Tell me what you know about Wah Gay."

"Well, maybe I can't tell you where he is right now," Chong Loo began thoughtfully, "but I can tell you what happened at 45 Catherine Street before he went away." He crushed the unsmoked portion of the cigarette on the ash tray, blowing streams of smoke out of his nostrils. "Last night he left his mah-jong game and went to 33 Catherine Street . . ."

"Wow your mother, it's 45 Catherine Street and not 33," said Ah Sing.

"Okay, number 45 then," resumed Chong Loo. "As fate would have it, Wah Gay ran into Ah Song as the latter was coming out of Ben Loy's apartment. When the old man saw Ah Song coming out of his daughter-in-law's apartment, his face got red and his ears got hot. He chased after Ah Song with an opened knife, and when he caught up with him, he cut off his ear."

"I wonder what the old man was doing in his daughter-in-law's building," said Ah Sing. "He seldom goes there. Maybe once in a long while . . ."

"What do you think?" said Chong Loo impatiently. "He went there to spy on his daughter-in-law. The way the rumors were flying it's even hard on a cow's ears. Ah Song is now at Beekman Hospital," continued Chong Loo with a sly smile. "I always say:

If you travel at night often enough, you will meet up with the devil, heh heh. If someone else had slashed at him, he might have been killed, heh heh. Wah Gay is a kind-hearted man. He only cut off his ear. If it had been your daughter-in-law he was running around with, what would you have done?"

"Go to hell," said Ah Sing indignantly. "Don't talk to me like that. If you say one more word, I'll stuff your mouth full of dung."

"Heh heh, what harm is there to talking?" said Chong Loo. "You're just superstitious. I've heard Wah Gay is now in New Jersey. If the cops catch him he could be in serious trouble."

Ben Loy didn't wait to hear any more. He paid his check hastily and stumbled out the door.

XLV

The brisk night air was good medicine for Ben Loy. A strong breeze lifted and dropped the front and side pieces of the rolled-up awnings of some of the stores. It began to rain.

Suddenly the surroundings took on an unfamiliar appearance. He was a stranger in a strange town. The black hand of darkness seemed ready to swoop down from the clouds to grab him. His emotions gave way to a vision. The winds began to howl around him. He began to walk faster and faster. As fast as his heart could carry him, but it was never fast enough. Darkness was everywhere, up and down the street. Faster . . . faster. But he could not shake off this darkness. Neither could he shake off the clouds. Nor the lightning. He began to run but it was no use, for he could not distinguish the roads and the causeways between rice paddies from the mass of blackness that surrounded him. Many times he lost his footing and stumbled onto the submerged fields. Each time he got back on the road he cursed himself violently but the rains never stopped coming. Another roar of lightning struck the skies, and there was no end to the downpour, like a cascade rushing down a valley of Five-Fingered Mountain. In a moment he was drenched. There was no place to escape. All the doors in the villages were locked and barred.

His eyes wearily searched the breadth and length of the street. All doors were closed and locked. In the obscurity of the night the contours of the stores looked only half-real. He felt himself being spied upon. What if someone should call the police to report a prowler?

Slowly he turned toward home.

As Ben Loy walked, he tried to formulate in his mind what to tell Mei Oi when he got home. In a way he was beginning to feel more sorry for her than for himself. He realized that, even if his father were found and his trouble cleared up, the relationship between his father and his wife and himself would never be the same again. His wife would be too ashamed to lift her head and address his father as *Lao Yair* the way she used to do. He himself would have the same problem about confronting his father. He would have no face left to make the meetings. Divorcing Mei Oi would suit his father fine. The old man would like to see that. He would probably finance a trip to China again if Ben Loy would take another wife. Or maybe he would be too disgusted with the role of father-in-law to try for a second time. But Ben Loy could not bring himself to consider divorcing Mei Oi.

He stumbled along Mott Street in a daze. He didn't feel like going home. He didn't care if he never got home. He hated himself. He hated the whole world. He hated Ah Song. He wanted to run a knife through him.

XLVI

Mei Oi was waiting for him.

"Is *Lao Yair* all right?" she asked anxiously. "Did you see him? Should I go and see him?"

At this question, all of Ben Loy's resentment toward his wife returned.

"No," replied Ben Loy curtly. "I don't think he would want to see *you.*"

After the initial surge of filial concern for the father, Mei Oi fell back into silence. The rebuff from Ben Loy was enough to unnerve her. She was puzzled but she did not dare speak. She felt grave apprehension. Hers was the task of cooking rice for her husband, to darn his socks, to comfort and nurse him in sickness. Not to talk back to him. She could sense the anger, the sarcasm in his voice. She decided to wait.

Without another word to his wife, Ben Loy walked to the kitchen and poured himself a cup of tea from the enamel pot which stood on the table. He gulped the contents down with one lift of the cup. He was thirsty and the hot tea helped calm his nerves. He began wiping the sweat off his forehead and the back of his head. He poured himself another cup of tea and downed it as he had done before.

When he finally returned to the living room, he found his wife softly sobbing. It pleased him to see her cry. He wished she would cry louder and longer. The useless bitch! He felt she had let him down. She had disgraced him. Made him the laughing stock of the whole town. The wearer of the green hat! He wrinkled his nose and sniffed again. His inside was seething with resentment and hurt.

"The police are looking for Wang Wah Gay," he said, "because he cut off the ear of Ah Song. It happened in the hallway of this building!"

"Maybe you want to leave home and live somewhere else," Ben Loy suggested sarcastically, trying to control the emotional turmoil in his voice.

"I don't want to leave home," Mei Oi cried. "This is our home, our marriage . . ." The sobbing became anguished cries. "I . . . I have been like a crazy woman . . . What I have done is the work of a crazy woman . . . I . . . I don't blame you if you disown me . . . but I still love you . . . You are my husband!"

Ben Loy glared at his wife. He scoffed at her protestations of love for him. Words are easy to flow out of one's mouth. Why should he believe her? As he stood glowering at his wife, his thoughts raced in a confused muddle. The scenes shifted from his rural village . . . his mother . . . the wedding in the market . . . to the Money Come club house . . . to his father . . . to Wang Chuck Ting . . . to Chin Yuen . . . to himself . . . and back to Mei Oi. He wished he hadn't married at all. Look at Chin Yuen, a carefree bachelor! He shouldn't have listened to his father . . .

He lit a cigarette and sank down on the upholstered chair, sticking his feet out carelessly. This was his thinking position, at least for the moment. There were intervals when his mind was blank. He closed his eyes and kept them closed for a long time. Then he sprang to his feet. He threw the partly finished cigarette down on the floor and crunched it with his foot. He had never done this before. He had always used an ash tray.

Behind this outward belligerence, Ben Loy would not admit that he was still in love with Mei Oi. He was still too hurt to offer a comforting word to her. But deep down in his heart he fervently wished the scandal would blow away and he and Mei Oi could return to a normal life. He hoped that after all this was over his father would refrain from further interference with their lives. Then his emotions got the better of him. To uphold his manly pride he snapped at Mei Oi, who was still sobbing in her own lonely world.

"If you should change your mind, it is still not too late to pack up and leave!" Then he stamped out of the apartment.

It was a calculated-risk challenge he hurled at her. Where could she go? She would not dare! She would not dare . . . she would be too ashamed to do anything but to stay home . . . she

210

has no other place to go!

As he walked toward Columbus Park, where he planned to sit and brood, he was heaving with self-pity. Why did she do this to me? he kept asking himself. But there was no tangible solution, no satisfactory answer. He sat on the park bench in solitude, hidden and protected by the darkness, gazing at the stars, at the clear blue sky. Seeing but not understanding. He had a feeling he was communing with some supernatural force. He was hoping that somehow his ancestors would extricate him from his marital impasse. From where he sat, he could see silhouettes passing in the distance, from one side of the park to the other, and then disappearing into the night. But Ben Loy was not interested in the rest of humanity. Under the veil of darkness little drops of tears flooded his eyes and he hesitantly wiped them off with his handkerchief. He wasn't crying and he wasn't sobbing. Just the free flowing of tears. He was certain nobody saw him. That Ah Song . . . he would kill him if his father had not got to him first . . .

When he was ready to go home, it was almost two o'clock. Mei Oi was not yet asleep when he tip-toed into the living room. His wife was relieved to see him back, for she had feared the worst. He could have walked out of her life when he stepped out of the apartment tonight. She had begun waiting for a husband who would not come back . . . and the baby . . . it would have no one to call father. Her eyes were still red from crying, her voice cracked and harsh from the terrible shock of exposure. She had been held up to shame. Her whole world tumbled before her. But the moment she heard the door opening, then followed by footsteps, her agony was momentarily forgotten and she became actually elated. She rushed to meet her husband.

"Loy Gaw, I'm terribly sorry for what I have done." She fell to her knees and clung to his leg with all her might. "Please . . . please forgive me . . . I . . . I'm so ashamed."

Ben Loy stroked her soft, silk-like black hair with one hand and gripped her shoulder with the other.

"All right, all right," he said. There was tenderness in his voice.

XLVII

That very night, after he had obtained Wah Gay's address from Lee Gong, Chuck Ting took the Hudson Tubes to Newark, arriving there about 9 P.M. From Penn Station he took a cab for the laundry on Court Street. When Chuck Ting entered the small laundry on the narrow, quiet street, Wah Gay was the most surprised man in all New Jersey. He and Mee Kee were going to close the shop in another half an hour or so.

"Oh, ah . . . ah . . . Chuck Ting Gaw!" fumbled the startled Wah Gay, as if he had seen a ghost. "How come you're over here?"

Then, recovering, he added, "You should have come a few minutes earlier. We've just finished dinner."

"Thank you very much," said Chuck Ting, removing his hat and glancing about the place. "I just ate before I came. No need to be ceremonious. Lee Gong told me where to find you and I asked him to be gracious enough to let me come in his place."

Wah Gay stepped forward to shake his hand. "This is elder brother Mee Kee," he said, turning to his host, "your little brother's old schoolmate. And this is Chuck Ting Gaw."

"I have heard of the name," acknowledged Mee Kee, interrupting his work at the ironing board, smiling and extending his hand. "But I don't think I've ever had the pleasure of meeting you." Chuck Ting grabbed the hand and shook it warmly.

"You have a very kind heart," he complimented Mee Kee, "the way you take care of my little brother."

"It's only a normal duty," said Mee Kee. "Anyone would have done the same thing. We are good friends."

The two men removed themselves to the small adjacent room, leaving Mee Kee to his ironing.

"Why didn't you let me know?" demanded Chuck Ting, his voice loud and soft at the same time. "Regardless of what has happened, you should have said some words to me about it!"

"I . . . I owe you an apology," admitted Wah Gay. "Everything happened so fast, I didn't . . . I didn't have a chance to think."

"What is done, is done." Chuck Ting sat down on a stool indicated for him. "Between brothers there is nothing to be afraid of. Nothing to hide."

"The tea is not so warm," Wah Gay brought in a cup of tea for his brother.

"That's all right. Never mind that. I'm not thirsty." But Wah Gay placed the cup on a corner of the small table, within his brother's reach. "I have thought this thing over carefully," Chuck Ting continued. "You'll have to come back to New York and give yourself up."

"Give myself up?" the shocked Wah Gay bellowed. "It can't be done. At my age, if I go to jail, I will die in jail!"

"You won't go to jail," calmly assured Chuck Ting. "Who said anything about your going to jail? Do you think your elder brother would trick you into going to jail? What advantage would I gain out of that? I'm advising you to do this for your own good."

"I'm going to kill that sonovabitch yet!" Wah Gay clenched his fist.

"You do nothing of the kind," said Chuck Ting firmly. "You're coming back with me."

"I don't think I can go back now," Wah Gay shook his head. "There's no turning back now," he added determinedly. "Maybe I'll go out west somewhere."

"Wah Gay, you listen to me, little brother," Chuck Ting tried again with added earnestness. "I will *not* let you go to jail. Do you think for a moment I would allow you to give yourself up so that you could go to jail?" Chuck Ting stared at him fiercely, his face reddened, and his mouth curled. "What do you think I am? Am I your brother or not? If tonight you agree with me that I am your brother, you must do as I say!

"I have been telling people what to do for thirty to forty years," Chuck Ting continued grimly, "and I have always been afforded some measure of face. But you I can't even get to listen to me. People will laugh at me now."

"That's not true," replied Wah Gay. "That's not true!"

"I suppose it's not true simply because *you* said so," roared Chuck Ting. "I know how people will talk. They'll talk a lot more if you don't give yourself up and the police happen to catch up with you later on. The charges against you are just a formality. The police had to charge you with something because Ah Song filed those charges against you."

"Give me a little time to think this over," said Wah Gay. "I'll think it over and let you know in a few days."

"A few days?" Chuck Ting's voice was fraught with disbelief. "A few days might be too late. In the meantime, the cops might come and take you away. In things of this nature, no one knows what is going to happen next."

"Well, I'll let you know tomorrow then," Wah Gay committed himself reluctantly. He sighed deeply, hoping that this would satisfy Chuck Ting. Chuck Ting asked him to sign a letter addressed to Ho Soon, president of Ping On Tong, requesting a meeting to deliberate the case of Wang Wah Gay versus Ah Song.

Wah Gay didn't want to sign it, saying that he did not wish to further humiliate himself before the public.

"But you have to sign it," Chuck Ting insisted. "If you don't file a complaint against him, he will surely file one against you. He has already filed one with the police, you know that. As soon as he comes out of the hospital, he will certainly go to the Tong president and say you tried to kill him. Don't you see that, as a matter of defending yourself, you will have to take the offensive?"

Wang Wah Gay read the letter over carefully. Reluctantly he affixed his signature. He gave Chuck Ting the club house key to take back to Lee Gong.

XLVIII

When George Dong arrived at Beekman Hospital to see Ah Song, the latter was resting comfortably in bed, with his head bandaged. Ah Song was not exactly happy to see the English-language secretary. In answer to the visitor's cheerful hello, he asked glumly, "What are you here for?"

George looked about the small but neat room, where four other patients were reposing in their beds. One bed by the corner was vacant. All the patients wore bandages of one sort of another, giving the whole room an effect of being swathed in white. After a brief glance about the room, George's eyes fell back on Ah Song. He had known Ah Song for many years but was never close to him. Their friendship was of a nodding acquaintance variety. George assumed that every year around election time, because of Ah Song's closeness to Wang Wah Gay via the mah-jong table, he must have voted for him, George Dong, who was tutored and originally sponsored for the job of English-language secretary by Wang Chuck Ting. But the winds of fortune were blowing differently today. Ah Song had charged Wah Gay with assault and battery. Solidly behind Wah Gay loomed the formidable figure of Chuck Ting. Without the slightest hesitation George Dong would align himself with Chuck Ting. And Ah Song knew that too.

"What are you doing here?" he repeated suspiciously.

This lack of sociability exasperated George. "How come you're so careless?" he asked, pointing a finger toward the bandaged ear.

"That sonovabitch Wang Wah Gay tried to kill me!" he shouted. "He must have gone mad. We are long time friends. Ten years . . . twenty years. Who would think he'd turn out to be such a scoundrel?"

"Are you sure it was Wang Wah Gay? Maybe you didn't get

215

a good enough look at him," George Dong suggested.

"Wow your mother," said Ah Song, annoyed at the visitor's insinuations. "You go sell your ass, little Georgie. What the hell are you talking about? Do you think I'm blind? Who do you think you're talking to—a blind man?" he snarled and sneered.

"Maybe it was dark and you couldn't tell who was who," persisted George. He had not intended to talk to Ah Song in this vein, but he got on the track quite accidentally when Ah Song's hostility became apparent. He remembered his mission and smothered his own personal feelings to assume an air of impartiality. "Anyway, you'll be out of here in no time," he tried to placate the irritated Ah Song. He didn't want to present himself as a Wang Wah Gay man. Personally he had no love for Ah Song, the lone wolf. He put himself in Wah Gay's son's place. If someone had come to his apartment and made love to his wife, he would . . . "What did you tell the police?" he asked.

"I told them the truth," growled Ah Song. "Everything as it had happened." Dong waited for him to continue but not another word came out of his mouth.

"So, what did you tell the police?" George pursued.

"Why don't you go and ask the police? Why come to me?" Ah Song's face was flushed with indignation.

"All right, I've already asked them," said George bluntly. "They said they would drop the charges against Wang Wah Gay if you would withdraw your charges."

"Withdraw my charges?" Ah Song exploded. "Do you think I'm crazy? Do I look crazy to you? Wah Gay tried to kill me and you want me to drop the charges!" He stuck out his lower lip and screamed: "You're crazy, not me!" The other patients stared at them in astonishment.

"I'll tell you why I'm here, Ah Song," George began in earnest. "Lao Chuck sent me to see you. You know how it is . . . he and Wah Gay are cousins. Naturally he wants you to let go of that hot air of yours and get back to normal. He doesn't like to stir up any trouble."

"Who's stirring up trouble?" Ah Song asked vehemently. "What are you talking about?"

"Lao Chuck says you're not to show up to press charges against his cousin . . ."

"It's all up to the police," replied Ah Song sullenly. "Let them do their duty. It's out of my hands now."

"That's just the point, Ah Song. If you don't show up to press the charges, the police won't hold Wah Gay."

"What do you think I am?" Ah Song bounced to a sitting position. "You must think I'm stupid like a pig."

"Don't talk so loud," cautioned George. "You're disturbing the other patients. Be quiet."

"Get out. Get the hell out of here. You go to hell. Go sell your ass . . . you sonovabitch!"

XLIX

The following day, after a night of painstaking reflections, Chuck Ting called Wang Fook Ming, the incumbent president of the Wang Association and explained to him the case of Wah Gay. He hinted to Fook Ming he wanted him to call a meeting of the officers of the Association. The president thereupon relayed the message to the secretary, who immediately sent out notices for a meeting the following Sunday at 7:30 P.M.

It rained all day Sunday. But Chinatown was not to be dampened by a little rain. Children and adults, young and old, whole families, climbed out of the BMT on Canal Street on their way to Chinatown. The Wangs came too, from Brooklyn, from Staten Island, from the Bronx, from Long Island. A few of the Wangs who had come to Chinatown this Sunday mounted the four flights of stairs at their Association headquarters for the meeting.

"Members of the executive committee," the president began in his native Sun Wei dialogue. He was a man in his late fifties who had recently inherited a grocery store from his late father. "We are meeting tonight because one of our members, Elder Brother Wah Gay, is at present in a little difficulty. We are here to help him, if we can. For what good is an association such as ours if we could not come to the aid of one of its members when he is in need of help? It is, then, to help devise ways and means to a solution of this matter which concerns brother Wah Gay that we are meeting here tonight. We have someone among us tonight who can tell you in detail what has happened in the past few days. I now call upon Elder Statesman, Mr. Cousin Chuck Ting, to review for us the events that led to Wah Gay's going out of town. I might add that in the past, as far as we have known him, Brother Wah Gay has been a faithful supporter of the Association, always ready with a donation, whether it be for a burial of a cousin or for a building fund in Havana. He has

218

performed whatever duties, as a member, that have been requested of him. It is fitting now that, when he is in need of our help, we should do all we can to help him. I now call upon Mr. Cousin Ting to instruct and guide us in this matter."

Beaming, Chuck Ting slowly got up. He was sitting at the other end of the long table, opposite the president. His coat front was unbuttoned and open. One corner of his coat was pushed back but his right hand stuck in his pants pocket. The left hand held a cigar.

"President and members of the executive committee, I first heard of this matter when . . .

"What we said here tonight should not be repeated outside of this room. If any of us had been in Wah Gay's place, I'm sure we would have done the same thing. Perhaps something more serious than cutting off Ah Song's ear might have taken place. Wah Gay is our cousin. We want to help him as much as we can. And in this case, I believe we *can* help him."

The president got up. "You've just heard Mr. Cousin Chuck Ting review the happenings for the last few days concerning the matter of Mr. Cousin Wah Gay. Little brother is of the same opinion, namely that we write and let Ping On Tong know of our feelings in the hope that they would carry out our wishes and have Ah Song withdraw these charges against our cousin." The president paused and glanced toward the ceiling, then continued. "These charges could be big or small. We should not take a chance on them becoming small when we can make an effort to do away with this chance by having Ah Song withdraw the charges." He looked about the room once more. There were several approving nods from the members.

"Do you have any other suggestions to the solution of this matter?" he asked. When no comments were forthcoming, he turned to the Chinese-language secretary, Ging Fong, more affectionately known as Third Uncle. "Third Uncle, will you draft a letter to Ping On Tong, outlining the justifications for the request to have Ah Song refrain from appearing in court to testify against Wah Gay. In the meantime Mr. Cousin Chuck Ting will be in touch with their president, Mr. Ho Soon. We will discuss our Spring Festival Banquet at our next meeting. We don't want to take up any more of your precious time. The meeting is now adjourned."

Wang Fook Ming, slightly bent and rapidly greying, hurried back to his grocery store on Pell Street, for it was very busy on Sundays.

L

The meeting of Ping on Ton had been called for 6:30 P.M. The conferees sat at a table forty feet long in the meeting room of Tong headquarters. The Chinese-language secretary, Ging Fong, sat at a little round table by himself, near the head of the table where the president sat. President Ho Soon began by reading the letter from Wang Wah Gay that Chuck Ting had persuaded him to sign when he visited him in Newark.

Dear Mr. President:

> *On the night of November 9th about 10:30 o'clock I caught red-handed a fellow member of Ping On Tong, Ah Song, emerging from the apartment of my insignificant daughter-in-law. This is my misfortune. Enraged, I tried to scare Ah Song with a small pocket knife, but in the ensuing struggle with him, I accidentally cut a piece off his ear. I now charge Ah Song with breaking up my home as well as the home of my offspring, Ben Loy. Ah Song's inhuman action has caused me great loss of face. His continued presence in the City of New York will add to this embarrassment. Other families will not be safe from a scoundrel like Ah Song. If he is permitted to stay in New York, what is to prevent him from breaking up other homes? He has the audacity to go to the police and . . .*
>
> *Respectfully submitted,*
>
> Wang Wah Gay

Next the letter from the Wang Association was read.

Then before the members were given a chance to discuss the matter, president Ho Soon called upon elder statesman Wang Chuck Ting to add to the letter.

Wang Chuck Ting rose slowly. He was glad of the chance to say something on this matter. He would do his utmost to further the cause of his cousin Wah Gay, whom he always treated as a younger brother. He had already conferred with President Ho Soon and the other officers of the organization privately. They were all friendly and sympathetic to his cause. All that remained was the formality of actually presenting the case to the members. Wang Chuck Ting raised his voice and continued.

"...We all have sons and daughters and daughters-in-law. Do you want your daughter-in-law to be raped by such a rascal as Ah Song? It is true that this Ah Song is a member of our organization, but we all know of his stinky reputation. We need not go into any elaborate details, for we do not want to keep you here and take away precious time. If we permit Ah Song to remain in our community, would this not be a license for him to continue his exploits? Who will be the next victim? Your daughter or your wife? Are we to keep our community safe from animals like him? What sort of community do we want to live in? If a case similar to this ever happens again, people will say 'He is a member of the Ping On Tong. He is free to do anything. He even got away with raping Wang Wah Gay's daughter-in-law!' The reputation of the man reflects upon our organization. We should make an example out of him so that no one will want to follow in his footsteps. Banish him from the streets of our community!"

Wang Chuck Ting had a clear, ringing voice. He looked from one end of the table to the other and he happily noted that everyone was listening to him intently. He beamed with the thought that here in this room, no one would come to the defense of Ah Song. "Ah Song was a lone wolf who operated by himself," Chuck Ting resumed. "If anyone could say he was ever close to him, that one man was Wang Wah Gay. Did not Ah Song take advantage of Wang Wah Gay's hospitality? Did he not visit him at the basement club-house everyday? Drink his coffee? Drink his tea? Wang Wah Gay treated him like a brother. Even better than a brother. And how did he repay him? He made love to his best friend's daughter-in-law! Is this the kind of people we want in our community?" Chuck Ting's face became flushed

222

and he gestured vigorously with his hands, pounding his right fist into his left palm. "I ask you: Ostracize this no good scoundrel from the community! Show him that we don't approve of what he did. I will not keep you much longer. I just want to add that this scoundrel who had dared to violate the sanctity of the home, now has the audacity to file a complaint with the police for the arrest of Wang Wah Gay. And why did he file the complaint? Because Wang Wah Gay objected to his making love to his daughter-in-law!" There was an outbreak of half-suppressed chuckles among the conferees. "What would *you* do? Would *you* like it if someone went into your home and made love to your daughter-in-law? Would *you* say nothing? Could you close your eyes to a thing like this? What kind of man would *you* be?"

He snapped his head one way and then another, looking fiercely into space. "There is only one thing we can do here tonight and I plead with you with all my heart to do it. First: Order Ah Song to withdraw the charges he has filed against Wang Wah Gay. Secondly: Ostracize him from New York for at least five years. This is for the good of the entire Chinese community."

During the speech there had been a tense silence. No one even coughed. Immediately following the speech, before the president got up to talk, the silence continued. Soon the quietness became awkward. Then all of a sudden a simultaneous applause broke out from among the members. A broad grin adorned Chuck Ting's flushed face and he nodded happily to a number of friends. Applause sounded good to his ears. Not that he hadn't been used to applause in the past; for frequently at meetings and conventions he had been given standing ovations. But tonight's meeting was different. It was a business meeting at which he pleaded a case, as an old friend and guest. The applause was overwhelming indication of support for his cause. Seldom, he rejoiced, was there ever such a burst of emotion equal to the one he had just witnessed. Gratification and good feeling coursed through his body. It made him feel that all the hard work that had been required to get him where he was today was worth the trouble. This was, first of all, a personal victory for him. He lit a cigar, stuck at a rakish angle in his mouth.

The president stood up and waited for the commotion to subside. He raised both hands and soon quiet was restored.

"You have just heard a detailed account of the case of Ah Song and Wang Wah Gay," he began when the room fell silent. "Are there any questions? Is there anything you want to say? Anything to add to what has already been said?" Only silence greeted his remarks. "In that case if there is no objection, I declare that Ah Song be ostracized for a period of five years and that he be ordered to withdraw the charges he filed against Wang Wah Gay with the Police Department. If there are no further business, the meeting is adjourned."

Wang Chuck Ting beamed happily and shook hands all around.

LI

President Ho Soon sent two of his aids, the English-language and the Chinese-language secretaries, to talk to Ah Song, who had been discharged from Beekman Hospital. George Dong and Ging Fong went directly to Ah Song's apartment when informed by the hospital that he had been discharged.

"H'mn," snarled Ah Song, opening the door in answer to the bell. "How come you're so kind-hearted to come and see me?" he asked sarcastically upon seeing George Dong and Ging Fong. Reluctantly he said: "Come in, come in." He bowed slightly and moved back out of the way, as if making a mockery of their entrance. His left side where the ear used to be was heavily bandaged.

The door opened into the kitchen. In the sitting room a small portable TV was on a stand in one corner, blasting away in the program's finale. Ah Song walked over to the set and turned it off. There were no sofa or upholstered chairs in the room. There were only three wooden chairs hugging the edge of a round table, one side of which was pushed against the wall, between two windows. Ah Song now pulled the chairs away from the table. "Sit down," he said. "What do you want?"

"The president has ordered us to come to talk with you," said George Dong. "Didn't you get the notice for the meeting?"

"What meeting?" said Ah Song. He feigned a surprised look. "I didn't get any notice."

"We mailed you a notice for the meeting," said Ging Fong. He was bespectacled and scholarly looking, in his sixties.

"I didn't get any notice," insisted Ah Song glumly.

"The notice was mailed to you several days ago," repeated Ging Fong.

"Well, I didn't get it," snapped Ah Song. He tried to recall what the card had said. Although the notice had not stated the

225

matter to be discussed, he knew it would deal with Wang Wah Gay. Never before had they sent him a notice for a meeting. He never expected them to send him one because he was not on the committee and was not an officer of the organization. He had decided not to show up because he didn't have anything to say. No one would listen to him anyway. He had no powerful friend like Wang Chuck Ting to speak up for him. "I look in the mail box everyday," he added convincingly. "There was nothing."

"Well, that's too bad," said Dong. "We had a meeting last night. You should have been there to defend yourself."

"We have been instructed to inform you the following," Ging Fong brought out a paper from his pocket and began to read from it. "The Tong orders you to withdraw the charges against Wang Wah Gay and you are to get out of town and stay out for a period of five years. After the five years are up, you can come back and reapply for membership."

"Five years!" screamed Ah Song, jumping to his feet. "You guys can go to hell...all of you!" He paced the floor and gestured with his hands. "What did *I* do? *I* am the injured party." He beat his chest with his hand. "Wah Gay slashed me!" He pointed a finger at his bandaged left side. "He tried to kill me. The way you put it, you think I was the attacker."

"It's no good telling us now," said Ging Fong. "You should have been at the meeting."

Ah Song shook his head slowly and grimaced when the wound pained him. He showed part of his teeth in a wan smile. "A big stone will crush to death a crab," he said. "My presence there would have served no purpose. You know that only too well or you must be blind. Who do I have on my side? Are *you* on my side? Are you?" He turned to the other. "Are you on my side?"

Somewhat taken aback the two visitors said nothing. What Ah Song said was the truth. His presence at the meeting would have done him no good. No one would have sided with him.

"Good-bye now," said the emissaries. "See you again. Have a good trip."

When the door closed shut again, Ah Song was in no mood to return to the television set. He aimed his foot at the two chairs that had just been vacated and kicked them over. He stopped and glared at his own chair. The right foot struck out again and that, too, toppled over. Sonovabitch . . . the goddamned sonovabitches . . . No, he would not get out of town.

He was officially directed to leave but why should he? He had not done anything wrong. Nobody was going to tell him what to do . . . He flipped the switch on the TV set and righted one of the chairs and sat down. But his mind was not on the screen.

Go away? But where could he go? He had been to a lot of places. Vancouver. . .Seattle. . .Montreal. . .San Antonio. . .San Francisco. . .Las Vegas. . .All the places he wanted to go in New York would be barred to him. .Money Come. . .Good Fortune. . .The Gold Mountain. . .

The next day he went to the Elizabeth Street Police Station and withdrew the assault and battery charges he had made against Wang Wah Gay.

LII

"Chairman," George Dong announced excitedly, "Ah Song has withdrawn the charges!"

"Good, that's good, my boy." The two men shook hands. "Thank you for your fine cooperation." Chuck Ting patted George on the back.

As soon as George left, Chuck Ting called Wah Gay in Newark.

"You can come home now," he said calmly. "That sonovabitch Ah Song has gone to the police and withdrawn the charges against you."

"Are you sure?" asked Wah Gay incredulously. "I don't trust that sonovabitch!"

"I told you Ah Song has withdrawn the charges against you," repeated Chuck Ting. "You can come home now."

The following day, instead of returning to Money Come, Wah Gay went to a hiding place in the Bronx. He was still too ashamed to see his friends and cousins. Although for the first time in two weeks he did not have to look furtively about before taking another step, he had made up his mind to leave New York. Before leaving, he had to make some disposition of his club house. He wanted to lose himself in a far away place. He summoned Lee Gong to his hideout.

"I have to go away," he announced grimly when Lee Gong arrived in his apartment in the Bronx. "I can't stay in New York any more."

"You stay," said Lee Gong. "I'll go away."

"I've made up my mind..."

"No, I'll go away. If it had not been for that no good daughter of mine..."

"All that is in the past," said Wah Gay. "It is best to forget it. It wasn't your fault."

"She's the cause of it all. I have no face to meet my friends." Lee Gong shook his head.

"You stay here and take care of the club house," said Wah Gay.

"No, I can't. I can't stay."

"I'm giving you the club house. It's all yours. I want no part of it."

"It's not right for you to do that," said Lee Gong. "I will not accept it. I think you should stay and continue your operations."

"No," Wah Gay shook his head. "I have to start a new life. I cannot stay in New York. The shame is too great."

"If you're going to leave New York, why don't you sell the club house?" asked Lee Gong. "You probably can get several thousand dollars for it."

"My idea is to give it to you..."

"Thank you very much but I can't accept it. I have to go away too."

"See if you can get someone to buy it," said Wah Gay. "You set the price. Whatever you do is all right with me."

That same night Wah Gay and Chuck Ting met in a Chinese restaurant in midtown New York.

"I hope you don't mind my asking you to come up here," said Wah Gay.

"It's quite all right," replied Chuck Ting. "I'm glad to see you. The main thing is that you're all right and well, with no one to bother you."

"I'm so ashamed of myself I cannot go back to Chinatown."

"You need not be. It was not your fault."

"Just the same, I have no face left."

"Where do you plan to go?"

"To Chicago. Aurora. My brother still has a restaurant out there. I can still do some work..."

"I wish you wouldn't go..." said Chuck Ting.

"I've made up my mind."

"How soon are you leaving?"

"As soon as Lee Gong sells the club house for me...I want to thank you for everything you have done for me."

"Don't mention such a thing," said Chuck Ting. The two men shook hands and Chuck Ting returned downtown.

Lee Gong had already written to Sacramento, inquiring if he could go out there and work in his cousin's poultry market. His cousin had answered that he would be glad to have him. But before he could leave, Lee Gong had to sell the club house for Wah Gay.

Within a matter of days the whole community buzzed with the news that Money Come was for sale. Many came to inquire about the sale price. They were mostly bargain hunters, and Lee Gong dismissed them without much ceremony.

One week later Kitchen Master walked in and made Lee Gong an offer.

"I offer you three thousand dollars for the place," he said in a business-like manner.

"Four thousand dollars," replied Lee Gong without hesitation.

"Three thousand is a good price," said the Kitchen Master.

"Four thousand is a conservative price, if that's what you mean," replied Lee Gong.

Lee Gong stood his ground and, after two days of haggling, the Number One Cook from New Jersey bought the club house for four thousand dollars and quit his job in the restaurant to devote his full time to Money Come.

For Lee Gong there remained a lingering nostalgia in the air. One does not forget many years' association in a matter of minutes. For more than fifteen years, he had spent practically every day at the club house. It no longer represented home to him. The club house was gone. The life and game of mah-jong were gone.

Following the sale of the club house, Lee Gong and Wah Gay had a last meeting together before each went his separate way. The two in-laws met at the New Moon Restaurant on Forty-Eighth Street.

"Just give me three out of the four thousand dollars," said Wah Gay. "You keep the other thousand."

"I can't do that," said Lee Gong firmly. "The money is all yours."

"You took care of the place for me and you should get something."

"No, I can't accept any money from you. It was no work for

me to stay there."

"Here, take the thousand." Wah Gay counted the money and pushed it into Lee Gong's hand.

"You keep it." Lee Gong refused the money. "Whenever I need money, I'll let you know," he said.

When the waiter brought out the meal, the two in-laws ate silently. There was so much to be said that neither of them could find words for their thoughts. When they had finished eating, Lee Gong permitted Wah Gay to pay for the dinner.

Out in front of the restaurant, they paused and looked at each other, speechless. They were choking with emotion. Finally Wah Gay stuck out his hand.

"See you again, grandpa!" he said.

Lee Gong heard himself called grandpa for the first time in his life. Astonished and taken aback, he quickly recovered sufficiently to grab the extended hand.

"See you again, grandpa!"

They set out in opposite directions and, when they were a few feet apart, each whirled and called out, "You have my address?"

They nodded to each other and continued down the street. With bowed head, unknown to the other, each took out a handkerchief and dabbed at his eyes. In their hearts was this grim thought: In all probability, we will never see each other again.

LIII

Facing his co-workers after the outbreak of the scandal was a continuously trying experience for Ben Loy. Finally he quit his job at the New Toishan. Though outwardly they were friendly and sympathetic, Ben Loy could not help but feel that his co-workers were talking about him behind his back. *The wearer of the green hat,* they would say. *His wife hooked another man.* Or: *His wife is very apt at knitting the green hat.* They don't tell you these things to your face but say them behind your back. They are making fun of you. Ben Loy knew it. If someone else was involved in a similar predicament, he supposed he would laugh behind his back too.

But with Chin Yuen it was different. He could confide in him. Although many years older than himself, Ben Loy regarded Chin Yuen as a contemporary. There was no other whom he could turn to. He was more inclined to talk over his marital difficulties with Chin Yuen than with Mei Oi. Up to now, he had refrained from discussing it with anybody. But having suppressed his explosive anxiety over the behavior of his wife for so long, he at last felt compelled to find an outlet for his bottled-up emotions. He had found such an outlet in Chin Yuen.

"Mei Oi has been playing around with someone," he confided to Chin Yuen one afternoon. "In a way I have myself to blame. I have ruined my health."

Chin Yuen had wanted to discuss the matter but, like a true friend, had refrained from mentioning it until Ben Loy spoke first.

"Do you think it is wise to continue to live in New York after all that has happened?" Chin Yuen asked, sympathetically.

Ben Loy made no reply.

What Chin Yuen didn't quite understand was why Ben Loy had failed to take any action in the face of mounting rumors about his wife. Now his father had gone and chopped the guy's ear off...Chin Yuen shuddered at the thought.

Chin Yuen reflected that Ben Loy was accustomed to doing as his father said in matters concerning his marriage and his job. Would this easy-going personality be able to begin a new life for his wife and himself in some strange city, without the old man telling him what to do?

Chin Yuen doubted it. Then the sly thought entered his mind again: If someone was going to steal his best friend's wife, why not Chin Yuen? All the farmers in Sunwei knew this much of philosophy: *Fatty water should not be allowed to flow into another's rice paddy*...Chin Yuen was quite intrigued by this ancient but true observation.

The former school teacher was faced with two conflicting philosophies: 1. *Fatty water should not be allowed to flow into another's rice paddy*. 2. *Male and female are not to mix socially*.

The fatty water in this case, of course, was Mei Oi, and the rice paddy represented Ah Song. On the other hand, because of his closeness to the family, Chin Yuen figured that the fatty water should rightly have gone to him. But such a wicked thought would violate the teachings of Kung-fu-tze. Besides, he didn't want to make a fool out of Ben Loy. He would think no more of it.

After Ben Loy quit his job, Chin Yuen had visited him at home twice within a few days. Each visit he had brought with him a few items of groceries. Each time he was asked to stay for dinner and each time he readily accepted the invitation.

This afternoon Chin Yuen, looking more chipper than usual, rang the door bell at four o'clock. Mei Oi got up eagerly from the sofa and hurried daintily toward the door. She had been looking at herself in the mirror, applying a light make-up on her face and a dash of lipstick to her full mouth. She had changed to a new maternity dress because she didn't want to be seen in the same dress all the time. Just before the bell rang, she had sprayed herself with a sweet-scented fragance. She had wanted to wear her gold bracelets and her large almond-shaped jade ring, both gifts from her father-in-law. Should she wear them? She craved to. What would her husband say?

What *could* he say? That's what they are for. Impulsively she had gotten them from the drawer and put them on.

"Oh, Uncle Yuen!" exclaimed Mei Oi. "It's you! Come in. Come in." She eyed the brown paper bag he was carrying. "What's that?" she demanded happily.

"Oh, nothing. Just a chicken," said Chin Yuen. The first thing he noticed when the door opened, even before his eyes fell on the dazzling gold bracelets and the jade ring, was the exotic aroma of the perfume. He inhaled appreciatively and let its fragance drift into his nostrils, tickling his senses, giving him a feeling of exuberance. He got as close to her as he dared without actually touching her. The perfume seemingly had the power to draw him ever closer to her, and no one realized this more than Chin Yuen himself. He allowed himself the luxury of thinking that the perfume and the jewelry had been especially put on for him. This thought gave him an overwhelming sense of inflated ego.

She put the chicken on the kitchen table. "Oh, you shouldn't have done that!" she exclaimed.

The good smell pleased Chin Yuen no end, and he smiled graciously at his hostess. He tried to recall if he had experienced this wonderful fragance during his previous visits. The answer was no. He had not recalled having had the pleasure. He asked himself: *Why should she go through the trouble of putting on the perfume for me? She is taking a liking to me...* He felt compelled to add a mild deceptive expedient to his visit. "Where is Ah Loy?" he asked solicitously. Usually he referred to Ben Loy as *Loy Gaw* in front of his wife, but this time he dropped the more formal form of address.

"Oh, he just stepped out," said Mei Oi. She guided the visitor to the living room. There Chin Yuen made believe he discovered the bracelets and the ring for the first time. If he had remembered seeing them before, he now gave the impression that he had not.

"The bracelets—they are lovely," said Chin Yuen breathlessly. The light, tastefully applied make-up on her face and the bright red lipstick glowed radiantly in the cone of subdued light from the table lamp.

234

"Sit over here, please." Mei Oi's palm softly gestured toward the chair next to hers. Chin Yuen went over obediently and sat down. He eyed the blue two-piece maternity dress, then the bigness of her belly, and calculated to himself how many more weeks before the baby would be due. He remembered the first time he had met her, right in this very apartment. The once long straight hair was now done up in a permanent. The rural-looking face was now adorned with make-up. The shy, self-conscious bride was now a woman who was going to have a baby. These past couple of years had seen many changes in Mei Oi.

She brought out a package of cigarettes and offered them to Chin Yuen, explaining that it was Ben Loy's pack and that she didn't smoke herself. "It is so unsightly for a woman to be smoking," she remarked candidly. "I never smoke." She smiled at her listener. "Maybe you want to smoke a cigar?" She tried hard to be a good hostess. "Let me get you a cigar." Actually there was none in the house.

"Don't be formal," said Chin Yuen. "I don't smoke cigars."

"Ben Loy said we are going to move out to San Francisco soon," said Mei Oi, relieved that she did not have to produce a cigar for her guest. "We are going to miss you," she added pleasantly.

"Oh, I'll miss you too," said Chin Yuen quickly, adding, as if the previous remark had sounded too overbearing, "Ben Loy and I have been old friends, long time friends."

"Yes, I know," smiled Mei Oi. "I hope you can come out and visit us some time. You can always find another job out there," she added wistfully.

"Yes, I guess I can," replied Chin Yuen, overwhelmed by his hostess's invitation.

Closely he watched Mei Oi's every moment. Her wave of the hand, her carriage in walking, her smile, her teeth, the curve of her lips—everything about her excited him. He was flattered that a young and beautiful woman like Mei Oi should have even a remote interest in him. He saw in her the embodiment of love itself. He recalled vividly an old saying of the Old Master: *One admires his own poetry but somebody else's wife.* Chin Yuen

235

was fond of discussing with his fellow workers the position taken by Kung-fu-tze that we love our friend's wife and our own poetry. He smiled slyly with the thought that it was natural for him to have a strong desire for his friend's wife. Kung-fu-tze said so.

"I will have Ben Loy send you our new address so you will know where to look for us when you come out," Mei Oi said.

"Yes, please do that," said Chin Yuen. "That's an excellent idea."

"Let me pour you a cup of tea." Mei Oi got up and headed toward the kitchen, with Chin Yuen watching her until she disappeared into the other room.

"Don't stand on ceremony," he called after her. "I'm not really thirsty."

"You don't have to be thirsty to sip a cup of tea," chided Mei Oi sweetly. She returned from the kitchen and offered the tea to Chin Yuen with both hands.

"I owe you an apology." Chin Yuen bowed slightly and accepted the cup of tea with both hands. The closeness of Mei Oi brought a strong fragance of the sweet-scented perfume to his nostrils once more. He stole a glance at the bulged areas where her breasts came up. The bigness of her belly did not show because the maternity dress draped over it well. As he sipped the tea he wrinkled his forehead trying to recall the brand of tea. "Is this Woo Lung?" he asked, to make conversation.

"Yes, I think so," laughed Mei Oi. "You know, I didn't even bother to look at the label on the box."

The two now sat facing each other, Chin Yuen on the chair and Mei Oi on the sofa. His eyes fell on her bracelets. "Five dollar gold pieces are a rare thing now," he commented.

"Yes, I suppose so," she said. "These cost nineteen to twenty dollars each. My father-in-law gave them to me." She hadn't wanted to mention her father-in-law but it came out inadvertently. After the words tumbled out, she felt self-conscious at the reference to her father-in-law.

"Do you want more tea?" asked Mei Oi.

"No, thank you." He looked up at her and an irresistible urge came over him. He got up and walked over to her and, bending, his hand gently lifted hers. "This is a beautiful brace-let." He felt the soft, smooth skin, holding her hand caressingly while pretending to examine the bracelet. A wonderful sensation coursed through his veins and he desired closer contact with Mei Oi.

Abruptly Mei Oi pulled her hand away. "I'd better go and prepare dinner," she said.

A few minutes later Ben Loy returned and the three of them had broiled chicken, sweet and pungent spareribs, beef with bok toy, and bean curd soup for dinner.

LIV

The phone in Chin Yuen's apartment rang. It was Ben Loy. He asked Chin Yuen to drop by to see him on something important. Something important, Ben Loy had said. What could that be? Is this a trap, asking him to come up? Will he be cut up just like Ah Song? Previously the only time Ben Loy ever called him was to ask: Can you work for me tomorrow? There was no such request today. In the excitement he had forgotten that Ben Loy was no longer working. But what could *he* have found out? The last time he was there Ben Loy had not come home until after he had spent considerable time with Mei Oi alone. Did Ben Loy find out that he was holding his wife's hand? Would Mei Oi be foolish enough to tell him? Maybe he had been put on the alert after the Ah Song episode. *Don't trust anybody, not even your best friend.*

Why should he, Chin Yuen, take the risk of showing up, only to be slaughtered? All he did was to hold Mei Oi's hand. Was that such a crime? He summoned his vast knowledge of the stories of the Three Kingdoms, learned and memorized from his school days—stories in which many distinguished generals had tried out their cleverly conceived strategies. Schemes that throughout the centuries had come to be accepted by the general reading public as strokes of genius. Chin Yuen asked himself: What would Kung Ming have done under these circumstances? After mulling over it for more than an hour, he decided to call Ben Loy back.

"Hello? Loy? this is Chin Yuen."

"What's the matter now Yuen *Gaw?*"

He was always happy to have someone call him elder brother. He reasoned that if Ben Loy were going to do him harm, he would not be so courteous. But still...

"Say, Ah Loy. Of course I'm coming. I might bring a friend

238

with me. Would you mind?"

"Of course not," replied Ben Loy. "Bring him up."

Chin Yuen let out a big sigh of relief. His fears had been unfounded. He laughed about bringing a friend. He would tell Ben Loy the friend had gone home and did not come with him. If Ben Loy had planned to do him harm, he certainly could not have wanted a witness to his crime.

Within half an hour Chin Yuen was at the Wang apartment. He had stopped by the Bowery Super Market to buy a few things for the dinner table. As he crossed the street near Chatham Square, he whistled a tune known only to himself.

Husband and wife rushed to the door when the bell rang. The door opened and Chin Yuen pushed an armful of groceries into Ben Loy's hesitant arms. Ben Loy awkwardly accepted the package with a feeling of embarrassment.

"You shouldn't have done that," Mei Oi repeated her previous complaint pleasantly. "Every time you come, you bring so much food."

"It's not much. What I bring I eat most of it myself," he chuckled.

"Sit down, old friend," said Ben Loy, just returning from the kitchen. Then to his wife, "Pour a cup of tea for Mr. Chin."

"I've asked you to drop by today because we want to tell you we're moving to San Francisco," said Ben Loy with a grin on his face.

"Leaving? When?" asked the surprised Chin Yuen. Although Mei Oi had mentioned moving to San Francisco the other day, he had not expected it to happen so soon.

"In a few days," replied Ben Loy.

"Ben Loy wants you to sell our apartment for us," said Mei Oi.

"In the meantime you stay here and pay the rent," chuckled Ben Loy, "Get whatever you can for it. Two hundred...three hundred...four hundred. Whatever you can get."

Chin Yuen nodded.

"When we get out there, we'll send you our address," said Mei Oi.

Chin Yuen said he wanted to see them off at the station but

Ben Loy replied that he wasn't sure of the train schedule yet. Before Chin Yuen left, Ben Loy gave him the key to the apartment, saying, "The next meal we'll have together will be in San Francisco."

The Wangs entrained for San Francisco the following Saturday, two days after Ben Loy had given a duplicate key to Chin Yuen. With his small savings to tide them over, Ben Loy hoped some of his wartime buddies would remember him and come forward with some job recommendations.

He had tired of playing the role of the dutiful son, keeping silent while his father told him what to do. He had no inkling of his father's plans to leave New York. Whether he did or not was of no importance to Ben Loy. He was going away himself, with Mei Oi.

The mere thought of going away with Mei Oi had given him new hope. He saw on the horizon a chance for a new beginning. The desire for vengeance had lessened with the passage of time.

LV

In San Francisco Ben Loy and Mei Oi had registered at the Pacific Hotel on Jackson Street in San Francisco's Chinatown. From his hotel room he started calling his friends one by one. After the initial surprise and enthusiastic greetings from his friends, he would say: "I'm looking for a job. Do you have any leads for me?"

The first few days were very discouraging. Some of his buddies refused to take him seriously. When he asked if they knew of an apartment available, they laughed and said they were in the market for one too.

Two weeks later Henry Kwong called. He had been in India with Ben Loy. "Loy," he said, "do you want to work weekends?"

"Sure," Ben Loy replied excitedly. "Sure, I'll work weekends. I'll take anything." Ben Loy was glad of the chance to work again. With the baby on the way he needed the money.

"It's at the Globe Cafe. It is only about a block from your hotel."

The next day Ben Loy reported to the manager of the Globe and was told to report for work Saturdays and Sundays. He worked diligently at this part-time job for four weeks. Then the manager asked him to work as a regular waiter. Ben Loy readily accepted the offer.

Mei Oi rested in the hotel room most of the time while her husband worked. Ben Loy had taken her to see Dr. Frances Moy, who had offices right in the hotel. There was no need to interpret for her and quite often she went to see the doctor by herself when Ben Loy could not accompany her.

Luck was with the Wangs. Another friend called to offer an apartment, and arranged for them to inspect it.

A week later Ben Loy and Mei Oi repacked the few things they had taken out of their suitcases and took a taxi to their newly acquired apartment on Mason Street, between Jackson and Pacific. It was just a short distance from the hotel, so that when Mei Oi went to see Dr. Moy there was no inconvenience. When Ben Loy went to work it was still only a short walk to the Globe Cafe.

One block below Mason Street, on Stockton, there was a store which Ben Loy passed every day on his way to and from work, with a big sign in the display window:

WE CAN CURE THE FOLLOWING:

ASTHMA · TUBERCULOSIS
CANCER · BERIBERI
BOILS OF ALL KINDS · IMPOTENCE
SLEEPLESSNESS · ULCERS
DIZZINESS · HERNIA
COMMON COLDS · HIGH BLOOD PRESSURE
LOSS OF APPETITE · LOW BLOOD PRESSURE

Impotence was the third one down on the right hand column and Ben Loy stared at the word silently for a full minute before passing on to the other illnesses listed on the card. His first reaction was disbelief. He recalled his visit to the herbalist in New York for a pulse examination. But perhaps he had not continued the treatment long enough. Now, everyday, day in and day out, he passed this herb shop on his way to work.

"*Moi Moi*," he said excitedly one night to his wife. "Down on Stockton Street there is an herb store and the herb doctor claims he can cure impotence. He has a big sign in the window." It was the first time he had willingly and, without ill feelings or reluctance, discussed his physical condition with Mei Oi. He no longer felt self-conscious.

"Well, what are you waiting for?" urged Mei Oi. "Go and pay him a visit. Maybe he can do you some good." For the first time, Mei Oi felt both a desire and a responsibility of sharing her husband's problems. She no longer felt the antagonism of old. Gone was the bitterness she had nursed against her husband since the beginning of his decline in masculinity.

In their place now, there were only understanding and sympathy. The ugly episode in New York had served to strengthen the bond between them. She now felt a sense of belonging, of belonging to Ben Loy. She realized that her husband could have disowned her but he chose to stick by her. In spite of what she had done, Ben Loy still wanted her. It made her feel proud to be wanted. "Loy *Gaw*," she implored him tenderly. "I want you to go. If you love me, you'll go, just for me."

The words elated Ben Loy. After all that had happened between them, Mei Oi wanted him to go, wanted him to get well and be a full-time husband again.

The next day at work, he kept remembering what Mei Oi had said to him. Neither could he forget the big sign in the herbalist window. All day long at the restaurant he glanced at his watch, impatiently waiting for quitting time. He barely got through the day's work without making mistakes in the customers' orders.

After work, he took a short walk to Stockton Street to see the herb doctor.

The herb shop had two display windows, each with an identical card listing the illnesses in English and Chinese. Otherwise the windows were bare; not even a single stick of gingsing was evident. As Ben Loy pushed open the door, a bell attached to the door clanged. Inside, arranged in a row, were several straight-backed wooden chairs on one side, now devoid of occupants. The emptiness and quiet reminded him of his early afternoon sessions with his father at the club house. A wooden partition separated the front section from the rest of the store, with a curtained doorway in the center. After glancing at the unpretentiousness of the place, Ben Loy sat down on one of the chairs uncertainly. He wondered if he should walk up to the curtain and part it for a quick informal investigation. But he was certain that the clanging of the bell had announced his arrival sufficiently. He waited anxiously for a few moments. Then a middle-aged man of medium build in a grey business suit came out with a big smile and an extended hand.

"Sir, what is your esteemed name?" he bowed slightly.

"Wang, insignificant Wang," said Ben Loy, accepting the

hand shake.

"Insignificant Suey," replied the man. He parted the curtain and bowed his patient in.

In the center of the room there was a large desk on top of which was the familiar small black pillow. The doctor took the seat behind the desk and motioned Ben Loy to take the other chair.

"Well, what seems to be the trouble?" asked the herbalist. His friendly manner made Ben Loy feel less awkward. He hesitated only for a moment.

"It's. . .it's my impotence," he blurted out. "I saw your sign and . . ."

"Yes, yes," nodded the doctor. "You're still very young. There's no reason why you should not be strong and vigorous."

"Do you think you can cure me?" asked Ben Loy anxiously, leaning forward in his chair.

"I'll do the best I can," replied the doctor. "Now tell me from the very beginning what has happened to you."

Ben Loy began by telling the doctor about his honeymoon and its abrupt ending when he was no longer able to have sexual intercourse. His days of loose women and his subsequent bouts with venereal diseases received the herbalist's close attention. The doctor listened quietly, interrupting here and there only with a question. When Ben Loy had finished, the doctor smiled and said, "I was young once. I understand." He pointed to the pillow on the desk, and Ben Loy obligingly placed his wrist, with palm up, on the tiny black pillow. The doctor proceeded to feel his pulse, first on one wrist and then on the other.

"Doctor. . .do. . .do you think. . .?"

"Eat a bowl of tea and we'll get you on the way to recovery," said the doctor.

"Eat a bowl of tea?" asked the skeptical Ben Loy.

"Yes, eat a bowl of tea," smiled the doctor. "Can you come back in about three hours? It takes that long to brew the tea."

"I'll be back in three hours," said Ben Loy excitedly and left.

244

LVI

Early in the morning a few weeks later, the baby's cries awakened its parents. The baby, named Kuo Ming, had been born to Ben Loy and Mei Oi fifteen days ago at the Chinese Hospital. All their free time was taken up now by this new addition to the family. With the arrival of the baby, the couple was blessed with a tie that drew them closer to each other. Sacrifices for the baby were made cheerfully and enthusiastically by the new parents.

Ben Loy himself had changed over from working in the dining room to assistant cook. He was rapidly learning to become a good cook. The change gave him new self-assurance. His old job of waiting on tables had subjected him to all sorts of pressures from the diners: *The tea is too strong. The chow mein is cold. Not enough shrimps. Where's my roast pork?* Now that he was working in the kitchen, this constant pressure was greatly reduced. He was learning a new skill. He expected to become a master at it.

The birth of Kuo Ming marked the beginning of a new era for him. He was now a proud father. It scarcely occurred to him to wonder whether he was the blood relative of this small person who was so dear to him and Mei Oi. It was enough that the baby was one of life's miracles and that it needed him.

This precious responsibility meant added expenditures, but he was prepared for them. His new job meant more money to take home. He was working hard to become number one cook at the restaurant.

He liked San Francisco. With the passing of each day, the New York chapter of his life was pushed further back in his memory. New York represented parental supervision and the reckless mistakes of youth. Now all this was being replaced by new surroundings and new attitudes. The proverbial parental shackle had been cut. For the first time Ben Loy knew and enjoyed emancipation. New frontiers, new people, new times, new ideas unfolded. He had come to a new golden mountain.

Except for one thing, he was happy. He tried to push this problem, this inadequacy, into the background. If he could have forgotten it, shut it off from his daily life, he would have done so. But it was impossible and his impotence plagued him with shame. Mei Oi was an understanding and sympathetic wife, but how long could he, as a husband, allow such a situation to continue? Even if his wife were not to make any demands on him, he would still hold his head in shame.

Outwardly, he gave no hint of this inner torture. And his friends said teasingly: "When is the next one coming?" He wished he knew. He would like nothing better than to become a father for a second time.

He had been going to the herbalist faithfully for many weeks. He was determined to do anything to regain his vigor. The thick, black, bitter tea was not easy to swallow, but he kept going back to the herb doctor uncomplainingly.

Mei Oi encouraged him to go, although she herself had not the slightest idea whether the tea would do him any good. As a native of China, where herb medicine was an accepted means of curing diseases, she should have some confidence in the use of herbs. But she could only hope...No matter how much she tried to tell herself that everything would be all right, that her husband's impotence was a temporary condition, there was apprehension behind the managed smile on her pretty face. She pretended she did not care; that her husband's inadequacy would not make her an unwanted or useless woman. But deep inside her, there was terror and resentment.

She wanted so much to be a good, worthy wife; to be a good, respectable mother. Above all, she was a woman. She would have been supremely happy if it had not been for her husband's lack of manliness. The change of locale had given her a fresh outlook. The move from New York to San Francisco was for her, as it was for Ben Loy, a break from the stern supervision of the parental eye. Her brief stay in New York was a part of her life she wanted to forget. She liked the sunny disposition of

California. She made new friends. The birth of the baby gave her a precious jewel the equal of which did not exist anywhere else in the world. She loved the baby. She could walk the streets of San Francisco's Chinatown with her head high. In spite of their marital difficulties, understanding and compassion drew husband and wife ever closer together, a relationship nourished by the birth of their son.

The sun shone brightly everywhere—except for the problem of incompatibility. In her own quiet, wifely way, Mei Oi tried to help. Unknown to her husband, she bought and scanned numerous Hong Kong periodicals and newspapers for advertisements which might contain the key to recovery of Ben Loy's vitality. If his present treatment failed, she would suggest sending for some medicines from Hong Kong.

After many weeks of eating the tea, Ben Loy continued to appear at Dr. Suey's. The doctor felt his pulse.

"The pulse has improved," said the herbalist. "It is much stronger and more regular."

Ben Loy heaved a sigh of relief. "Do you think I am...do you think I am strong enough now?" he asked.

"You are much stronger than before," replied the doctor. "Don't over-exert yourself and rest as much as possible."

"Do you think I am ready...I am ready for a test, doctor?"

The doctor chuckled. "Young man, no one can tell you when you are ready. You know that better than anybody else," he smiled at the puzzled Ben Loy. "When the time comes, you'll know." And he winked at him.

For many weeks he had wanted to test his masculinity; but in the back of his mind there was always the fear of failure. The doctor's answer to his query offered him no solution or encouragement. He realized that, if he failed in this challenge, he faced a very bleak future with Mei Oi. He was like a man who had a new house without a key.

He had delayed the test long enough. Fear was the constant companion of indecision. Lately, though, he had been encouraged. Upon rising in the morning, he felt his body pulsing with vigor. It gave him a sense of elation and hope.

LVII

When Kuo Ming had passed the first months of life, Ben Loy and Mei Oi decided to celebrate the baby's birth by inviting their friends to the Globe Cafe for Kuo Ming's haircut party. Most of the guests were from Ben Loy's army days. They did not invite Wah Gay or Lee Gong because they did not particularly care to let them know about the baby. The two older men would eventually learn of the baby's birth from Ben Loy's mother, whom Ben Loy had already informed of the event.

The haircut party was nothing like the affair they had at the Grand China Restaurant in New York, where Wah Gay had invited hundreds of people. Here in San Francisco, the Wangs had a quiet party of only thirty people, including Ben Loy's boss and co-workers.

That night when Ben Loy and Mei Oi got home with the baby, they were aglow with the excitement of the party. Ben Loy's face was flushed from the few sips of Ng Gar Pai he had taken upon the insistence of his buddies and to the consternation of Mei Oi. Tonight Mei Oi had presented a picture of the beaming, happy bride, crowned with the confidence of the new mother, and Ben Loy was justly pleased with her. In her clinging, long Chinese *sar* gown, Mei Oi was indeed a beautiful woman. Ben Loy had hardly taken his eyes from his wife during the entire party. He felt himself falling in love with her all over again.

When his buddies stole glances at Mei Oi, he felt a twinge of jealousy. At the same time, their admiration made him feel a surge of pride that he was her husband. He had a tantalizing impulse to stroke her silk-soft black hair, to touch her face. He leaned over, put his arm around her waist and held her tightly. He was discovering in Mei Oi a quality new and exciting, unknown and delightful. Like the blossoming of a new romance. He exulted in the ripe fullness of her hip against his

248

thigh as he politely acknowledged the congratulations of his friends.

For a time he had wondered impatiently if the party would never end.

Back at the apartment, Ben Loy stared with sensual pleasure at Mei Oi's half-exposed breasts as she bent in her slip to change the baby's diapers.

When Mei Oi had finished with the baby, she turned and looked steadily at Ben Loy a long moment. Ben Loy saw in his wife's gaze a mingling of shyness and longing, question and challenge, invitation and animal urgency.

He responded with an impulse to take her brutally and cruelly and he remembered that she was his wife and he was immediately ashamed and then the chill of fear pervaded him and he waited as his senses struggled between terror and desire and as he sat, torn and hesitant, Mei Oi dropped her eyes and walked into the bathroom.

Ben Loy paced the floor in an agonized cadence of despair and anticipation as he waited for Mei Oi to finish her bath. Then he persuaded himself that he should take a shower.

Mei Oi had considered Ben Loy's tacit rebuff as she lingered in her bath. For the first time, she did not respond to his hesitance with her usual feelings of injury and withdrawal. She had seen her husband's pride and pleasure in her womanly allurement earlier in the evening at the party and she had felt his sheathed power and she resolved that tonight she would rediscover the husband that Ben Loy had been meant to be.

So she had bathed and put on only her night gown over her perfumed skin. She felt clean and refreshed. Her lips showed pale and colorless in the mirror and she quickly ran over them with lipstick. She knotted the sash around her nightgown. Her breasts bulged through the flimsy material, big and round and full of milk for the baby. She smiled at the happy, carefree girl in the mirror and began to hum a tune...*When is my husband coming home?* She had learned the song in the village as a school girl during the Sino-Japanese War...*When is my hus-*

band coming home? She thought it was a beautiful tune and liked it very much.

The soft, melodious tune drifted to the bathroom.

"I'm coming!" shouted Ben Loy from the bathroom. He hurried into the bedroom, still dripping from the shower.

"You're all wet!" gasped Mei Oi. "Here, let me dry you."

She sponged him tenderly with the towel. Abruptly she stopped and knelt at his feet.

"Loy *Gaw*," she murmured, hugging his legs to her face. She nuzzled his thighs with her lips. She was no longer apprehensive, only elated and bubbling with the vitality of her youth. "My dearly beloved husband," she whispered tenderly. Ben Loy's eyes met hers. "I love you so very much..."

She kissed his body in a rush of feeling from which had vanished all trace of the shy maiden of her native village. This time Ben Loy responded with a blind thrust of passion and his wife's urging, melting body was there to claim it.

No longer was there any fear, any doubt...ten thousand battles, ten thousand victories...

For this hour, all creation existed solely for them. Their bed was the universe, the stars, the sun, the moon, the air, heaven and earth. The room was incandescent ...

A long while later, the baby whimpered from the crib.

"Let him alone," said Ben Loy. "He'll be all right."

The baby quieted after a few more wails.

"We must invite *Lao Yair* to our second haircut party!" whispered Mei Oi.

"Yes," agreed her husband. "We won't forget to invite your father, too!"